THE BREAKABLE PROMISE

Richard Hawke gave Cassie his most dazzling smile and mocking look as he declared, ''I shall not demand my rights as your husband until you wish it.''

She looked up at him, making no effort to hide her satisfaction. ''Then I thank you. I can only hope for your sake, Mr. Hawke, that you are a most patient man. Because nothing will ever, *ever* induce me to be your wife in fact as well as in name. Indeed, I fear it will not be many days before you will discover that you have made an extremely bad bargain.''

But rather than looking discomposed, Mr. Hawke still smiled down at her. ''I have learned, my dear, that no one can accurately foretell the future.''

CHARLOTTE LOUISE DOLAN attended Eastern Illinois University and earned a masters degree in German from Middlebury College. She has lived throughout the United States and in Canada, Taiwan, Germany, and the Soviet Union. She is the mother of three children and currently makes her home in Idaho Falls with her husband and daughter.

The Unofficial Suitor

by

Charlotte Louise Dolan

A SIGNET BOOK

SIGNET
Published by the Penguin Group
Penguin Books USA Inc., 375 Hudson Street,
New York, New York, 10014, U.S.A.
Penguin Books Ltd, 27 Wrights Lane, London W8 5TZ, England
Penguin Books Australia Ltd, Ringwood, Victoria, Australia
Penguin Books Canada Ltd, 10 Alcorn Avenue, Toronto, Ontario, Canada M4V 3B2
Penguin Books (N.Z.) Ltd, 182-190 Wairau Road,
Auckland 10, New Zealand

Penguin Books Ltd, Registered Offices:
Harmondsworth, Middlesex, England

First published by Signet,
an imprint of New American Library,
a division of Penguin Books USA Inc.

First Printing, July, 1992

10 9 8 7 6 5 4 3 2 1

This book is dedicated to my great-great-grandfather, Nicholas Richards, who was a tin miner in Cornwall. He brought his family to America so that his daughter, Mary Ann, my great-grandmother, would not have to work in the mines as so many young girls were forced by poverty to do. And I also wish to dedicate this book to my grandfather, William Nicholas Baker, who first told me the stories about his mother and grandfather and their journey from Cornwall to Wisconsin.

I wish to thank Peggy Summers and Charlotte Baker for reading my manuscript and making suggestions for improvements.

Chapter One

Mr. Carneby kept a well-run, albeit modest establishment in Falmouth. Returning from a short business trip, he was therefore not expecting the door of his town house to be flung open and his housekeeper to hurry down the steps to meet him, her normal manner of quiet dignity and reserve quite forgotten.

"Oh, sir, I am so glad you are home at last. There has been a strange man coming around for three days asking for a Richard Hawke. I have told him over and over that he must have the wrong house, for there is nobody living here but our Mr. Carneby, and no one in this household has heard of anyone by the name of Hawke, but he wouldn't listen. He . . . he . . ." She was unable to continue, as if afraid of his reaction to what she was trying to say.

Not wishing to satisfy the idle curiosity of casual passersby, Mr. Carneby left his companion to pay the coachman and bring in the luggage, and taking his flustered housekeeper by the arm, escorted her back into the house. He smiled calmly to reassure her. "Now then, Mrs. Roberts, just what did this man say?"

"He wouldn't take no for an answer, Mr. Carneby." Her voice trembled, but she managed to go on. "I told him you was a gentleman as likes your privacy, and you didn't care to have strangers coming around uninvited. I told him you didn't even make me privy to your comings and goings, and I had no idea if you would be home today or next week or not for a month, but he insisted . . ." Her voice ended in a self-pitying wail.

"He insisted on what?" It was getting harder and harder to mask his impatience with the housekeeper, who by now should have calmed down but who instead was wringing her

hands and looking as if a sharp word from him would make
her fall entirely to pieces.

"Oh, sir, he insisted, and there was nothing I could do,
what with you being gone and Tuke with you, and no one
in the house but Betty and me, and her with no more backbone than a wet sponge, going on and on about what a
handsome gentleman he was. And then when he said he was
Viscount Westhrop—I couldn't stop her, sir, indeed I
couldn't! And I told her I wasn't to be blamed, and I told
her it would be all on her head, and she said it didn't make
her no mind, it would be worth it and all, just to have a
chance to look at a real lord."

He weighed the odds of being able to get some sense out
of his housekeeper, and decided they were minimal. It was
obvious he would have to seek out this Viscount Westhrop,
whoever he was, and discover the nature of his business with
Richard Hawke. "Did you manage to find out where this
handsome lord is staying, Mrs. Roberts?"

She looked at him in dismay. "But that's what I've been
telling you—Betty let him into the house! He's been in your
study since ten o'clock this morning, and he refuses to
budge!"

"The devil you say!" What had been idle curiosity before
rapidly became rage. The idea that someone had been
sequestered alone all day in a room containing his private
papers—even if the said papers were safely hidden in a wall
safe—the possible consequences of such a rash act did not
bear contemplating. "Send Betty to me at once." He stalked
down the hall to confront the waiting stranger.

Having cast her fellow servant to the wolves, the housekeeper apparently had some slight twinges of conscience.
"You won't be punishing Betty too hard, will you, sir? She
means well, and she's a good worker, just that she's a bit
of a pushover for a handsome smile and charming tongue."

There was no point in telling the silly woman exactly what
he thought of her part in this whole affair. All it would
accomplish would be to cast her into hysterics, which he
definitely did not need at this moment. He contented himself,
therefore, with a scowl, which was adequate to stop the

housekeeper's babbling and send her scurrying to the kitchen in the basement.

Opening the door of his study quietly, he stood ready to catch the intruder in the act of riffling his desk or tapping the walls looking for a secret panel. But at the first glimpse of the young man dozing in an easy chair by the fire with his long buckskin-clad legs stretched out in front of him, the man calling himself Mr. Carneby forgot all worries for the safety of his business papers.

With a relaxed smile replacing the scowl of moments before, he shut the door gently behind him. "Well, Perry, so now you have become a house-breaker. I always predicted you would come to no good end."

The other man was instantly alert and on his feet. "Richard, you wretch! I knew that stubborn old woman was lying through her teeth, claiming she didn't know you!" He closed the space between them and they stood there for a moment grinning, each inspecting the other until, unable to resist, they pounded each other on the back in an exuberance of good feeling.

The first intense emotion spent, they returned together to the chairs by the fire, where Richard seated himself calmly and the younger man threw himself back down in the same relaxed sprawl he had favored earlier, giving a great sigh of relief.

"Confound it, Richard, I've been worried for days that you might be dead or in trouble. All Captain Rymer would say when I asked him your direction was that I should look for a Mr. Carneby in Falmouth, who might be able to give me word of you."

"Ah, I was wondering how you tracked me down. And how did you find Captain Rymer?"

"It's more a case of his finding me—in New Orleans—brought me a letter from the family lawyer informing me of my inheritance."

Before he could go on, there was a light knock, and a very anxious face appeared around the corner of the door. Then the slight figure belonging to the face slid into the room, her head tilted down so that all they could see was her mobcap. "You wished to speak to me, Mr. Carneby?" she whispered.

"Yes, Betty. Send my valet up with some brandy for my guest and tell Mrs. Roberts he will be staying for dinner."

Her head jerked up, and she stared at him dazedly, her mouth hanging open in disbelief. Then she seemed to grasp the reality of her reprieve and scurried out before anyone could snatch her luck away.

"So *you* are the mysterious Mr. Carneby," his friend mused. "What is the point of this masquerade?"

"I prefer to keep my business dealings private. I find it simpler if people know only as much about me as I choose to let them know."

"So everyone here knows you as Mr. Carneby?"

"In Falmouth? Yes."

"Something about the way you say that makes me wonder who I should look for when I am not in Falmouth."

As Richard had anticipated, Perry did not even bother to glance up when the door opened and the "valet" entered with a tray containing a bottle of brandy and two glasses. At the sight of the visitor, John almost dropped the tray he was carrying, but he made a quick recovery, pouring them each a glass of brandy as neatly as if he were indeed a servant.

It was all Richard could do not to spoil the coming surprise by laughing out loud. "Well, that would depend on where you were looking, to be sure. In Portsmouth, it might pay you to look up the ever-so-respectable Mr. Rawlynson. Or if you happened to be in Dover, there is a Mr. Hanchett there who some people suspect of being a bit of a Frenchie but who others insist must be part Spanish or Portuguese. He frequently knows my direction."

"And in London?"

"In London? I do not believe that there is anyone in London for you to ask. The time is not yet ripe for London to know of me."

As Richard watched, his young friend became aware that the "servant" who had handed him the glass of brandy was still standing there, intruding on their private conversation.

Perry looked up in sharp annoyance, which was immediately replaced by amazement and then sheer delight. "Tuke? John Tuke? I can't believe it. I thought you cocked up your toes in Baton Rouge, after that wily little Frenchman carved you up like a piece of cheese."

"As you can see, my dear Peregrine, I am still here, but I would not waste any time looking for that little frog. Hawke has his own ideas about who is to stay and who is to depart this world."

"And you have become Richard's valet? Shame on him for treating an old friend thus."

John Tuke retired to stand leaning negligently against the mantel. "It suits me to play the role."

"It sounds as if you, too, have come up in the world, Perry," Richard drawled. "Or were you also using an alias when you told my housekeeper you were a peer of the realm?"

"No, it's true, for my sins. You see before you the ninth Viscount Westhrop."

"You never mentioned you were in line for a title."

"Didn't think I was. With two uncles, three cousins, a father, and one older brother ahead of me, there were no objections when I was ten and my mother's younger brother offered to take me to America with him and give me a start in life. After all, there were seven apparently healthy men between me and the title, none of them given to taking the slightest risk."

He laughed. "To be sure, my cousin Gerald managed to scandalize the entire family by falling into the Thames while returning from an evening drinking with his cronies at Vauxhall, but other than that, they all managed to die peacefully in bed. It's a good thing they did, or despite the fact that I've been in America for the last fifteen years, there would probably be whispers that I'd dispatched them all in order to inherit the title."

Perry sobered up. "And the truth is, I don't want to have anything to do with that wretched title. I intend to give it up as soon as possible. I'm an American now. That's the way I've thought of myself for years. I've still got one cousin left over here. Edmund was always a self-righteous prig when we were growing up, and a tattle-tale of the worst sort—let him play lord of the manor.''

"So, why did you come back, if not to accept your *rightful* place in society?''

Richard heard the slight touch of mockery in Tuke's question, but luckily their young friend appeared not to notice.

"Mainly because of my grandmother, Lady Letitia. She sent a tear-stained note along with the lawyer's letter, piteously begging me to come home. I was halfway across the Atlantic before it occurred to me that such maudlin sentimentality is totally out of character for her. She is probably laughing up her sleeve at having tricked me, but not even her clever scheming can make me stay in England. There is no way I can give up what I've found in America.''

"And what is that?'' Richard asked, giving Tuke a sharp look, which silenced whatever sarcastic remark he was about to make.

"Freedom to do as I please, and . . . and room to do it in, I suppose you could say. It's hard to explain—everything is so big there, and so cramped and crowded together here. Do you know, I own twenty thousand acres of virgin land in Kentucky, and they expect to tempt me to stay here for the sake of an old manor house and a few hundred acres of used-up land. It's incredible country, Hawke—I wish you could have gone upriver with me to see it. I'll wager that Kentucky alone is almost as big as England, and yet I doubt if there are as many people in it as there are in this little corner of Cornwall. And it's a glorious country, teeming with game—I could shoot a deer every day if I were so inclined, and nobody to say me nay, and there are bears and foxes and wild turkeys—''

"Be that as it may, I confess I fail to see the advantage of living in a country with no people,'' said Richard.

"You're joking!'' Perry exclaimed. "You've been to America—you've seen its beauty—and the continent is so vast, we haven't even begun to find out what's there. How can you be content to live in stuffy old England when there's a whole new world to explore? Where's the spirit of adventure you used to have?''

"I am not aware that I ever had any spirit of adventure," Richard replied.

"You must have had, to do the things you did. You took more chances than any man I've ever known."

"It seemed the only way to achieve my goals." Richard did not bother to explain that having started with nothing, he had needed to seize every opportunity that came his way, no matter what dangers were involved—and it had paid off royally.

"You can't be serious." Perry was looking at him in amazement, but then Perry had started with a silver spoon in his mouth, and a name and a family behind him. For him the risks had been attractive options, to take or not as the mood seized him.

"I am completely serious. I have had enough of what you choose to call adventures for any ten people. And contrary to what you may think, the only dream I have ever had has been to live the quiet life of an English country gentleman. Having now acquired sufficient wealth to turn my dream into reality, I intend to have a thoroughly peaceful life—no excitement, no adventures, no unexpected surprises." He glanced at Tuke, and their eyes met in silent agreement. Richard knew that the older man understood him as no one else ever could.

Tuke had been with him from the beginning, and as a young ensign, had been the only ship's officer to take pity on the skinny boy impressed into the merchant marine, helping him over the rough time he'd had adjusting to the hard work and privations of life at sea.

And the fates in return had decreed that only the two of them should survive the pirates' attack on their ship. As a result, and more to the point, only Tuke shared the memory of what it felt like to be sold into slavery.

For a moment Richard could smell again the stench of sweaty, unwashed bodies in the stuffy slave quarters, hear the rattle of chains as someone shifted in a futile effort to find a comfortable position on the hard-packed dirt floor that served as a communal bed.

As if it were yesterday, Richard could feel the utter exhaustion of his body, driven beyond the limits of endurance. He could feel the never-ending hunger twist his belly unmercifully, hear the crack of the overseer's whip, feel its sting across his shoulders . . .

From a great distance he heard Tuke conversing with Perry, and in his rational mind Richard knew he was safe in England and half a world away from the Caribbean island where they had been forced into slavery. But it was hard to shake off the memories.

He thanked God once again for John Tuke. If their mutual experience was not enough to bind them together, there was also the knowledge that neither of them alone could have found the means of escaping from slavery and then from the island that was actually a more effective prison than the plantation had been.

He had been the one to formulate their plan of escape, but it had been Tuke's strong right arm that had enabled them to carry it off.

"How utterly boring such a life sounds. Every bit as tedious as what my family plans for me." Perry's mouth curled in an impish grin. "It's too bad I can't give you my title, Richard. You would undoubtedly make a superb lord. Far better than I would, I'm afraid. You have the natural arrogance for it."

"As to that, I would not accept the title if you could give it to me instead of to your cousin. I have about as much use for the English aristocracy as I have for unnecessary risks— both are utterly pointless. I suppose in that respect, some of my experiences in America have changed me. I can no longer judge a man according to his rank, as opposed to his achievements."

"I would have thought that would be the logical next step in your dream—first buy a nice manor house, then marry a lord's daughter."

"Me? Marry into the aristocracy? Don't be ridiculous."

"Of course you. Any woman, no matter how high her

degree, would be lucky to have you for a husband, Richard.''

''Ah, but you miss the point Perry. I, on the contrary, do not feel your titled ladies are good enough for me. I admit, I have decided it is time I married and started acquiring heirs, but I have no need of a frivolous wife—a spoiled, feather-headed society miss who would do her best to squander my hard-earned riches and would expect me to be grateful for the privilege of providing her with the blunt to buy herself enough bonnets and dresses and shoes for any ten women.''

''So? What more can you expect from a woman than that she be pleasing to the eye? They are, after all, the weaker sex.''

''That is where you are out, my boy. I think, if the truth were known, many of them are far stronger than us mere males. I knew an incredible woman once. Her name was Molly—'' He caught Tuke's look of surprise that he should mention her name for the first time in years.

''Sounds like a comely Irish maid my uncle used to have. She was well worth remembering, too—biggest, softest blue eyes—''

''She was not Irish.'' Richard did not explain that she had been a mulatto and a slave and far from beautiful. There was no way that Perry's understanding would stretch that far. ''But she was the bravest person I have ever met—and the strongest, and the most practical.'' And the most loving, he added to himself. She had become like a mother to him and had stolen extra food for him from the kitchens where she worked, thereby saving him from the gradual starvation that was the fate of most of the slaves. It was due to her efforts that he had not ended up weak and stunted, but had grown to a man's full size and strength. ''And I am afraid she spoiled me for lesser women.''

''So why didn't you marry this paragon, then? Or wouldn't she have you?''

Richard answered simply, ''She died,'' and Perry's light-hearted smile was wiped from his face. Richard did not go on to explain how she had died, sacrificing her life for him when the escape attempt had almost failed. He had thought he could get all three of them safely away, and when it had become obvious that he could not, she had turned back and sent him on with Tuke. He had never failed at anything since then, but his successes had come too late to help her. Even though he now owned the plantation where he had once been a slave and had freed his fellow slaves as soon as he became their owner, their number did not include Molly.

But he had adjusted years ago to the loss of the only woman who had ever really loved him, and it was pointless to turn this reunion with Perry into a wake. "So what about you? Have you actually come back to England to see your grandmother, or are you secretly hoping to find yourself a suitable wife—perhaps one of those lords' daughters you were trying to foist off onto me?" He had genuine affection for the younger man and he let it show in his smile, which very few people had ever seen.

Perry laughed. "Now that I think of it, I see your point about frivolous society beauties. I misdoubt any of them are ready to appreciate what Kentucky has to offer, nor do I think I would want to waste my energy dragging along any such useless baggage as a wife, no matter how beautiful and enticing she might be."

"You are sure then that you mean to give up the title?"

"I'm sure. I'm an American now. There's no way I could go back to being an Englishman. I'm here for a few months to pay my respects to my grandmother, and then I am set on returning to Kentucky—taking with me as many good Irish horses as I can afford, of course," he added with a grin.

"They will try to talk you out of it, you know."

"I know. But in the end, they'll give in. If worse comes to worst, I shall merely confess—" he hesitated, then continued, "—that I was on the winning side at the battle of New Orleans."

No one spoke for a moment, and Perry looked as if he were already regretting his confession. Finally Richard said mildly, "It might be best for your family if you used some other argument to convince them you are serious."

"I fully intend to. But I am also determined on my course. I . . . uh . . . would be more than pleased if you had the time to accompany me to London—for old time's sake."

"Ah, Tuke, now the truth comes out as to why he has wasted three days trying to find me."

Perry leaped to his feet. "Blast it, Hawke, you're being insulting. I had no ulterior motives for coming here. I just wanted to see an old friend again."

"And having seen me again . . . ?" Richard tried to keep his countenance stern, but he had the feeling he was failing. Tuke, on the other hand, was making no effort to hide his amusement.

"Ah, well . . . ." Perry sat back down again with a sigh. "Having seen you again, I am reminded of how adept you are at getting your friends out of tight spots."

"And?"

"And I think I would sooner face a bear in Kentucky with nothing but a pen knife than sit in a drawing room with my grandmother and tell her I do not intend to stay in England."

"I doubt I would be of much use to you in a social setting, thwarted grandmothers not being in quite the same category as drunken backwoodsmen or riled-up gamblers."

"In the case of this particular grandmother, I must agree—she's much more terrifying. But don't tell me you cannot cope with the social niceties. Remember, I have seen you wooing the mam'selles in New Orleans. You're as dangerous in the drawing rooms as you are in the dueling field, so say you'll come with me—for old time's sake," he pleaded.

"For old time's sake? Or to protect your back when you are routed by superior fire power?"

Perry grinned sheepishly. "You sound as if you've already met Lady Letitia."

"Not I, but I am beginning to believe it might be an interesting experience to meet someone who can cause you to think twice before throwing yourself into a new situation."

"Then you'll come? I'll make it worth your while. I promise to do my best to show you a good time in London."

"Ah, so 'tis a good time you are after. I am sorry to disappoint you, but for that you have come to the wrong place. Our Mr. Carneby would never dream of being involved in anything the least bit amusing. He is much too dour and staid, and thinks of nothing but his ships and counting houses. On the other hand, there is a certain Jasper Trelawney in Penzance, thought by some narrow-minded souls to be a smuggler but actually not a bad sort if his reputation is to be believed, and he definitely knows how to show his friends a good time.''

"Jasper Trelawney, do you say? He does sound like someone I would enjoy meeting, especially if he has gained your approval.''

There was a muffled sound from Tuke, and Perry looked up at him sharply. After a pause he turned to Richard and said wryly, "So that's the way it is . . . . Would this Trelawney perchance be a very near and dear relation to Mr. Carneby of Falmouth?''

There was a chuckle from Tuke, and Hawke smiled, inviting Perry to share the joke. "Some people, if they were to see the two of them together, a most *unlikely* occurrence, to be sure, might remark a certain family resemblance, although the similarity is superficial, Jasper being a wild Cornishman of uncertain background and moderate means.''

There was another pause, and Perry studied him with a considering look upon his face. Finally he spoke. "You know, Richard, if Napoleon were not safely tucked away on St. Helena, I would be suspecting you were a French spy. Surely your business dealings do not demand that you use so many aliases?''

"Have you been gone so long from English society that you have forgotten the very cornerstone upon which it rests? What do you think would be my chances for social acceptance in any proper English village, were it to become widely known that I am merely an adventurer with a murky background?''

"Blast it all, Hawke, you're not simply an adventurer.'' Perry again leaped to his feet and stood glaring down at Richard. "You've a dozen ships, and more than one plantation, and who knows what else. And you've earned it all honestly, whatever crazy risks you may have taken to achieve your success.''

"Ah, Tuke, with that resounding oratory the lad has truly convinced me he is an American, heart and soul.''

Turning away, Perry stalked over to the window and stood staring out.

"Come, come, my dear Lord Westhrop, admit the truth. In England a man is admired only for the wealth he inherits, no matter how he squanders it; it is therefore better for all concerned if society thinks I am a lazy, good-for-nothing scion of a wealthy family than that I have earned my brass by honest toil."

Perry turned back to them, a scowl on his face. "Then I think you had better come back to America with me and let all these hypocrites have the joy of each others' company."

"But I prefer to live here," Richard replied mildly, "so stop scowling and tell me if you have a few days at your disposal to sample the delights of Penzance before you must be off to face the rigors of London."

Perry could not hold back a smile. "I can spare a few days for merry-making with your Jasper Trelawney. Perhaps he would be interested in meeting my grandmother, since I cannot persuade you."

"Ah, but Trelawney, I regret, is more at home rubbing shoulders with smugglers in disreputable dives than he is sipping cups of tea with dowagers in elegant drawing rooms."

"Then I shall use the few days I have here in Cornwall to best advantage, to entice you to London."

The unseasonable warmth of the February day had fled with the setting of the sun, and Cassie hunched her back against the wind, which was now reaching its fingers under her cloak to steal the last warmth from her body. She tried to pull the threadbare fabric more tightly around her, but it was a difficult job to do with only one hand. Yet if she let go of Dobbin's mane, she would be in danger of sliding off his broad back.

It was really too bad that the only saddle they still had was her mother's sidesaddle, while the only horse left in the stables was an ancient plow horse, too old to work in the fields and too broad in the beam for any saddle. He was kept

on only because his four legs could still give her a degree
of freedom and mobility she would not otherwise have had.
Whether from age or inborn good nature, he went willingly
wherever she directed him, although his pace could not be
speeded up, no matter what stratagems she tried.

It would have been easier to endure her present discomfort
if her errand of mercy had been more of a success, but she
had been able to offer nothing —not food nor money, as she
had none herself, nor relief from the pain of the bruises that
covered the woman's arms and face and undoubtedly her
body as well, and that Cassie was positive were the result
of a beating at the hands of the woman's own husband, an
out-of-work miner who wasted what little the family had on
hard drink for himself.

Lost in her thoughts as she was, she made no effort to guide
the ancient horse, but relied on him to get her safely home
as he had so many times before, and was only alerted to the
fact that they had reached the stables when he stopped his
plodding steps and stood waiting patiently for her to
dismount.

But where was Digory? He usually heard them approaching
and was standing ready to help her down. "Digory? I'm
home!" Her voice shattered the stillness, but there was no
answering greeting.

Well, she did not want to wait in the cold any longer, not
when she knew Seffie would have some water heated against
her return. Grasping Dobbin's mane with both hands, she
rolled to her stomach and started sliding toward the ground.
She was about to let go and drop the last little bit, when hands
caught her roughly around the waist.

"Here we go, my pretty. I ain't Digory, but whatever you
wants from him, I can give you."

She was jerked back and held against a hard body that gave
off a rank aroma of stale sweat, beer, and horses. Her
struggles to free herself from the arm that was locked around
her waist were in vain, and in the space of seconds she
acquired a full understanding of what it truly meant to
be a woman at the mercy of a man stronger than she
was.

"Oh, my, it's a feisty one we've caught here. Let's have a look at what'cher hiding under your cloak."

Her hood was jerked off and she opened her mouth to scream, but thick fingers twisted in her hair and forced her head backward until she stopped struggling and stood quietly, her neck bent so far she was afraid if she moved it would snap.

Chapter Two

The man holding Cassie started dragging her toward the stables, telling her in explicit words she only halfway understood just what he intended to do to her once he got her there. She was tensing her body to make one last effort to escape if he even momentarily slackened his grip when she caught a glimpse of a green and gold coach standing in the stable yard.

"I presume my brother the earl is now in residence?" She somehow managed to croak the words out and was released so abruptly she almost fell. Regaining her balance more easily than her dignity, she turned to face her attacker.

Only her brother could have hired such a man as a groom. Mere inches taller than her own five feet, he was squat and broad and resembled nothing so much as a toad. An honest traveler, meeting him upon the road, would doubtless mistake him for a highwayman, in spite of his ill-fitting livery.

The humble, subservient manner he now adopted was spoiled by the hostility that still radiated from his cold eyes.

"I asked you a question," she snapped out, trying to make her voice sound haughty and hoping the cloak hid the fact that she was trembling all over from reaction to the near rape.

"Yes'm, m'lady. The Earl of Blackstone is in residence, if you can call it that." His lip curled slightly, and he made no attempt to hide his contempt for the decaying manor house that stood behind her.

She knew she should not let his insolent manner go by without correction, but she was willing to wait for another day before risking a direct confrontation, since she was not at all sure how long invoking her brother's name would protect her. Nor was she at all certain just how much control her brother had over his minion, who would have seemed more at home in a novel by Mrs. Radcliffe than in this forgotten corner of Cornwall.

"See to my horse," she snapped out curtly. By exercising her total willpower, she was able to retreat in a dignified manner, when all she really wanted to do was run as fast as she could away from her attacker. It was a relief when she slid through the French doors into the library and knew she was hidden from his view.

Her relief was short-lived, however, as it took her only a moment to realize something was amiss there, too—the room was warm.

Her immediate awareness of the fire in the normally unused fireplace gave her a second's warning, enabling her to school her expression and react calmly to the voice that came out of the shadows beside her.

"Ah, my dear sweet sister, I presume. Yes, the resemblance to your mother, God rest her dear departed soul, is even more pronounced, now that you have . . . uh . . . developed, shall we say? And I must say also that I am so glad you came to find me, my dear, before I was forced to the trouble of having you fetched. Indeed, I have been wondering about the strange household you keep here. So far, you are the first living, breathing inhabitant of this pile of damp stones that we have set eyes on since we arrived here. If we had not found these doors open, we might still be waiting on the stoop. Have you given all your servants the same day off by some miscalculation?"

Geoffrey was still the most handsome man she had ever seen in her life. In face and form he resembled their father, who had always been held to be a fine figure of a man, but Geoffrey's light brown hair and hazel eyes came from his mother, the earl's first wife.

She, on the other hand, had her midnight hair and deep blue eyes from their father, but in all other respects was the spitting image of her mother, an accredited beauty who had reigned supreme in London society before becoming the second wife of the Earl of Blackstone.

"The servants left years ago, when you neglected to pay them." Cassie clenched her hands to keep them from trembling.

"One is scarcely aware of the seasons coming and going when one is in London," he said lazily. "Let me see, how long has it been since I was last here?"

"Father died seven years ago in May."

Her brother had not even made a pretense of mourning, but had left for London the day after the funeral, never writing or returning until now.

"So long? My, my, I fear I have neglected you and our dear sister shamelessly." Abruptly, his manner became brusque. "But what is past is past, and we must look to the future. I find I have suddenly developed a tremendous interest, nay, a preoccupation with your well-being. Chloe!" he bellowed suddenly, striding over to the ruins of a once-elegant sofa, which still boasted three legs and undoubtedly at least one or two unbroken springs.

"Chloe!" he thundered again, whacking a pile of scarlet satin and orange feathers that was crumpled there. "Bestir yourself, you lazy slut. I've a job for you."

Slowly the red heap sat up and straightened and adjusted itself until Cassie could see it was a well-padded woman with hair as orange as her feathers, and cheeks as impossibly red as her dress.

"Give me a moment or two, guv, to get me wits about me, and then we can oblige."

"None of that now, you've work to do." He grabbed her hand and jerked her to her feet. "See that?" He pointed to Cassie, who still stood by the window. "Take that upstairs, clean it up, and put a decent dress on it. I want to see what I have to work with, but I find my senses so revolted by the stink of the stables and that depressing rag it's wearing, that I am quite unable to think straight."

There was such an improbable aspect about everything that had happened since she had slid off Dobbin's back, thought Cassie as she was half dragged up the stairs, that she might be excused for wondering if she were still on horseback plodding along toward home, her mind totally involved in a daydream that now had more similarity to a nightmare than to her usual fantasies.

The tub of water was still steaming slightly, and Cassie

knew the unexpected visitors could not have arrived much before herself. Apparently Seffie and Ellen had had enough warning to hide, as there did not seem to be any sounds of hysteria in the background.

"So, you're his lordship's sister." Chloe undid the strings of Cassie's cloak with one quick tug.

"Don't you *dare* touch me!" Cassie backed away, fending off the other woman's hands. "I can undress myself."

Without even losing her smile, Chloe slapped Cassie hard across the face. "Now then, ducks, I'm not too good at explaining things, so let's hope you catch on real quick. Your brother told me to clean you up and make you presentable, and I always do what he tells me to do, and that way things go along nice and smooth. So you don't get to decide whether I give you a bath or not, you just get to decide how you wants it to be—hard or easy—and if you make things hard for me, I can make things real unpleasant for you, don't think I can't."

Her cheek stinging from the impact, Cassie stared at the woman, too stunned to respond.

When Chloe reached out again and started undoing the buttons on Cassie's dress, the younger girl stood quietly, staring straight ahead, her teeth clenched so tightly her jaw hurt.

"I'm not so bad as a lady's maid if I do say so myself. I had me a job once, as abigail to a rich lady. She thought I had real talent, too, especially with her hair." While Chloe talked, her fingers fairly flew, stripping off Cassie's dress. "But then madame found me in the master's bed playing tickle and squeeze, and I was out on the street, although not for long. The master had me settled snug in my own cozy little house before the week was out, he did."

She finished stripping Cassie to the skin, and no amount of pretending on Cassie's part could lessen her embarrassment at finding herself naked in front of another person. Not even her sister had ever seen her without her shift, at least not since they had been very small girls together. As quickly as possible she stepped into the metal tub and sat down, grateful for the meager covering offered by the water.

Chloe poured a dipperful of water over Cassie's head and began rubbing her hair vigorously with soap. "I found the gentlemen much easier to please than the ladies, so I gave up my aspirations to become a dresser."

"So, you prefer to be mistress of a man like my brother, rather than to do honest work?" Cassie was rewarded for her impertinence with a vicious yank on her hair.

She glared at the other woman while the bath water continued to cool slowly in the tub.

Finally Chloe spoke again. "I prefer being an honest whore to being a dishonest hyprocrite like many a fine lady." She smiled at Cassie with patently false good humor. "You do know what a whore is, don't you, ducks? It's a woman what sells herself to a man." Then she threw back her head and howled with laughter.

When the bath was finally over, Cassie was relieved to be left to the task of drying herself while the red-haired woman looked through her wardrobe. "Three dresses? This is the extent of the clothes we have to choose from—three dresses? One black, one brown, and heaven knows what color that rag on the floor is intended to be. And all three of them long-sleeved with buttons up to the neck—what are you, a nun?"

"At least I am not a . . . a . . ." She could not bring herself to use the word the other woman had used. "A *fallen* woman!" she finally blurted out. Even before the other woman reached out and gave her an expert pinch on the arm, Cassie knew that retaliation was sure to be swift and unpleasant, but she had reached the point that she no longer cared.

"Appears like you'll have to wear a dress of mine." Chloe abandoned her attempt to find even one slightly suitable garment hiding itself somehow in the darkest corner of the wardrobe, and started digging around in the bandbox that Cassie had not even noticed on her bed. "Yes, this will do." Chloe pulled out a piece of shimmery blue fabric, so beautiful that Cassie could scarcely hold back an expression of delight.

Any pleasure she might have had at wearing a dress made out of fabric the likes of which she had never seen was destroyed, however, when she slipped it over her head.

"It's a good thing fitted waistlines are not in style these days, or as skinny as you are, we could never adjust a dress of mine to fit the likes of you." Chloe grabbed a handful of the extra material at the waist of the dress and pulled it tighter. "Although you're well enough endowed up front where it counts. Yes, indeed, I do think your brother's going to be in a proper good mood when he sees you in this dress."

Cassie stared at her reflection in the mirror. "Well, think again, because my brother is not going to see me in this dress. I would kill myself before I would allow anyone, even a relative, to see me wearing a garment that makes a mockery of all that is decent and respectable."

All of her brother's servants must have trained under the same master, because Chloe yanked viciously on Cassie's hair until she collapsed backward onto a small stool. A great many pinches on the arm later and she stood once more in front of her mirror while Chloe efficiently pinned up several inches at the bottom of the gown.

As fogged as it was, with the silver peeling off the back in great patches, the mirror still reflected back a tantalizing image of a beautiful young woman, standing straight and slender like a shimmering blue flame, her hair arranged elaborately on top of her head, with one long ebony curl artfully escaping to emphasize the pure whiteness of her neck and shoulders.

Unfortunately, the dress was cut so low in front that Cassie was afraid to take a deep breath for fear she would pop right out. "I refuse to wear this dress one step outside my room," she said in the voice she reserved for telling her sister and her step-mother that she was done listening to any arguments. When she spoke with such authority, they knew it was pointless even to try to change her mind.

Chloe evidently did not recognize the futility of continuing to present her case. Finishing her task, she stood up and, hands on her hips, glared down at Cassie.

"Will you stop arguing! Talking back to me has earned you an arm that's black and blue and still you won't be reasonable. Well, this is the last warning you're going to get from me. If you're stupid enough to cross your brother, then you'll *really* rue the day you were born, and I guarantee, if you make him come fetch you, then don't be surprised if he drags you down the stairs backward by your hair.''

Doing her best not to pay any heed to the woman's threats, Cassie remained standing where she was, staring at the image of herself in the mirror, an image she could not in any way relate to the person she knew herself to be. She might have been staring at a total stranger, so alien did she appear. Nor could she take pleasure in the way the blue fabric shimmered when she moved, because of the horrible expanse of—of chest that was displayed.

In the end it was not Chloe's warning that induced her to overcome her reluctance to leave her room, but the memory of her brother's petty cruelties when they were children that caused her to decide it would indeed be folly to provoke him into a needless display of temper.

The shawl she found to drape around her neck was also a factor in her decision to do as she had been told, and it was actually only a few minutes after Chloe's descent that Cassie found herself entering the library, which was now brightly lit with dozens of candles in the wall sconces. It would appear, in fact, that every candle in the house had been brought into this one room, in an extravagant waste unparalleled since the days of her father's entertaining.

Staring at her brother from a few feet away, Cassie realized she had been wrong to think him still as handsome as ever. In the better light now available she could see the marks of dissipation that were already quite evident on his face, and she was willing to wager that not too many years in the future only a memory of his good looks would remain.

''So, Geoffrey, what brings you home at last? Come on a repairing lease? Or hiding from your creditors?'' Her voice was light and mocking, her resolve not to antagonize him forgotten.

''Why, my dear, I was forced to come. My man of business wrote me the most extraordinary letter. Said there was nothing left here to sell. So of course I was obliged to leave my rather pressing engagements in town to travel down here and see for myself.''

Now her brother was running true to form again, thinking of himself first and foremost—in fact thinking of no one's wishes but his own.

"And having seen for yourself that your long journey was in vain, I assume your visit will not be unduly prolonged." Her voice held only a faint echo of the bitterness she'd felt for years at the repeated visits of Jackson Thwaite, her brother's man of business, an apologetic, cringing little worm of a man, who had nevertheless managed to ferret out and remove everything that could possibly be sold, not concerning himself unduly with such niceties as differentiating between items belonging to the estate and items Cassie had inherited directly from her mother, the second wife of the late earl. The only things not carted off by Thwaite were a few broken pieces of furniture that Cassie and Ellen had retrieved from the attic.

"In vain? But my dear Cassiopeia, whatever gave you the idea that my trip was not successful? On the contrary, the results have exceeded my wildest expectations, and I fully intend to be handsomely rewarded for the jolting about I had to endure to come here."

"Rewarded?"

"Why, yes. I find Thwaite has quite overlooked the most valuable asset left at my disposal."

"Not—not the house!" All the anger and resentment drained out of Cassie, leaving her limp with fear. "But what could we do—where could we go if you sold the house?"

He smiled at her with genuine mirth, as if he were amused by some secret joke. "No, no, Cassie, there is no money to be had from the house. It is mortgaged to the hilt, I am afraid. In fact, were the truth known, I have mortgaged it twice over, and I am afraid that mortgaging it a third time would be pushing even my luck a little too far. Guess again."

Cassie was not about to fall into his trap. She knew full well that his present amiability was only skin-deep, and that even now, as a grown man, he would not pass up any opportunity to tease and torment her the way he had done so regularly during her childhood.

Instead of continuing to try to divine his purpose in coming to Cornwall, she walked carefully over to the tall French doors through which she had entered earlier and stood pretending to look out into the darkness. Actually, she was watching her brother's reflection in the glass and was therefore not caught by surprise when his voice spoke behind her, only inches away from her ear.

"Don't wish to play guessing games anymore, little sister? I have to admit, I have found other games much more interesting, also."

His reflection did not show the ravages of time, and Cassie again saw the handsome older brother who had seemed so godlike in her childhood. Why she had been taken in then by his superficial good looks, she could not say, since her memories of him were uniformly unpleasant. Try as she might, she could not dredge up the memory of even one small act of kindness on his part, not for her nor for their little sister nor for any of the servants, who at that time had still run the house with clockwork precision.

The best she had settled for then had been to be ignored, so that was the most she could hope for now—that he would take whatever he had come for and depart, leaving them to manage as best they could.

And really, they could manage without him. They were, thanks to Digory's willingness to supply what they could not grow themselves, reasonably well fed, which was, after all, the most basic necessity. And they still had an attic full of broken bits of furniture to burn in the fireplace.

With one finger under her chin and absolutely no force, her brother turned her to face him. "You see, Cassie, what Thwaite quite overlooked . . . " His finger slid down her neck and tugged until he managed to dislodge the scarf from its place.

Somehow she found it less demeaning to let the scarf slither to the floor than to make a futile grab for it, which would undoubtedly have afforded her brother a good laugh at her expense. But no amount of willpower could stop the flush that crept up to her shoulders and beyond to her face, and it was only by clenching her fists that she was able to keep her hands from automatically covering the expanse of rosy skin now exposed to his view.

"Is you," he finally concluded.

She looked at him blankly, her mind in total confusion, unable to make any sense out of what he had just said.

"I am sorry, I do not quite understand what you . . ." her voice trailed off, as her brain suddenly grasped the meaning of his words.

"What do you mean, me?" she whispered, her throat tightening up so much she had trouble talking.

His laughter rang in her ears. "Why, my dear, sweet, saintly sister, is it not obvious? I intend to take you back to London with me and sell you to the highest bidder."

Cassie clutched at her brother's sleeve in desperation. "What do you mean? You cannot sell me—I am your sister. I am the daughter of an earl. Even your reputation would not survive such infamy."

"Ah, so you have heard of my reputation even here in the back of beyond. Not to worry. I am sure the old biddies in London will thoroughly approve of my actions. After all, what could be more suitable than a loving brother sacrificing to give his beautiful sister a Season in London and doing his best to help her form an eligible connection? And if you think they would disapprove of a very large marriage settlement being the sole criterion for eligibility, then there you are out. On the contrary, I could be sure of receiving their censure were I to allow you to throw yourself away on a penniless nobody."

"You would marry me off to anyone with enough money to line your pockets?"

"Not as things now stand. I admit, I had not planned on taking you to London. I had thought to take you directly to Leeds or Manchester, where I could have conducted a private and very discreet auction among some of the merchants, whose pocketbooks are as fat as they are, and whose desire to hold onto what they have accumulated through trade is secondary only to their desire to marry above their station."

"You would marry me off to a . . . a tradesman?" Nothing Cassie had experienced this evening shocked her as much as her brother's last statement. She might be forced to live on the brink of total proverty with very few hopes of the situation's ever improving, but one thing had always given her the strength to go on, and that was the knowledge of who she was—she was Lady Cassiopeia Anderby, daughter of the Earl of Blackstone, and as such she could hold her head up in the most exalted company.

Never, *never* could she bring herself to stoop so low as to marry into trade, not even to enrich herself, and certainly not to enrich her brother. She would—she would throw herself into the pond, before she would do anything so degrading.

Her brother was still smiling, as if her reaction had amused him. "You're not paying proper attention, my sweet, delectable sister. I said that was what I had *intended* to do, before I made the acquaintance of your not inconsiderable charms." His eyes dropped to her bosom, and this time she was unable to prevent her hands from flying up to cover the parts of her anatomy left exposed by that awful woman's dress.

"No, no, my dear sister, with beauty of face and form such as you possess, and with a name as old and respected as ours, we can aim as high as we wish—in fact, money and title are not enough. A mere baronet need not apply, for example."

For a moment Cassie was tempted. The thought of a family—of having children and security—made her think such a bargain as her brother was proposing would be as much to her advantage as to his, but then she remembered what it really meant to be married.

She had seen too many women mistreated by their husbands—women beaten, abused, neglected. She had heard too many stories of wives cast aside when their husbands lost interest, of women married for their money and then forced to endure the humiliation of their husbands' mistresses.

Ellen, her step-mother, had once even confessed that in some ways it was a relief to be a widow. She had immediately retracted her statement, of course, and assured Cassie that the married state was truly the only one a woman should aspire to.

Even were Cassie to accept without question that any marriage was preferable to spinsterhood, still Chloe's mocking words echoed in her mind. "Do you know what a whore is? It's a woman who sells herself to a man."

That is what she would be if she allowed Geoffrey to carry out his scheme, Cassie realized. She would be selling herself to a strange man, giving him the right to see her naked, to touch her—to *paw* at her—to do heaven knows what unspeakable things to her, in return for giving her his support and the protection of his name. An unknown man would be buying her body for the price of a few pretty frocks and bits of jewelry, and she would be nothing more than his legal whore, bought and paid for.

"No, I will not do what you are proposing." She spoke flatly, with no emotion in her voice. "And you cannot make me participate in such a revolting plan, either. I shall make faces at any man who looks at me twice." She crossed her eyes and let her mouth slack open.

Her brother laughed. "Then you prefer Manchester? I am sure I could find a rich factory owner there who is willing to take an old sow to wife if the porker only has a title."

"Then I shall . . ." Cassie cast her mind around desperately, trying to hit on some weapon that could be counted on to quell the ardor of the most persistent suitor. "I shall start a rumor that the doctors are certain my spells of insanity will gradually increase as I grow older." She could not keep from smiling in triumph at the beauty of her plan.

Her brother sighed, but something about his sigh seemed phony, as if he were not yet ready to concede defeat. "Then I am afraid you leave me no other choice." Before she could congratulate herself on the ease of her victory, he continued, "It will have to be your sister, then."

"There you are out, also," she said smugly. "Seffie is too young. You may have forgotten, but she is a full five years younger than I, and she is only now just turned fifteen. And," Cassie added, "she is terrified of her own shadow, and could not possibly manage to attract a husband."

"Who mentioned anything about a husband for her? Living

here as isolated as you have, perhaps you did not know that there is quite a good market on the Continent for terrified fifteen-year-old virgins? I assure you, I have it on good authority that in certain cultures a bonus is paid for blondes, and I have a vague memory that sweet little Persephone is quite fair, am I not right?''

Cassie had known her brother was not a particularly nice person—that he was self-centered, inconsiderate, greedy, and mean—but she had not had any inkling of how low he had sunk into depravity. At some time he had evidently crossed the line into real wickedness, of the sort she had only heard about from the pulpit on Sunday.

"No answer, my dear Cassie? I leave the choice to you, then. You may have your Season in London and marry a man of my choosing, or you must let your sister take her chances on the open market.''

"You are despicable. You are the most miserable excuse for a gentleman that it has ever been my misfortune to meet.''

His complacent smile was not dislodged by the most dreadful things she could think of to say to him. "Come, come, my dear," he said finally. "We must not waste any more time discussing my character. What is it to be then? Will you join me in London, or shall I start making arrangements—''

"Yes, yes, I will come to London," she interrupted, not wishing to hear again what could happen to Seffie if she herself refused to cooperate.

"And you will smile sweetly and not try any tricks to discourage your suitors? I must warn you that one chance is all you will get, and if you have not managed to snare a rich title by the end of the Season, it will be off to Leeds with you. I am presently but one step ahead of my creditors, but they will be more than willing to hold off a little longer when they see what a lovely asset I have in your person.''

Before Cassie could utter another protest, the orange-haired woman returned.

"I have checked all the rooms, m'lord, like you asked. There is nothing here that I'd give two shillings for, nor yet there isn't. Thwaite has been most thorough.''

"Then, my pet, I think it is time for us to be off." He started for the door where Chloe waited.

"You are going back to London?" Whatever Cassie had expected, it had not been this calm leave-taking.

Her brother paused at the door and looked back at her. "Surely you do not expect me to spend even one night in this rotting mausoleum, do you, my dear? I have already reserved rooms at the Red Goose, and I shall return on the morrow to make the final arrangements."

With that he was gone, leaving nothing behind to show that he had actually been there and that she had not merely dreamed the whole episode except the dress she was wearing, the candles burning down, and the fire crackling in the fireplace.

In this instance Cassie found it hard to enjoy the pleasant experience of being able to see clearly, since all the myriad tiny flames did was show the dismal state of abandonment and decay that had destroyed a once magnificent room. Not a single one of the many books that had formerly lined the shelves now remained, and the only furniture left in the room besides the broken sofa was a very shaky end table, which now gave precarious support to two candelabra.

Unable to hold back a bitter thought of what the morrow would bring, Cassie moved quickly to snuff out the candles nearest her. The light her brother had enjoyed tonight would be paid for by an endless string of lost evenings, when having no candles at all would force them to retire to their beds with the setting of the sun.

But no, there would be no more evenings here. Geoffrey was taking them to London, where the darkness would be banished by hundreds of candles—wax candles, undoubtedly, not tallow like these—and every one of them paid for by the sale of her person.

Leaving the rest of the candles burning, she picked up one of the candelabra with a hand that trembled in spite of all her efforts to control it and went in search of her step-mother and sister. She delayed only long enough to pull the pins out of her hair and change back into her own dress, leaving the exotic gown in a silvery-blue puddle on the floor.

She passed room after empty room on her way—rooms that once had served a purpose, rooms now stripped to the bare walls to feed her brother's voracious appetite. And soon she herself would be a living sacrifice to his insatiable greed.

Chapter Three

Finally reaching the abandoned schoolroom, Cassie tapped gently on the panel that concealed the priest's hole. "Everything is all right, Seffie. It is safe to come out now."

The panel slid open the merest crack—only far enough for the people hiding inside to be sure it was she, and that she was alone, but upon ascertaining this, her sister emerged and threw herself into Cassie's arms.

"Oh, it was awful. Some strangers came and pounded on the door, and then they broke into the house. They have been wandering around through all the rooms. We heard their footsteps. It is indeed fortunate you did not return earlier, for you would of a certainty have fallen into their clutches."

There was little point in relating to her sister and her stepmother what had passed between Geoffrey and herself. Ellen was totally ineffectual in any situation that called for positive action, and she had raised Seffie to be equally ineffectual. So instead, Cassie forced a smile and tried to keep her voice cheerful, hoping her step-mother would not notice anything was wrong.

"It was no strangers, my dears, but rather Geoffrey, come home to see us at last."

"Geoffrey? Here?" Ellen's dubious tone of voice was an indication that she had not entirely forgotten the spiteful ways by which her step-son had indicated his disapproval of his father's third wife.

"Yes, he has come to take us back to London so I may have a Season."

"London—he has come to take us to London for the Season?" There were tears forming in Ellen's eyes. "We are saved, Seffie. Saints be praised, we are saved." She took a dainty handkerchief out of her sleeve and wiped her face.

"Where is the dear boy? I must thank him myself. He has come to rescue us from this desolate place. And to think I have so misjudged him all these years." She hurried to the door.

"There is no need to rush. He has gone to the Red Goose for the night and will be back tomorrow, or so he says."

"Oh, of course, of course, to be sure. One could not expect him to manage on such meager hospitality as we can offer him here. London! Just think of it, Cassie—you will have a Season. Oh, how I have racked my brains to try to come up with a way for you to be presented, and now, like a messenger from heaven, Geoffrey has come to offer you your chance. Oh, my, did he say when we would be leaving? Are we going with him or by post? Has he rented a house for the Season?"

Any unrealistic expectation Cassie might have had that Ellen would make a push to help her escape from the untenable position her brother had put her in was dashed by her step-mother's obvious readiness to forgive Geoffrey anything, so long as he was willing to take them back to London and away from Cornwall, which Ellen had always stigmatized as being a barbaric place, totally unfit for civilized people.

Cassie finally escaped from the fluttering excitement of her step-mother and went to find the one person she knew she could count on to be on her side. Wrapping herself in her cloak but not bothering to light a lantern, she resolutely made her way out of the house and back to the stables, the moon providing her with all the illumination she required to pick her way across the paving stones.

She was a little afraid that Digory might have gone out on another smuggling run, but was reassured to find him rubbing down Dobbin, who was placidly chewing his ration of oats.

"Digory, my brother has come back."

"So I noticed. His groom was sniffing around the stables this evening like a blooming exciseman."

"He did not find your room?" Involuntarily she glanced at the rough wall that Digory had built across the end of the stable years ago. It looked no different from any of the other walls, but concealed behind it was a room that, although not large, was adequate to meet his needs.

"It would take a sharper eye than his to notice the discrepancy between the outside of the building and the inside. But on the other hand, it was indeed our good fortune that there were no kegs of brandy under the straw for him to find."

"Oh, I had not thought of that. He might have notified the preventatives."

"More likely he would have merely helped himself to a keg or two. But as chance would have it, there was nothing for him to find in the stable but Dobbin, so you needn't get upset about what trouble there might have been."

"That is not precisely why I am upset." She had not realized it would be so hard to ask Digory for anything. They'd had a private agreement for years, that Digory could use their stables as his headquarters, and in return he would supply them with meat for their table, but this was the first time she had attempted to alter what had been essentially a business relationship between them. "I was wondering if I might perhaps ask you . . . a favor?"

"I cannot promise anything until I know the nature of the favor, but you may feel free to ask, and I will do what I think best."

Her relief was overwhelming, as she did not doubt for a minute that he would be able to think of some way to thwart Geoffrey's plans. Never did she anticipate that having heard what Geoffrey had in mind for her, Digory would think it best for her to go to London and try her utmost to make a reasonable match.

"But he is only forcing me to do this in anticipation of the funds he expects to wring from my future husband. He sees me as the means of settling his debts."

"For whatever reason, 'tis the best opportunity that is likely to come your way for you to catch yourself a respectable husband."

"But I do not want a husband. I do not want to get married. I have never wanted to get married." She truly did not, but how could she get a man to understand that a woman might prefer to remain single?

"Then what do you want? How do you plan to support yourself if not by taking a husband? And how do you intend to find a husband if you refuse to go to London? What marriage prospects do you have, living here as isolated as you are?"

"I do not know," she admitted, feeling physically ill at the mere thought of a husband. "I just want things to go along as they are until something—"

"Until what?" Digory interrupted her. "Until your stepmother dies, and even her meager jointure is cut off?"

"How can you talk so casually about Ellen dying?"

He ignored her remark and continued his attack. "By then you will probably be middle-aged and beyond the point of being able to attract a man."

"I will not need anyone to support me if I get a job."

"And if the streets were paved with gold, we would all be rich. Just what job do you think you can do?"

She considered for a moment. "I know how to manage a household. I could become a housekeeper."

"You have not the faintest clue as to how to run a house. All you know is how to survive on next to nothing, which would be of little help to you in directing servants. Besides which, unless you found an establishment consisting solely of females, you would be seduced within a sennight."

"Then I shall be a smuggler. I know how to sail a boat. You taught me yourself." She eyed her companion with disfavor as he leaned against the broad side of the horse and shook with silent laughter.

"I took you sailing a few times when you were fourteen," he finally managed to say. "Not quite the same thing as teaching you to sail. You could not begin to handle a boat on your own; there simply is not enough of you."

"I am bigger now than I was then. Indeed, I have grown immensely since then."

"Aye, you have grown all right," he looked at her with open approval, "but you are not an inch taller today than you were then."

She crossed her arms defensively in front of her chest, annoyed that everyone seemed to have decided that the best topic for discussion today was how far she stuck out in front.

"I thought you, of all people, would be willing to help me."

"I, of all people? What makes you think I, *of all people*, should want to help you?"

"Because I have always thought that you are really . . . that I am your . . ." She started over again. "I have thought for years that you are probably my . . ." She looked to him for help, but he waited impassively for her to say it. "When you are clean-shaven and all dressed up in your fancy clothes, you look so much like the portrait of my father taken when he was a young man, that I just assumed . . . that you are my brother," she finished in a rush.

His glance was shuttered, and she could not read his thoughts. "So you have figured that out, have you? Well, it has never been any secret who my father was."

"I thought, perhaps, that with the relationship between us—"

He interrupted before she could go on. "I am afraid you have been laboring under a misapprehension. Although I will admit to having found our association beneficial, it has been as much to your advantage as it has to mine. But in truth, the fact of the matter remains that I feel no more responsibility toward you than I do toward any of the other numerous progeny of our illustrious parent."

"Other?" Cassie looked at him in bewilderment, which changed to shock as he went on.

"Surely you do not think your father limited his activities to my mother, do you? I assure you, he did his best to scatter his seed far and wide. Were I to feel responsible for all my brothers and sisters, I would be supporting half the country-side." At her shocked reaction, he relented a little. "I exaggerate, my dear. Actually, I doubt if there are more than a dozen or so bastards in the immediate neighborhood who can properly call the late earl papa."

"A dozen?"

"Or thereabouts. Interesting, is it not, that he only

managed to have three legitimate children, and it took him three wives to accomplish even that much?''

The humor of the situation escaped Cassie, since she now realized she could expect no favors from Digory, at least none based on their relationship. And she had nothing else to offer to induce him to come to her aid.

Unable to think what to do, she remained silent, until finally he said quietly, ''It is not such a bad future your brother has lined up for you. You really have no choice, you must realize, but to marry to advantage. You will come to like the married state well enough, I am sure, and it will also put you in a position to help your sister find a husband of her own when the time comes. Have you considered your obligation to provide for her?''

''Of course I have considered her. I told you what Geoffrey threatened to do if I did not cooperate. Do you think I would even consider going to London if not to save her from Geoffrey?''

''The best protection you can give her is to marry a husband willing to let your sister and your step-mother live with you. Then in a few years, you will be in a position to sponsor her come-out.''

''And suppose my husband is someone like Geoffrey?''

''Then marry him and put poison in his soup. If you do it right, you can end up a rich widow while you are still young enough to buy yourself the husband you want.''

''But I do not *want* a husband. Men are all beasts.'' She turned and ran out of the stable, leaving a very thoughtful ''beast'' behind.

Picking up the currycomb from where he had dropped it in the straw, he began once more to groom the old horse.

He had not been telling the truth when he had told Cassie he did not care what plans her brother made for her. He cared very much. On the other hand, he had not been lying when he said he felt nothing for his other assorted half-brothers and half-sisters. For the most part they were a common lot, although none of the others quite reached the depths of depravity that Geoffrey had managed to sink to.

Cassie alone had always been special to him, partly because

of her courage and intelligence, but also because of her capacity to care for other people. In that way she had reminded him of her mother, whom he had twice had occasion to meet before she had died, and whom he had never forgotten. She had been a lady in the truest sense of the word, and along with the kind of beauty that could stop a man dead in his tracks, she had also passed on to her daughter a degree of courage and compassion that were a rare combination.

From a discreet distance he had watched Cassie growing up, in some inexplicable way proud to be related to her, but he had not actually gotten involved in her life until the old earl had died and he had heard rumors to the effect that the new earl had run off to London, abandoning Cassie to her own resources, her step-mother being more of an encumbrance than a help.

In a moment of sentimentality, he had stepped into her life and had taken upon himself the responsibility of seeing to it that she had sufficient food to eat and that she did not suffer the usual fate of a young girl alone in the world with no male protector.

His bargain with her to use the stables in return for providing her with meat for her table had served its purpose, and she had arrived at a marriageable age with her innocence intact, and without realizing that she could ride safely around the neighborhood only because the word was out that anyone bothering her in any way would have to answer to him.

Unfortunately, having successfully managed things so far, he had found himself at a standstill for the last two years. He had been trying ever since she turned eighteen to figure out some way to find Cassie a suitable husband, and while he would not have thought to approach Geoffrey on the subject, he could not but think it was providential that the wayward earl had appeared so opportunely on the scene.

Cassie might think she would be happier living alone, but Digory had no doubt that once she got to London she would like it well enough, just as he had no doubt that with the proper husband she would adjust quickly to the married state.

On the other hand, despite Cassie's earlier self-confidence that she could tackle any job, she was, in fact, remarkably young and inexperienced in the ways of men, and Geoffrey seemed quite prepared to marry her off to an old lecher, provided said lecher's purse strings were adequate for Geoffrey to hang on.

"It would appear, Dobbin my boy, that the time has come for me to go to London myself, to see about investing some of my ill-gotten gains in a more reputable business."

The horse turned his massive head and stared at Digory.

"So you think that sounds rather tame? Well, to be honest, so is smuggling, now that old Boney is safely locked away and Englishmen are again running tame around Paris."

Moreover, Digory considered while he fetched some fresh hay, if he went to London now, he would not only have the opportunity to watch over his little Cassie, but he would also have the pleasure of observing her discover her own talents for setting the hearts of all the young lords in turmoil.

He wondered if she had the faintest idea how beautiful she was. He had done his best to avoid emphasizing the fact. In spite of the temptation to see her in garments designed to enhance her beauty, he had resisted giving her any of the silks he smuggled in, deeming the made-over dresses her step-mother provided her with to be an additional deterrent to the local bucks.

"Digory?"

He turned to see Cassie standing calmly in the doorway of the stables, no sign of her earlier emotions on her face.

"Yes?"

"Will you please take care of Dobbin for me while I am gone?"

He nodded his head briefly. "I will make whatever arrangements are necessary."

"Thank you." She turned and vanished again into the night.

Yes, all things considered, he had definitely earned the pleasure of watching her emerge from her chrysalis and try her wings. And if anything happened to her—if someone decided to try clipping her wings—why then he would be on hand to give them a lesson in the proper way to treat a lady.

* * *

"What say you, John, shall we accompany the reluctant Lord Westhrop to London?" The evening had been an enjoyable one for all concerned, replete with good food and pleasant reminiscences. Having tucked their most welcome but by now slightly inebriated guest into bed, Richard Hawke and John Tuke were enjoying a last few moments of relaxation beside the fire before they too retired for the night.

"I would not be averse to the idea. I confess, I have always had a certain fondness for our young friend, and might wish he could be content to remain on this side of the Atlantic."

"He is not that much younger than we are."

"In years, perhaps not, but in experiences . . ."

"Ah, if experience is to be the measure of a man's age, I doubt not but what I am eighty in the shade."

There was a comfortable silence between them as they contemplated the flickering fire, each lost in his own thoughts, before Richard spoke again. "Yes, I am inclined to think that the time is right for Richard Hawke to emerge from the shadows and begin his life as a proper English country gentleman, enjoying the sights of London with his friends as any provincial hick might be expected to do."

"I find the label 'provincial' an incongruous one when applied to you, Richard, never having seen you at a loss, no matter what the setting."

"Not even when I was a callow youth on board the good ship *Golden Dreams*?"

"Not even then. You had something that set you apart from the others. I do not know what to call it other than a kind of determination. And my early estimates of your abilities have proven to be correct, although even I am sometimes astounded at how far you have come."

"We have come together, my friend, and our journey is almost over. Yes, I do believe the time has come for the last step. We can use our time in London to build acceptable backgrounds for Richard Hawke and John Tuke."

The silence that greeted his last remark was no longer

comfortable, and Richard turned to see a look of distress on his friend's face.

"If you mislike the plans I make, you have only to say so, John. I would not like to think I am forcing you to go against your own desires."

His companion smiled wryly, as if in self-mockery. "I suspect that in this case, you will deem it in my best interests to apply a little gentle coercion, which will nonetheless be impossible for me to withstand."

"I had not known you thought me such a fearful ogre. Pray enlighten me as to what absurd ambitions you cherish that I must talk you out of."

The older man stared into his glass for several minutes before he finally spoke. "I wish to continue as your valet in London." Receiving no response to his statement, he finally looked up and met Richard's amused glance.

"Ah, John, how well you know me. I do believe you are the only person alive who can predict what I will do."

"Then you do intend to dissuade me?" At Richard's nod, John continued. "Is there nothing I can say that will convince you I am serious in this request?"

"Perhaps if you explained yourself more fully?"

"It is not easy to explain, and I am not sure how well I understand it myself, but I will make an effort. My father was a vicar, you see. He is dead now. I made inquiries when we returned to England. I have no doubts but what he was sincerely mourned by his little flock when he passed on to his reward. He was a very *good* man, you see, who managed to find some goodness in everyone around him.

"I am not completely sure he even believed in the existence of true evil, and such petty sinners as he had to deal with in his parish were assumed by him to be merely misguided, rather than fundamentally bad. He wished me to take orders also, but I was mad for the sea, so he made the necessary arrangements to secure me a position on a merchant ship."

"Perry was right. I have dragged you down unforgivably."

"No, Richard, on the contrary. You have not only saved my life on numerous occasions, but you have also saved my sanity. I confess, I thought of nothing much those first few weeks of captivity except finding the necessary means to put a period to my existence.''

"I would never have allowed you to do that.''

"I was aware of that, and it played a large part in my decision to cast my lot with you, young as you were. And I have never regretted that decision.''

Staring into the fire with unseeing eyes, his friend became silent, as if his thoughts were in a distant place, and Richard realized that the stripes on their backs and the marks of the irons on their wrists and ankles were not the only scars they both carried. And sometimes the scars on the mind were the slowest to heal.

"But I am getting ahead of my story now,'' Tuke continued softly, "and I must go back to when we first met on board ship. There was more of my father in me at that time than I was willing to admit, and on first meeting you, I immediately placed you in the category of misguided sinners, and I determined to lead you back into the paths of righteousness.''

He turned toward Richard with a rueful smile on his face. "I was not so blind to reality, you see, as to think that you were a total innocent when you were dragged on board. I was reasonably certain you had not spent your early years entirely on the right side of the law.''

"In that you were correct.''

"Where I erred was in my belief in a world without true wickedness. I have since discovered that there is such evil in the world and it is ofttimes so much more powerful than the good that it frequently makes me doubt my father's unshakable belief that the righteous will triumph over the unrighteous, and justice prevail over the unjust.''

"While I appreciate your taking me into your confidence, John, I am unable to see how this relates to your wishing to continue as my valet.''

"As to that, I fear it is sheer cowardice. I simply feel more comfortable continuing under your protection, and I do not yet have any great confidence in my ability to survive long on my own in such a wicked world as this one.'' The self-mocking smile on his lips was not reflected in his eyes, which were dead serious.

"You wrong yourself when you admit to cowardice. Remember, I have already seen numerous examples of your bravery."

His friend shook his head sadly. "Ah, Richard, it is one thing to face physical danger bravely. It is another matter entirely to face evil with no spiritual armor. Were my father alive today, and did I explain myself fully to him, I am sure he would denounce me as a wicked blasphemer, for, truth to tell, I would sooner have you as my shield and defender than our Savior himself."

"Nevertheless—"

"As I predicted, Richard? The iron hand in the velvet glove?"

"As you predicted. I cannot allow you to continue in such a subservient role as my valet, and the sooner you accept the equality that is your due, the better it will be for both of us. As I have always told you, the half of such wealth as we have acquired belongs to you, and I have fully meant what I said. We can, however, compromise to the extent that I might introduce you to others as my secretary—perhaps a distant relation? That would not utterly limit your options and would make your later rise to riches more credible.

"I do not doubt but that the day will come when you see me as a mere mortal, with all the normal human weaknesses, rather than as . . . er . . . your savior, as it were. . . . Confound it, John, that image you have of me is too much to swallow. Now I must strive to keep my boots on in your company, lest you discover my feet of clay."

"What do you mean to do, my dear?" The cook paused in her packing and looked at the newest addition to Lord Parkhurst's household.

Annie Elizabeth Ironside did not answer for a moment. Then she shoved aside some clothes and sat down on the bed. "Do? Why, continue on in service here, of course."

"You should not even think of staying in this household, now that the wicked Earl of Blackstone is taking over the premises for the Season. I have always said that gambling is evil, and this certainly proves the case. I cannot think what

Lord Parkhurst was about, wagering the use of this house on the turn of a card. And then to have included all of us servants in the bargain—work of the devil, that was, and the devil was in the cards that night, too.''

She folded another voluminous apron and stuffed it into her bag. ''Well, take my advice and find yourself another job. Lord Parkhurst may have gambled us away like so many shillings, but we are not slaves to be bought and sold like that. I advise you to come away, also, and find another position in a more respectable household.''

''I think I must stay and take my chances,'' Annie replied simply.

''Well, it shall be on your own head, then,'' the cook muttered. ''I, at least, have done my Christian duty by warning you.'' She forced the bag shut and with Annie's help, fastened the straps. Pausing in the doorway as if she were going to say something more, the cook only shook her head sadly before she departed.

Left behind, Annie threw herself down on the bed and contemplated the unfortunate situation in which she now found herself. The cook was not the only servant leaving the household. In fact, only a mere handful were intending to stay.

Annie's reason for not leaving was as valid as any. Married at sixteen to her childhood sweetheart, she had left the Highlands to follow the drum in Portugal and Spain, only to lose her husband at the Battle of Waterloo.

Since then she had lived a precarious, hand-to-mouth existence in London, the small number of sewing jobs she was able to take in only slowing down the gradual process of starving to death. The position here as an upstairs maid had seemed an incredible piece of good luck, and she had thought it meant her worries were over.

Unfortunately, Lord Parkhurst had gambled her future away. With no letters of recommendation from previous employers, she could not, like most of the others, simply apply for another position. And having worked here only a fortnight, she could not impress any potential employer with her vast experience.

The same thoughts kept going around and around in her head, as she tried to think of some way out of the mess she was in. Finally she drifted off into a light doze.

She was not sure what woke her, but when she opened her eyes a strange man was smiling down at her. It did not take the cook's description of him for Annie to recognize the wicked earl, for his depravity was clearly written on his face.

"Well, well, what a delicious morsel Lord Parkhurst has left behind for me. I am only surprised he did not see fit to take you with him. I, on the other hand, have never been one to resist temptation, and I have always had a particular weakness for red hair. Yours is an especially enticing color, my sweet. Tell me, have you a temper to suit your fiery locks?"

He reached out a hand to touch her hair, but Annie was up off the bed in a flash. Unfortunately, the earl managed to keep himself positioned between her and the door, blocking her escape. When he took a step toward her, she immediately made a feint to the right, then darted to the left.

The room was too small and the earl was too quick for her, and he easily caught her around the waist. "You may struggle all you wish, my sweet. It just makes the pleasure sweeter."

Annie had no intention of struggling ineffectually. Her husband had taught her a better means of defense, which she had used on several occasions since his death.

In a second the knife she always carried concealed upon her person was in her hand, the tip pressing against the earl's ribs.

Shock and surprise intermingled on his face when he jerked away from her. He looked down at the slash in his jacket, as if not believing the blood that oozed out. Then he began to curse dispassionately.

Holding the knife the way her husband had taught her, Annie waited for his next move.

"You should not have cut me," he said, cold anger replacing the hot lust in his eyes.

"It is nothing, a mere scratch. But you may consider it

a warning. The next time I shall not hesitate to drive it home.'' Annie forced her voice to be as cold as his.

''Do you think I cannot take that knife away from you?''

''Perhaps. You may try, in any case. Do you think I cannot come into your room some night and slip a knife between your ribs while you are sleeping?''

Unexpectedly, he smiled. ''We are more alike than I had realized, my sweet. I think we will do very well in bed, once you are over your girlish reluctance. It is fortunate I am a patient man. I can wait awhile until you realize we are two of a kind.''

To her relief, he took his departure, holding one hand to his ribs to stop the bleeding.

Without hesitation she rushed to bolt the door behind him.

Chapter Four

The stagecoach hit a larger bump than usual, and Cassie was thrown against the man to her left. She immediately jerked herself back into an upright position and clutched her cloak more tightly around her.

London was going to be an absolute diasaster. Any slight hopes she may have had to the contrary had been dispelled virtually as soon as the trip began, and nothing that had happened during this interminably long day had given her cause to change her mind.

It had been bad enough when her brother had refused to let them travel with him in his coach. Despite her objections, he had vanished back to London, only very grudgingly parting with enough money for them to take the stage. His obvious selfishness had been almost enough to disillusion even Ellen as to Geoffrey's near-sainthood, but in the end her step-mother had managed to justify his odious behavior as "pressing business in London, of a most urgent nature, which precludes his kicking his heels here while three giddy females make preparations to embark on the greatest adventure a woman can dream of having."

Cassie privately suspected that the urgent business consisted of a rackety set of cronies and a deck of cards. She was, in fact, firmly convinced that it was pure meanness on Geoffrey's part that had caused him to abandon them to their own devices.

As for London being the greatest adventure—stuff and nonsense. She was about as willing to be convinced that being thrown on the Marriage Mart was an experience greatly to be desired as Marie Antoinette would have been willing to agree that facing the guillotine was an experience she would not wish to forgo.

On the other hand, to be fair, Cassie had to admit that her present uncomfortable situation was partly her fault. Having made the acquaintance of Geoffrey's groom and mistress, she had bitten back the arguments she might have used and had not insisted upon a place in her brother's carriage.

She had realized her error as soon as the door to the stagecoach was thrown open for them to climb in. The coach seemed at first glance to be filled to capacity already, but a second look had shown her that it was occupied by only three men. They were such a disreputable looking trio, however, that they should not have been allowed to ride even as outside passengers. They had possession of three of the four corners of the coach, and their long legs, moreover, were taking up far more than their share of the room between the seats, leaving the three women to insert themselves carefully into the small amount of space remaining.

It would not have surprised Cassie if the three men had only bided their time until they were crossing an isolated section of moor before pulling wicked-looking pistols out from beneath the greatcoats they wore and holding them all up for their valuables. Although their pickings would be slim indeed if she and her companions were to be their intended victims.

Before the morning was over, she would have welcomed even an attempted hold-up to break the monotony. She had assumed, naturally enough, that she and Ellen and Seffie could have a comfortable coze during the trip.

The atmosphere in the coach, however, did not lend itself to the sharing of girlish confidences, and it would have taken a braver woman than Ellen to prate about dresses and balls and parties and suitors in such company.

The atmosphere, in fact, reeked of strong spirits, and the only thing Cassie could even be slightly thankful for was that the men had spent most of the day sleeping off the effects of the alcohol they had evidently imbibed freely before the trip. They had only roused themselves briefly at noon, when the stage had stopped barely long enough for the passengers to snatch a quick sandwich and a cup of hot tea—

although she strongly doubted that the three scruffy men had had tea in their mugs.

Shortly after lunch, Ellen and Seffie had also settled down, being able, as they were, to lean against each other and so achieve a modicum of comfort, and had joined the three men in the land of nod. Now only Cassie was left wide awake and sitting rigidly upright, her back aching both from the jouncing of the coach and from the effort it took not to touch either of the two men beside her.

The temptation was growing stronger, moreover, simply to lean over and rest her head against the shoulder of one of the men sitting beside her and thereby escape the tedium of the ride by falling asleep. She might even have given in to temptation if the seating arrangements had been a bit different, she thought, trying unsuccessfully to hold back a yawn.

Although at first glance the three men had seemed identical, with their rough clothes and unkempt hair, the hours she had spent watching them while they slept had enabled her to differentiate between them.

The oldest man, whom the others called Tuke, was by far the kindest looking of the three. In spite of his obvious physical strength, he had an air of gentleness about him. In fact, were it not for his disreputable appearance, she would say that he had an air of quiet dignity about him. She could picture herself making use of his shoulder to lean on if she became tired enough. Unfortunately, he was seated opposite, so that option was denied her.

The youngest man, who was sitting on her right side, was by far the most handsome, with blond good looks and a practiced smile, the effects of which he was obviously aware. Unfortunately, it had not taken long for him to notice her and make her the object of his attentions. She had been forced by the roaring fire in the inn where they stopped for lunch to put off her cloak, and no sooner had she done so than the mild interest he had shown in her previously had become quite pronounced.

He had turned the full force of his smile on her and stared at her quite openly. She was not a stranger to such bold looks, and even in her limited experience with men she knew enough to read the masculine desire that was in his gaze and to know exactly what the source of his interest in her was. Just remembering his bold appraisal of her attributes was enough to make her now pull her cloak more tightly around her.

The third man, whose age seemed to fall somewhere between that of the other two, was by far the most dangerous looking. She had heard the others call him Hawke and deemed it a suitable name for him.

She turned to look at him now. His nose, while not disproportionately large, was definitely aquiline. His jaw was angular, his eyes, when they were open, were piercing, his complexion swarthy, although it was hard to tell in the dim light whether it was actually his skin that was dark, or whether it was the several days' growth of beard that made it appear so.

From where she was now sitting she could not see the short scar by his left eye, which added to the aura of danger and violence that surrounded him, but even without a scar, the right side of his face could not by any means be called handsome.

He was uncompromisingly male, without the slightest touch of any of the softer, more feminine traits. Even in sleep his face did not relax, but remained as strong and forbidding as when he was awake. In a word, he was the embodiment of everything she most distrusted in men.

Cassie yawned again, then stiffened her back. The trip, which had seemed long before they even set off, began now to seem interminable, as if somehow they were all destined to ride onward for the rest of their days, trapped together in the confines of the coach. Her initial hope that perhaps the other three would not be accompanying them for the entire trip had been dashed earlier, when she had overheard one of them mention London.

To make matters worse, even the weather was conspiring against her. It had started snowing almost as soon as they had set their trip forward after lunch, and from the muffled sound of the horses' hooves, the snow was already piling up enough to slow their progress considerably. Such a storm, coming so late in the winter as it did, was quite unusual. Perhaps it was an omen that they should not be going to London?

While she sleepily debated the wisdom of waking her stepmother and trying to convince her that they should give up this wild adventure and return to their home, Cassie's eyes finally drifted shut.

Richard Hawke only gradually became aware of a warm body cuddled up against him, and it took him a few more moments to become sufficiently awake to identify where he was. His eyes opened only enough that he could recognize John sitting across from him, snoring softly. Shifting his glance a bit to the right, Richard gradually remembered the older woman and the young girl who had gotten on the stage in Truro. By turning his head slightly, he could see Perry, who was also lost to the world.

Which left whom? He had a vague memory of a third woman—of deep blue eyes and black hair and a forehead that seemed perpetually creased in a worried frown . . . a little figure struggling to sit up straight. He smiled to himself, pleased that she had finally relaxed. He doubted that he made a very soft pillow, but apparently she had no complaints. And he definitely had none.

With that thought, he allowed the rocking of the stagecoach to lull him back to sleep.

With a sway and a creaking of harnesses, the coach made a sharp turn and lurched to a halt. Cassie woke up abruptly to find her shoulder tucked behind Hawke's arm and her cheek pillowed against his shoulder. With deep dismay she pulled herself upright, then was reassured to realize the other five occupants of the coach were still sleeping, and no one else was aware of her lapse in decorum.

Even so, she could not keep a blush from creeping up her cheeks at the knowledge of how intimately she had been pressed up against a strange man.

Suddenly the door was thrown open with a crash, the wind catching it and jerking it out of the coachman's hands. The resulting noise woke up not only Ellen and Seffie, but also the three sleeping men.

"What's amiss?" the man beside her asked, and at the sound of his deep voice, Cassie recalled the warmth of his shoulder against her face. She was grateful for the chill wind, which cooled her overheated cheeks.

"I thought we could make it through to the next stop, guv, but the snow is blowing so fierce, 'tis nigh impossible to see the road. I'm for halting here, where we're sure of shelter for the night."

"How far is it to the next staging house?"

" 'Tis a good four miles, but it could easily take us several hours to get that far, assuming we didn't end up in a ditch with a broken wheel."

Cassie listened to the men's discussion in growing horror, not really upset by the obvious impossibility of arriving in London on schedule, but truly stunned by the financial impossibility of paying for an extra night's lodging and the additional meals. Geoffrey simply had not made any allowances for such an eventuality when he had doled out the pittance he had deemed adequate for their trip.

With great reluctance Cassie emerged with the others from the coach into a biting wind that whipped snow into her face with stinging force, and fought her way across the short stretch of open ground to the inn. At one point a sudden gust caught her and might have whirled her to the ground, but for a large hand that seized her by the elbow and virtually dragged her the last few feet into the haven that was the inn.

As a haven, it left much to be desired, the low ceilings and small windows giving the room a mean appearance. Cassie turned to thank the man who had helped her, but the words died in her throat when she realized it was the man called Hawke. Not that he seemed to notice her lack of manners, since he released her arm as soon as they were inside and directed his attention to the innkeeper, who stood swaying in the doorway of the taproom.

" 'Ere, 'ere, you can't come in. We're closed. No one 'ere to look after you. Go on somewhere else. No one 'ere. Not a staging house. Can't stay. Go away."

The coachman was not one to be put off by lack of welcome. "Look lively, man, and send someone out to help with my horses."

"No one 'ere. That's what I'm tellin' you. Wife's gone to m'daughter's. First gran'chil' coming. M'son drove her. No one 'ere but me. Can't 'elp you. Shelebrating. First gran'chil'. Be a boy. Told m'wife. Got to be a boy. Name 'im after me. Can't stay. No one 'ere to cook. Go somewhere else." He took another hearty swig from his mug and unexpectedly beamed at them. "Goin' to be a boy." Then he slid slowly down to the floor and started snoring loudly.

The coachman swore under his breath, then went back out himself to help the guard take care of the horses, but the other three men seemed unaffected by their strange reception. They calmly stepped over the landlord's prone body and proceeded into the taproom where without any by-your-leave they proceeded to make themselves at home.

"I cannot approve of this place."

Her step-mother's petulant voice startled Cassie almost enough to make her blurt out her own misgivings about their lack of finances. Only by exerting the greatest effort was she able to say calmly, "I am afraid the weather has taken the decision as to where we stay out of our hands. I realize these are not the accommodations we were expecting, but we must make the best of the situation."

"Very well, if you are so set on it, we will stay, although I will be very surprised if the sheets are not damp. Please have someone show us to our rooms, and then ask the maid to bring us something to eat."

Cassie would have been irritated by her step-mother's haughty attitude if she had not heard the tremble in her voice, and known that this was just Ellen's way of trying to cope with a situation that was beyond her capabilities. Ellen was sweet and kind-hearted, and Cassie loved her dearly, but unfortunately Ellen had not the least particle of resolution, and she had never been able to handle the slightest adversity. Cassie had, in fact, become quite accustomed to taking care of her step-mother as if she, Cassie, were the mother and Ellen were the child.

So instead of reminding her that none of them really wanted to stay in this miserable place, but the weather made it impossible for them to go on, Cassie merely said matter-of-factly, "They are a little short of help now, so I will take us upstairs and together we can pick out a suitable room. Then I will see what is available in the way of a meal."

There was not much to choose from upstairs—four rooms, each with a double bed, all of them cold and damp with no fires lit. It was a relief, however, to leave her querulous stepmother in the largest of the rooms, with Seffie delegated the impossible task of cheering her up, while Cassie addressed herself to the only slightly less impossible job of securing wood for their fire and food for their stomachs.

Pausing in the door of the taproom, she evaluated her three potential helpers, the coachman and guard evidently still being occupied with the horses. She had already made up her mind to approach the oldest of the three, in hopes that she was not mistaken in her belief that he possessed at least a modicum of kindness in his make-up.

Unfortunately, the only one facing the door was the youngest man, who, as soon as he caught sight of her, started smiling in a way that made her thankful she had not yet put off her cloak. She did not need his smile to know any request she might make of him would undoubtedly be interpreted as an invitation to share her bed. On the other hand, unless she actually entered the taproom, which she was loath to do, she could see no way of attracting the attention of the man with whom she *did* wish to speak.

The young man chuckled out loud as she hesitated there, then said something in an undertone to his two companions, which caused them both to turn and stare at her.

For Cassie, it was the final burden that proved too much for her to bear, and she turned tiredly away from their mockery and went down the narrow hallway in what she hoped was the direction of the kitchen.

Her thin shoes were soaked through from the snow, her feet felt like blocks of ice with the rest of her not much warmer, her stomach was tied in knots from hunger and anxiety, and every muscle of her body ached from the hours of jolting about in the carriage. All she wanted was a hot bath, a bowl of soup, and a bed to lie down on.

Most of all, she wanted to be home where she belonged and not on her way to London. There was no doubt in her mind but that this day was a good indication of what was to come.

The kitchen, when she found it, was as cold as the rest of the inn.

"Are you in need of some assistance?"

Even before she turned around she knew from his voice that it was the man called Hawke who had followed her. They all three had slight accents, as if they had not lived their entire lives in England, but his voice was the deepest of the three and as such unmistakable. Turning reluctantly, she stared up a long way into a harsh face that had become entirely too familiar to her in the course of the day.

There was no way she could ask a favor of this man, because she had no way of knowing what he might demand of her in return. On the other hand, she might well be able to deal with him if she were the one to strike the bargain in the first place.

"I would be interested in making an arrangement with you that would be mutually beneficial." She continued with more assurance in her voice than she actually felt. "Since we seem to be left to our own devices here, I propose that you and your friends see to the fires, and I will endeavor to provide food for us all."

"Agreed," was all he said before he turned abruptly, leaving her alone in the kitchen.

She could not suppress a shiver at her temerity, and she wondered briefly if she had been wise to make a bargain with such a man. Unwillingly she recalled the stories she had heard about people making pacts with the devil, but then she shook off her silly fancies and set to work to inventory the available food.

In that respect they were fortunate, since the absent landlady appeared to keep a well-stocked larder. There was half a leg of lamb, some cold tongue, a few apples that were still firm, and the beginnings of a kettle of chicken soup still hanging from the iron by the fire, evidently abandoned by the landlady in her haste to go to her daughter's bedside.

Carried away with the unaccustomed abundance of ingredients, Cassie prepared far more food than was necessary, adding the requisite vegetables to the chicken soup and starting three apple pies baking in the oven before slicing the lamb and tongue to make an enormous stack of thick sandwiches.

Having left the food for the coachman and his helper and the three other travelers on the table in the kitchen, she felt a slight twinge of guilt as she carried a tray upstairs to share with Ellen and Seffie. Not guilt because they might be sitting in the taproom expecting her to serve them, which she had never had any intention of doing, but guilt at the quantity of food she had prepared. She consoled herself with the thought that anything not eaten tonight would keep for several days and would probably not actually be wasted.

The fire in the fireplace had already done an adequate job of heating the room, Seffie had done a remarkable job of calming Ellen's anxieties, and the abundant food was all that the three women needed to help them recover from the stresses of the trip. Of necessity they slept in their shifts, their luggage, such as it was, still on the coach, and they shared the double bed, also. It was a tight squeeze for three, but far, far better than one of them sleeping alone in another room, especially as that one would undoubtedly have been Cassie.

She lay awake a long time after the other two had fallen asleep, worrying at first about how much they would have to pay for their room the next day, but then gradually becoming soothed by the rumble of men's voices coming up from below, which were audible now that the wind had died down. Every now and then she heard the deeper rumble that was the man called Hawke, and occasionally a burst of laughter, before finally she also drifted off to sleep.

In the taproom Richard Hawke paid only the bare minimum of attention to the conversation of his companions. The bulk of his attention was directed to the women upstairs, or rather, to one of the women.

Thanks to the great quantity of brandy he and his friends had imbibed the evening before, he had not paid any special attention to the three during the day. In fact, were he to have been asked earlier to describe them, he would merely have said three women, assorted ages and sizes.

To be sure, Perry had ogled the black-haired one at lunch, and could probably have described her in great detail. His interest had achieved him nothing, but had merely revealed his youth quite clearly. Richard had long since passed the stage where he assessed a woman on the basis of how well nature had endowed her. Although he had later been intrigued with the same young woman, it was not her looks that had attracted him, but rather her attitude.

In a word, she reminded him of Molly. She had fussed over the other two women with the same loving concern Molly had once shown for him, and he suspected this girl could be as fiercely protective of the people she loved as Molly had been. Not only that, but Cassie, as he had heard the other two females call her, had pushed herself to the limits of her physical endurance to provide for them. When he had turned to see her standing in the doorway of the taproom, he had seen the same bone-weary exhaustion that had been a daily part of his life as a slave.

Following her to the kitchen, he had expected to be met with tears, pouts, fluttering eyelashes, and other obvious bids for sympathy—all designed to elicit from him the required offer of assistance. From the start, he had been prepared to send her up to join the other women, and to set John to fixing the food while he and Perry carried in the wood.

Instead, she had faced him squarely, almost managing to hide the fear she had of him, and had made her proposal. She had gotten less by bargaining than she would have obtained simply by ordering him to fetch the wood and fix the food, did she but know it.

He had not sent her up to her room as he had planned. Somehow he felt it would be belittling her simply to brush aside her efforts to manage, especially when she had shown such courage in asking, and so he had simply agreed to do as she requested.

Nor had she stinted on her part of the bargain, either, as many women would have done. Richard added that to her list of virtues and was impressed with the total. He would have to search far and wide to find someone who more closely fit his requirements for a wife. There was something to think about in that.

The other thing to think about was a puzzling memory of the girl sleeping snuggled up next to him, but that memory was so vague, he was not sure if he was remembering what had actually happened or something he had merely dreamed.

Chapter Five

In the morning Cassie slipped out of bed without waking her companions and hurriedly pulled on her dress, forcing her feet back into her shoes which, although dry, were stiffened by the soaking they had received the day before.

The room was marvelously warm in spite of the fact that the fire had died out during the night, and a glance out the window confirmed the message the sun was trying to communicate—the snow had vanished, to be replaced by a day that was as unexpectedly balmy as the day before had been unseasonably cold. It was the kind of day when one could expect to see the first daffodils poking green shoots above the ground, and Cassie longed to be home in her own garden.

Upon descending to the ground floor, she found she was the first one to rise. The innkeeper was no longer sprawled in front of the door to the taproom, but was now snoring as loudly as ever on a wooden bench by the fire. In the kitchen the table was littered with dirty dishes, but to her amazement, not a single scrap remained of the food she had prepared the night before.

Cassie felt not the slightest responsibility to clean up after the others, but after a short debate with herself, she decided that even though breakfast had not been specifically mentioned in the bargain she had made, it would be petty to fix food for Ellen, Seffie, and herself without fixing anything for the men at the same time, especially when she found a supply of wood stacked conveniently on the floor beside the fireplace.

She had no idea what the men might be accustomed to in the way of breakfast, but from the quantities they had consumed the night before, the important thing would seem to be providing an ample amount. First she mixed up a batch of scones, and while they baked, she cooked some rice and made a huge pot of kedgeree, although the thought of such a heavy breakfast turned her stomach. For herself and her companions, she coddled three eggs, buttered some of the scones, and made a pot of hot tea.

Meeting the man called Hawke on the stairs as she was going up, she was surprised when, without asking, he took the heavy tray she was carrying out of her hands and preceded her back up the stairs. She wracked her brain for something to say to him, but remained tongue-tied when he handed it back to her at the door to her room and thanked her formally for the food she had prepared the night before.

Emerging with his friends from the taproom after a satisfying breakfast, Perry was treated to the sight of the shy little miss from the day before arguing resolutely with the landlord, who was obviously feeling the effects of the brandy he had consumed the day before. Quite a battle it was, too, with the outcome, at least in Perry's opinion, a foregone conclusion. It was doubtful if the landlord, even without a splitting headache, would have been a match for the chit, who was in a fiery temper.

"See here—you have charged us for the use of two rooms and a private parlor. That is outrageous. You are a scoundrel and a cheat, for you do not even have a private parlor in this entire inn, and if you had not been spending the night in a drunken stupor, you would also know that we have occupied only one room. And furthermore, I refuse to pay one penny for a meal I not only had to cook for myself, but which I also cooked for your other guests, and a sorry landlord it is who so shamelessly neglects his guests the way you have done. I've a good mind to stay and tell your wife exactly how you behaved behind her back."

It was an empty threat, thought Perry with amusement, since the girl called Cassie would by necessity have to leave when the stage did or be stranded in this hedgerow tavern, but apparently the mention of his wife coupled with the hammers that, from the looks of him, were pounding behind the landlord's eyes was enough to make him give up the struggle. Muttering to himself, the poor man took the amount of money Cassie was willing to pay, though the look he gave her was not such as would cause anyone to think she had made a friend of him.

"Now there's a suitable candidate for your wife, Hawke," murmured Perry, as the chit retired triumphant from the field of battle. "At least you will have to admit, she knows the value of money."

"I do believe you are right," his friend replied, his attention still on the outer door through which she had vanished.

"Richard, you can't be serious. I was merely funning. Why, she's nothing but a servant girl. Haven't you seen how she waits on the other two, who are obviously of gentle birth?"

"Yes, I have noticed the way she takes care of them, but I have seen nothing subservient in her manner. And as you have pointed out, a proper appreciation for the value of money was one of my criteria for a wife."

"I'll admit she's as tasty a morsel as I've ever seen, and I could understand any man wanting to mount her, but—"

There was an abrupt silence as Richard turned to him with such a menacing look that the words he had been about to say died in his throat. Perry had never before felt the impact of Hawke's anger directed at him, and he realized that his estimation of Hawke's natural power over other people had been woefully inadequate. He was silenced more effectively with one look than he would have been if another man had grabbed him by the neck with both hands and shaken him into submission.

"Perhaps I did not make my meaning clear. I intend to marry that young lady in the near future, and I will take it amiss if anyone displays the slightest disrespect toward her or her companions."

Perry turned automatically to Tuke, not sure what he was seeking from the other man, whether confirmation that Hawke was serious, or some kind of support in his attempt to make Richard see the light of reason. But he could read nothing more in Tuke's shuttered gaze than he could in

Hawke's, and any urge he might have felt to dissuade his friend from committing such an act of folly died before it was even born.

He expected Richard to make a push to attract the attention of the young lady in question. Being well acquainted with the charm his friend could produce when the occasion warranted, Perry had not the slightest doubt that Richard would be successful.

To his surprise, however, other than insisting that the three of them share one of the seats so that the three ladies could sit together, Perry could discern nothing in Hawke's demeanor that would indicate to an uninformed observer that he had the slightest interest in any of the three women. By the end of the trip Perry had almost convinced himself that his friend had reconsidered the entire matter and now realized how inappropriate such an unequal match would be.

It turned out to be wishful thinking on his part, as no sooner had the stage arrived in London than Richard set Tuke to follow the three women, who had waited only as long as it took to collect their baggage before setting out in a hired hack for an unknown destination.

Perry held his tongue as long as he could while he and Richard made their way to the discreet hotel he had decided to make his headquarters while in London, chosen to forestall any attempt on his grandmother's part to insist that he live in her town house, which had come to her from her third husband, and which therefore was not part of the entailed estate temporarily belonging to him.

But once they were in private, Perry could keep silent no longer. No matter what the consequences, he felt an obligation to do everything he could to save his friend from what he was sure would turn out to be a disastrous mistake. "It won't work, Richard. You must see that the whole idea is preposterous."

"You do not think I can convince her to marry me? Do not let these rough clothes fool you. I assure you, I clean up quite nicely, even though I can never aspire to your good looks."

"Don't joke, Richard; this is serious. Of course she will

accept if you're fool enough to offer, but that's hardly the point. You cannot simply close your eyes to the problems that will be the inevitable outcome of this mad start of yours. You have said you don't wish to marry a title. Very well, but there is no need to go to this extreme. That young woman, although her speech is not broad and she is comely enough, is just a servant, no matter what you may say to the contrary. It is equally obvious she has no breeding, or she would not have argued with the landlord like a shrew. It's one thing to know the value of money, but it's quite another to cause a scene in public the way she did. There is simply no way she could fit into the kind of life you have planned for yourself. All you would be accomplishing would be ruining your own life and hers in the process. She would never be comfortable as the wife of a landed gentleman and would only be made miserable if you attempted to force her into such a position.''

It would have been easier to argue if Hawke had attempted to refute his statements, but Richard offered nothing at all in defense of his choice, just listened quietly to everything Perry had to say. Perry had exhausted all his arguments and was reduced to frustrated silence by the time John Tuke reappeared with an air of quiet satisfaction and the suspicion of a smile lurking about his eyes.

''Did you find out her direction?''

''Did you think I would lose her in London?''

''And?''

''And,'' the smile that had been hovering now emerged full-blown, ''she is the Lady Cassiopeia Anderby, daughter of the fifth Earl of Blackstone and sister of the present earl.''

Perry was not sure who was more disconcerted by Tuke's information, himself or his friend Richard Hawke.

''Cassie, they've come, they've come!'' Seffie erupted into the library like a small whirlwind.

''Who has come?'' Cassie felt her insides tighten at the thought of meeting strangers.

''Not who, silly. Two of your new dresses have come and three for Mama. She says it is not too late to pay a few calls, now that you can be made to look presentable. Oh, hurry, do." Seffie grabbed Cassie's hand and pulled her to her feet, knocking the book Cassie had been reading off onto the floor. "Oh, is this not exciting? It is your new blue sarsenet and the peach sprigged muslin. Which will you wear? Oh, do wear the peach." Unable to control her excitement, Seffie danced from the room.

Cassie could not share her sister's raptures. After a week's reprieve, during which they had spent virtually every waking hour ordering clothes and being fitted, the moment she had been dreading was finally at hand. She was about to be thrown onto the market and sold to the highest bidder.

Retrieving the fallen book, she looked at it with regret. *The Castle of Otranto* by Walpole was written to terrify its readers, but Cassie would sooner meet a praying skeleton or a bleeding statue than face a roomful of unknown ladies . . . and perhaps even some gentlemen would be there to consider her attributes. Consider? No, they would be inspecting her the same way she had been inspecting fabrics and ribbons and bonnets these past few days. After all, they could not be expected to purchase a wife without checking her for defects and shortcomings.

Reluctantly climbing the stairs to her room, she repeated over and over again like an incantation, "I am the daughter of an earl; I do not need to be afraid. I am the daughter of the Earl of Blackstone; I am the equal of anyone."

She was not especially successful in controlling her fears, and so to give herself something else to think about, she made polite conversation with Annie, one of the few servants who had been included with the house her brother had rented for the season.

"How did you become so proficient at fixing ladies' hair?"

"In Spain and Portugal I was able to earn a little extra money by helping some of the officers' . . . wives."

The hesitation was slight, and Cassie decided it would be prudent not to call attention to it. But then it struck her that perhaps Annie had been one of them—one of the loose women who could always be found following behind any army. But surely not even her brother would have hired a fallen woman to work as a maid in his own household. Or would he? "You were in Spain?"

"My husband was a sergeant with Picton's Highlanders. I followed the drum for three years on the Peninsula."

"And your husband . . ." Cassie could not think of the proper way to phrase it, but the maid answered the unstated question.

"He was wounded at the Battle of Waterloo. I nursed him as best I could, but he died four days later." Her tone was matter-of-fact, but her eyes met Cassie's in the mirror, and there was a depth of pain there that Cassie had never encountered before.

Luckily for her, since she could not think of a thing to say in response, her sister chose that moment to interrupt them. "Do hurry, Annie. Mama is ready for you to fix her hair. Oh, Cassie, you look most elegant. I wish I were old enough to go with you. It is vastly unfair that I must stay at home with nothing to do. You must, you absolutely must remember every detail about what everyone is wearing and what everyone says and tell me all about it when you get home."

With no more talk of battle and dying soldiers, Annie finished with Cassie's hair and left her alone with her thoughts. As a way of taking her mind off her fears, the conversation with the red-haired Scottish girl had worked wonders. How could Cassie be afraid of something as trivial as a few morning calls when Annie had struggled in vain to save the life of her dying husband? A few gossipy women were nothing compared with that.

But the men she might also meet? The ones in the market for a beautiful, titled wife? Perhaps her unknown husband to be? What would they think when they saw her?

She looked in the mirror, and her heart sank. Although much more modest than the silvery blue dress belonging to her brother's mistress, the peach sprigged muslin was indeed vastly becoming. Too becoming, in fact, especially with her hair pulled back in ringlets, leaving her neck exposed.

"You look quite delectable, my dear."

At the sound of a man's voice from the doorway, Cassie jerked around to see her brother lounging there.

"I must confess, modesty enhances your type of beauty even more than brazenness. Perhaps I should raise your price to one hundred thousand pounds?"

All too soon the hired hack pulled to a stop in front of a beautiful town house. Not wishing to reveal her reluctance, Cassie immediately prepared to alight, but her step-mother caught her arm and held her back for a moment.

"Now you must be on your best behavior today. Promise me that you will remember all the rules I have been teaching you. Lady Letitia is one of the most powerful women in London. If she takes you in dislike— Well, I shudder to think what might happen in such a case. We may count ourselves fortunate that my grandmother made her come-out the same year as Lady Letitia, and although they were not bosom bows, still she is inclined to look kindly on me and mine."

Already Cassie was feeling a strong antipathy toward the unknown Lady Letitia, but she dutifully enumerated for Ellen a long list of things a young lady being introduced to the *ton* was not allowed to do.

Finally satisfied that Cassie would not thoroughly disgrace them, Ellen decided they could not delay any longer, and she led the way up to the imposing front door. Waiting at her step-mother's side, Cassie prayed that Lady Letitia would not be at home, but moments later the butler was ushering them into the sitting room. "Lady Blackstone and Lady Cassiopeia Anderby."

It was not hard for Cassie to determine which of the three ladies already seated in the room was Lady Letitia. In some subtle way she seemed to be the focus of everyone's attention, although she was not at all the imposing, full-figured battle ax that Cassie had been expecting. Instead, she was of only medium height, quite trim, and despite her white hair and lined face, her back was ramrod-straight.

"Oh, my dear Lady Letitia," Ellen gushed, "it is so wonderful to be back in London. Cornwall is so tedious, it is beyond bearing. But now that my daughter is of an age to make her come-out—or I should say, my step-daughter, since I am not at all old enough to have a daughter old enough—that is to say, may I present my step-daughter, Lady Cassiopeia?''

Lady Letitia held out her hand and Cassie obediently took it. Giving her hand a slight squeeze, Lady Letitia said with a kindly smile, ''You have the look of your mother, my dear.''

At her words, Cassie felt something in her heart shift, and she looked in the old lady's eyes for the first time. What she saw there was not only intelligence but compassion, and somehow Cassie gained the impression that this woman, who was separated from her by a vast gulf of generations, might very well become a good friend.

Turning to the man standing beside her chair, Lady Letitia continued, ''May I present to you my grandson, Edmund Stanier?''

Despite Ellen's description of the various types of gentlemen she could expect to meet, Cassie was almost undone by her first sight of a true London dandy. She had thought that the cartoons she had seen in London shop windows were merely caricatures, but it would appear that they were not as wildly exaggerated as she had assumed. Standing before her was quite the silliest looking man she had ever seen.

Dressed from head to toe in green, he could easily have gone to a costume ball as a stalk of broccoli. Wearing shoes with such high heels that he was in danger of breaking his neck if he stumbled, he was also draped with so many fobs and seals, it was no wonder his back was curled over almost like a question mark.

''Grandmama,'' the fop said in a languid voice, ''must I remind you again that I am no longer a plain mister?'' Turning his gaze to Cassie, he explained, ''My grandmother is getting old, and she continually forgets that I am now Viscount Westhrop. Delighted to meet you, my dear,'' he said, holding out his hand to Cassie as if he were royalty instead of only a viscount.

She was not particularly impressed by his limp handshake, and she could not help thinking that Lady Letitia must also be disappointed with such a namby-pamby grandson, titled or not.

Behind them the door opened again, and the butler announced, "Mr. and Mrs. Willard Craigmont."

Nudging Cassie in the side, Ellen indicated that they must move on and yield their places to the newcomers. Following her step-mother's lead, Cassie seated herself on a small ribband-back chair near the window, where she had a good view of the room.

The two ladies who had arrived earlier were just beginning to take their leave when the door opened a third time. "Viscount Westhrop and Mr. Richard Hawke," the butler announced, his face carefully deadpan, as if he were unaware of the consternation his words had produced.

Cassie, who had thought never again to meet the man called Hawke, felt her heart race at the sight of him. One look at that familiar face and she would have run from the room in total panic, except that her brother's words came back to reassure her: "A mere baronet need not apply."

Lacking any title at all, Mr. Hawke was totally ineligible as a suitor for her hand, no matter how elegantly he was now dressed. She need have no fear that she would be forced to marry him. Unfortunately, even though she knew rationally that this man could not possibly affect her life, she could not keep her heart from racing wildly when she observed that he was now staring directly at her.

His glance was bold, and his eyes held recognition . . . and something else that she could not identify from such a distance, something that made her feel as if she were a frightened hare, paralyzed by the intent gaze of a marauding fox, and for a moment the entire room and all its occupants seemed to fade away, leaving only the two of them.

But then Ellen clutched her arm and whispered, "I thought the other man was the viscount! Did he not say he was?" She gaped openly when the first Viscount Westhrop leaped to his feet, his entire body radiating outrage.

"How dare you! Grandmama, who is this impostor? Owens, throw this man out!"

Ignoring him, Lady Letitia rose to her feet and moved with stately grace toward the newcomers. "Perry, my dear, why did you not let me know you had arrived in London? And do not try to persuade me you are just come, because your clothes betray you. You will never make me believe that jacket was cut by anyone other than Weston.''

''But . . . But . . . you are supposed to be dead!'' the fop declared.

''Many men have tried to effect my demise, dear cousin, but so far I have led a remarkably charmed life,'' the new Viscount Westhrop said smoothly.

Taking a different tack, the original and apparently superceded Viscount Westhrop turned to Lady Letitia and said flatly, ''This man is not my cousin. He is an impostor, who is only pretending to be Peregrine in order to steal my title.''

''Do not be such a nodcock, Edmund. You do not have a title for anyone to steal, and you never did. Perry has always been ahead of you in the line of succession,'' his grandmother replied.

Jumping up and down in his rage and looking, to Cassie, quite like a little puppet being jerked with strings, Edmund Stanier repeated, ''But this is not Peregrine! Peregrine is dead! He has to be! I do not know how you can think this—this *American* is the real viscount. Why, he even speaks with a horrid colonial accent! Somewhere there is proof that my cousin is dead, and I intend to find it even if I have to travel to America,'' he said wildly before stalking out—if one could call the mincing steps he took stalking, thought Cassie, suppressing a smile.

''Come sit down, Perry, and tell me about your journey.'' Lady Letitia linked her arm with her grandson's and led him back to where she had been sitting.

''All in good time, Grandmama, but first I would make known to you my best friend in all the world, Richard Hawke.''

Suddenly grabbing Cassie's arm in a grip so tight it hurt, Ellen whispered frantically, ''Oh, we are undone! All is lost!''

''Why do you say that?'' Cassie asked.

''Those two men—they were on the stage with us from Cornwall!''

''Why yes, did you not recognize them?''

"They have seen us—" Ellen was white as a sheet and appeared to be in danger of fainting.

"Well, of course they have seen us. We traveled together for two days." Cassie was thoroughly bewildered by her step-mother's reaction. During the trip, Ellen had barely acknowledged the men's presence and had not actually spoken a single word to any of the three men. So why was she now in such a taking?

"No, no," Ellen said with a moan, "that is nothing to the point. They have seen us dressed in mere rags—in those hideous dresses and shabby cloaks, without even a decent bonnet. Oh, I have never been so mortified in all my life! They will tell the world, and we will be the laughing-stocks of London. I shall never live down such ignominy! I might as well throw myself into the Thames, since my life is now thoroughly ruined."

"Surely the matter is not that desperate," Cassie replied calmly. "If they were to spread such tales around London, they could expect us to retaliate by telling everyone they were in a drunken stupor for half the trip."

Ellen looked at her in disbelief. "You are indeed foolish beyond permission if you think that would stop them. Pray, what is the harm of a gentleman being in his cups, compared to the shame of a lady appearing in public in an out-of-date frock?"

Acknowledging to herself that there could be no meeting of minds on the subject, Cassie forbore to press her arguments. As ridiculous as it might seem to her, her step-mother was truly terrified out of her mind at the mere thought of what the two men might say. Clearly, it was Cassie's responsibility to do what she could to avert disaster. She could only regret that Mr. Hawke looked every bit as formidable in fashionable attire as he had in his buckskins.

Catching his eye, she stared directly at the man, then shifted her eyes to the left, then back to him, then to the left, repeating several times until she was sure he must have understood her silent message. Then she stood up and moved a few feet away and pretended a great interest in a little china shepherdess on the mantel.

Her ploy worked, and after a discreet interval, Mr. Hawke joined her. "My step-mother is most distressed," Cassie murmured without preamble.

"So I had noticed," Mr. Hawke said quietly. "Is there any way I might be of assistance?"

Fighting off the urge to move at least a foot or two away from this overpowering man, Cassie said bravely, "I am afraid you are the problem."

"I? What have I done to distress Lady Blackstone?"

"You have seen us dressed in—" She could not say rags, because that, of course, was an exaggeration. "You have seen us wearing garments that were not precisely fashionable," she explained, then waited for him to laugh mockingly. Really, she felt remarkably foolish voicing such a silly anxiety.

To her relief, he neither laughed nor mocked. "You may tell your step-mother that she has nothing to fear. I shall never by any word or action indicate that I have seen the two of you before this afternoon."

"And your friends? Can you speak for them also?" she asked, amazed at her own temerity.

"They will neither of them say a word."

"Thank you," she whispered before moving away to rejoin her step-mother. "It is all right, Ellen," she said reassuringly, "Mr. Hawke has promised neither he nor his friends will say anything."

Ellen was not completely reassured. Twisting her handkerchief into a knot, she said weakly, "Oh, I do wish we could quit this house immediately. That man makes me so nervous."

"I am quite willing to return home at once."

"No, no, we must not leave before our allotted time is up. That would be a dreadful insult to our hostess!"

Cassie sighed. So many rules, and most of them so totally absurd, it might be better if more people did ignore them.

"Mr. Oliver Ingleby and Miss Cecily Ingleby," the butler intoned.

The newcomers were obviously brother and sister, both tall, attractive, and positively radiating exuberant good humor. After an affectionate greeting for Lady Letitia, the girl immediately made her way to Cassie's side.

"Oh, I am glad there is someone here under the age of fifty! Aunt Letitia—actually she is my great-aunt—is popping me off this year, although she has told me if I do not meet anyone who suits me this Season, I may wait for next year without worrying that I shall be thought on the shelf. Is this your first Season, too?" Without waiting for an answer, Miss Ingleby continued, "Aunt Letitia is a dear, really, but she has so many *old* friends—" here Miss Ingleby rolled her eyes, "and I was beginning to think I must be the only young lady being presented this year. I have spent so many hours being fitted for clothes, I vow, I shall be quite exhausted before the Season even begins. Tell me, have you discovered Madame Argenteul? Is she not the most clever modiste?"

By this time Cassie had realized it was pointless to attempt to answer any of Miss Ingleby's questions, but Ellen was more experienced with such fluent conversationalists, and she simply began speaking at the same time as Miss Ingleby.

"She is a treasure, is she not? I have had two dresses of her—

"Did you see that lovely blue silk she has—"

"—and I am quite pleased with the results—"

"—which is shot with silver threads. I am sure it is smuggled—"

"—and I have already told her I shall be happy to—"

"—in from France—"

Trapped as she was between the two chattering ladies, Cassie's head was beginning to ache. She looked across the room and discovered Mr. Hawke was watching her again. This time, instead of returning his stare, she dropped her eyes modestly, as her step-mother had instructed her to do. It was unfortunate that Ellen seemed to have forgotten another of her rules, namely that they must hold their visit to thirty minutes, because Cassie was finding it harder and harder to convince herself that Mr. Hawke embodied no threat to her peace of mind.

Richard watched the three ladies conversing by the window. Or rather, he could not keep his eyes off the one whose tongue was not flapping away at top speed. Although he had not previously considered it a necessary requirement for a wife, he now realized that he had no desire to wed a chatterbox. Lady Cassiopeia, fortunately, did not seem to suffer from that affliction.

"Pay attention, Richard." Perry clapped him on the shoulder. "Ingleby here has just promised he will put our names up for White's and Brooks's."

"But not Boodle's," young Mr. Ingleby said with a grin. "That club's for the dandies, so if you want a membership there, you'll have to apply to Stanier. Ecod, but I'd give a bundle to have seen his face when you was announced. I'll wager his nose was bent out of shape when you turned up alive. Don't quite know how he got it into his noggin that you had to be dead. Quite a few people have gone to the Colonies and returned alive."

"The United States," Perry corrected.

"Beg pardon?"

"Not the Colonies anymore. We won our independence," Perry said quite seriously. "Twice now."

"Oh, to be sure, to be sure. But you said 'we.' Don't you mean 'they' old chap?"

Perry must be the total lackwit, Richard decided, to speak in such a revolutionary way before his grandmother. Although she appeared to be deep in conversation with one of her cronies, Richard was willing to lay odds she was listening intently to every careless word her grandson was saying.

Before Perry could say anything else that might prematurely reveal his plans to return to America, Richard took his elbow and gave it such a hard squeeze that Perry winced. "It is time we were on our way," Richard said smoothly.

Perry did retain a modicum of good sense, and without any objections, he took his farewell of his grandmother, who then held out her hand to Richard. Bowing over it, he said all that was polite, and moments later he was safely out on the street with his companion.

"Were you deliberately trying to stir up a hornet's nest in there?" Richard asked.

"My wits must have gone begging," Perry admitted. "I can't believe I spoke that carelessly in front of my grandmother. Thank goodness I at least had enough common sense to drag you along to London with me. Well, no harm done."

Easy to say, thought Richard, but he doubted Lady Letitia had missed the implications of the word *we* even if Perry thought she had. Excusing himself on the grounds that he had pressing business to look after in the City, Richard waited until he was safely seated in a hack before opening the note Lady Letitia's butler had slipped to him along with his hat.

Chapter Six

Lady Letitia wasted no time. As soon as the butler had left the room after serving them their dinner, she began her attack.

"My grandson has mentioned you in many of the letters he has written me. You are not precisely the English gentleman of leisure you are now pretending to be."

Now is the time, Richard thought, to prove I am as adept at getting out of a tight spot as Perry thinks I am. "I am English, at least," he replied mildly, "and not at all a savage. You will notice I am quite adept at eating with a knife and fork." He held up his utensils in mute testimony.

His hostess took another sip of her wine. "But you are not a gentleman born, nor are you a man of leisure. Wealthy, I will grant you, but none of it appears to have been inherited, which you must agree is the mark of a true gentleman."

"Delicious salmon," Richard said. Perry's grandmother was turning out to be every bit as formidable as he had said. It was too bad Perry had written such informative letters.

"I do not think my grandson has any idea of your past," she continued, "other than the part of it with which he was involved."

Reminding himself never to play cards with this old lady, Richard continued eating as if Lady Letitia's words had not bothered him. Just how much did she know?

"You were, I believe, a member of the crew of the ship *Golden Dreams,* were you not? Which ship was lost in the Caribbean during a storm?" Her expression gave away absolutely nothing of what she was thinking, but for some reason he could not define, Richard began to suspect that she might not be an enemy.

"You did not hear that from Perry," he said.

"No," she admitted. "But I have many sources of information."

"And," he continued, "you did not hear that as part of idle gossip. Which leaves me to believe that you have deliberately hired someone to pry into my life."

"I am afraid," she said, and this time she allowed a smile to show on her face, "that prying is one of the things I do best."

"Has no one ever told you that curiosity killed the cat?"

This time her smile was genuine. "I am in no danger from you. The reports I have received from Perry and from my other—shall we say merely, from my other sources?—have all been in agreement that you are a man of honor."

"But not a gentleman of honor?"

"No, not a gentleman. An adventurer, a risk-taker, and, if I may quote my grandson, 'a devilishly good friend to have at one's back when one is in a tight spot.'"

"So, since you know I am a fraud, do you intend to destroy my standing in society?" Richard asked, pushing his plate away and making no further attempt to act as if they were merely engaging in idle small talk—as if his whole future were not held firmly in this old lady's hands.

"That depends," she replied, "on what you are trying to achieve by pretending to be a gentleman. Perhaps you would like to say a few words in your own defense?"

How much to tell her, that was the question. And how to phrase it so that he would not give away Perry's plans. "As I have said, I am an Englishman. And having acquired sufficient wealth, as you have discovered, I now wish to purchase an estate and settle down to the life of a country squire. When I do that, it will be much easier to gain acceptance if my neighbors do not know that I have been in trade."

She nodded, as if satisfied with his answer, then casually moved to cut his legs out from under him. "I have always felt that half truths are better than lies when one wishes to deceive someone. It would appear that you have come to the same conclusion, because you have quite neglected to mention your intentions in regard to Lady Cassiopeia."

Richard had not, however, come this far in life without learning a few tricks about disarming his opponents. "I intend to marry her," he replied.

"I can prevent that," Lady Letitia said. Her voice was still casual, as if she were simply inviting him to have more wine.

"You can make it more difficult for me, but you cannot prevent it," he replied.

"Or, under certain circumstances, I can make it more easy," she countered.

He did not ask what those circumstances might be. She would tell him in her own time, but asking would only turn him into a supplicant, which would make his position weaker, and he fully intended to win this duel of words.

"My grandson does not intend to stay in England, does he." She said it as a statement, not as a question, so Richard did not bother to confirm what she had already deduced for herself. "I do not think I will be able to persuade Perry to change his mind. You, however, have considerable influence on him."

"I? I have never been able to persuade him to use the slightest caution before rushing into a dangerous situation."

"I believe, however, that in this case he would listen carefully to whatever you might have to say. Do you deny that?" The old lady was really a ruthless opponent, giving no quarter at all.

"No, I admit I have some influence with your grandson."

"And will you use that influence to help me persuade him to keep his title and estates and remain in England?"

"In return for which you will help me win the hand of Lady Cassiopeia?"

Her eyes fixed steadily on his face, she nodded.

"No," Richard replied bluntly, "I will not."

Lady Letitia leaned back in her chair and stared at him for long moments. Finally she spoke again. "I am beginning to have the feeling that whatever I were to offer you, you could not be bought."

For a moment he could not speak. Her words had conjured up a memory of the time when he *had* been bought—when he had been a tall, skinny boy of fourteen with bruises covering his arms and legs, and with his back striped by a cat-o'-nine tails. Dragged ashore in heavy chains, he and John had been forcibly stripped of their clothing, placed on a block, and auctioned off as if they were horses. No, not like horses—horses were treated with more respect.

Forcefully banishing the memory of that dark hour, Richard asserted in a flat voice, "No, I cannot be bought."

"Then," Lady Letitia said, "I shall help you court your fair lady, and in return I shall ask just one thing—a favor, if you would, not a bribe or a payment."

The old lady was full of surprises. Richard, however, had never liked surprises, since nine times out of ten they turned out to be nasty, even dangerous surprises. Nor did he have any faith in the altruism of people in general. "First you must tell me why you are willing to help me, since I am admittedly not a gentleman."

"Has my grandson ever mentioned to you that I am a confirmed matchmaker?"

Richard shook his head.

"I am successful in my chosen avocation because I have learned to see behind the masks people wear, to see the real people with all their shortcomings as well as their strengths. And I have also become adept at matching the people themselves—not their titles or their property. I have had very few failures—and I am referring to failed marriages, not failures to marry. Lady Cassiopeia has much of her mother in her, and knowing what I do about you, I believe that you and she will have a very long and satisfying marriage."

"Because she needs to marry a wealthy man? One who is also strong enough to protect her from her brother?"

"Ah, so you have already heard of Lord Blackstone's reputation?"

"I am afraid what I have learned about *his lordship* goes beyond a tarnished reputation. Despite his title, he has collected a wealth of enemies, which is hardly surprising, considering the fact that he appears to have no redeeming virtues."

Lady Letitia nodded. "Quite accurately described. But

actually Lady Cassiopeia's needs were not my primary consideration. I was thinking more about what your needs are.''

"Why should you worry about me, a veritable stranger?"

"If it has slipped your mind that without your intervention on several different occasions my grandson would be lying in an unmarked grave in America, I assure you that I, at least, will never forget the debt I owe you.''

"And yet you tried to bribe me into helping you?"

The old lady smiled, a very satisfied smile.

Richard groaned. "Why did Perry not inherit any of your deviousness?''

"Deviousness?" she asked, her expression now all innocence.

"You were never trying to coerce me, you were merely testing me." He should feel some anger at having been manipulated so easily and so effectively, but all he could feel was admiration. It was not often someone bested him as neatly as she had done.

"I do not read minds, Mr. Hawke, although I delight in giving people that impression. I also do not accept any one else's evaluation of a person I am interested in. And you, I must admit, are quite the most interesting person I have met in months. Which brings us back to the favor I was going to ask of you.'' She paused and looked at him expectantly.

"If you are waiting for me to say, 'whatever you wish,' then you shall have a long wait. I never agree to something without knowing what I am agreeing to.''

"All I ask is that you satisfy an old lady's curiosity."

"If I am to forgo styling myself a gentleman of leisure," he said with a laugh, "then by the same token you cannot be allowed to call yourself an 'old lady.' ''

"But I am old, and I am a lady, and those two things have restricted me more tightly than the iron shackles that once bound you.''

Richard caught his breath, and for a moment it seemed as if the world had tilted beneath him.

"There are marks on your wrists," Lady Letitia said simply. "And I recognize them for what they are. Scars like that are only made when manacles are worn for an extended period of time.''

Looking down, he saw that she was correct. He must remember to have new shirts made with sleeves an inch longer.

''Perry gets his love of adventure from me,'' she continued. ''But unlike my grandson, all my life I have had my freedom curtailed, my activities limited to what a well-bred English female was allowed to do. I was married off at seventeen to a man I had been introduced to only once, and by the time he died, when I might have had the freedom to travel the world and seek the adventures I craved, I had four small sons to take care of. Even though over the years I have adjusted to my 'captivity' and have learned the exact length of my ''chains,'' I have never learned to love my cage, and it would be a kindness indeed if you would tell me of your adventures in great detail, so that I might experience a little of the world beyond my bars, even if only vicariously.''

Looking at her sitting there, her back so straight, Richard's admiration for her increased. How many years had she endured her ''chains,'' always maintaining an inner integrity, refusing to grovel? A lesser person would have gone mad, or battered herself to death against the bars of her cage. How could he refuse her such a simple request?

Apparently taking his silence for acquiescence, she said, ''To start with, you can tell me where you were and what you were doing in the six years between the time your ship was lost and the time you appeared in New Orleans with the beginnings of your fortune.''

Of all the things she had said to him, this last remark cut the deepest. Everything else he was willing to talk about freely—all his other adventures traveling around the world he could relate to her in as thorough detail as she was willing to listen to.

But not those missing six years—not the years that had been stolen from him. He had never discussed that period of his life with anyone, not even with Tuke. By tacit agreement, they never mentioned their time as slaves. Even now, more than a dozen years after they had escaped from captivity, the memory was still too painful.

Did Lady Letitia know that she had brought him to his knees with that one remark? She was not obtuse or stupid—she must know what she was doing to him by her "simple request." But looking into Lady Letitia's eyes, he saw no triumph, no morbid curiosity, no pity—only great compassion and deep understanding.

"I may look old and frail," she said softly, "but my shoulders are still strong enough to help bear the burdens of my friends."

Slowly and without conscious decision, he began to speak. "Our ship was not lost in a storm—it was attacked and sunk by pirates."

"I would feel so much better if we had a man to escort us," Ellen repeated for at least the twentieth time since their hired hack had joined the line of carriages waiting to disgorge their passengers, who were all bound for the opening ball of the Season, being held this year at Sefton House.

Privately, Cassie thought that nothing would make her fel better except, of course, somehow miraculously being transported back to Cornwall. After several weeks of purchasing extensive wardrobes—always on credit, to be sure—interspersed by occasional morning visits to other ladies who were also deeply engrossed in preparations for the coming Season, the moment had finally arrived that she had been dreading ever since her brother had informed her he planned to support his hedonistic life-style by selling her.

Tonight she would be introduced to dozens of men, and the pre-sale inspection would begin. She felt positively ill at the thought of all the eyes that would be trained on her. "I think I am going to be sick," she said.

Ellen patted her hand. "I felt the same way before my first London ball. But you need have no worry that you will be a wallflower. Believe me, the men will flock around you like bees around a honey pot."

Before Cassie could explain that she would much prefer to sit out all the dances, the door to their carriage was opened.

After more than an hour of inching their way forward, they had arrived at their destination.

Half an hour later, when they were only halfway up the stairs, Cassie realized she had been overly optimistic. At the rate they were progressing, it would almost appear that by the time they reached the ballroom, the evening's festivities would already be drawing to a close. Only one good thing had come of the long delay—her anxiety had gradually been replaced by boredom.

But they did, finally, arrive at the door of the ballroom, where they were announced with great ceremony. Such was the noise in the room, however, that Cassie doubted anyone standing more than five feet away could have heard their names.

Someone had noticed their arrival, however. No sooner had they passed through the receiving line than Ellen clutched her arm and murmured, "Oh, how fortunate! Lady Letitia is signaling us to join her. Did I not tell you I have some influence with her?"

Slowly, stopping frequently to acknowledge the greetings of old friends, all of whom expressed their delight at seeing her in London once again, Ellen began working her way around the edge of the room toward the place where Lady Letitia was sitting in solitary splendor. They were halfway to their goal before Cassie realized with horror that Lady Letitia was not actually alone, but was instead a member of a small party. Indeed, why should she have come to such an event if not with an ulterior purpose? Her "ulterior purpose" in this case was apparently her grandniece, Cecily Ingleby, who although boring, was not in the least bit threatening.

The danger, however, lay in the other members of the party. Lord Westhrop was now handing his grandmother a glass of liquid refreshment, and beside him—*loomed* was the only word that came to Cassie's mind—the ubiquitous Mr. Hawke.

Catching her step-mother's arm, Cassie pulled her behind the nearest pillar and hissed in her ear, "Wait! I do not wish to join Lady Letitia's party."

"Not join her? Are you insane? To disregard her summons would be tantamount to social ruin," Ellen replied, starting to pull her arm away.

"But only see who is with her—the very men who you yourself said can destroy our reputation."

After a quick glance around the pillar, Ellen smiled reassuringly. "We have nothing to worry about, my dear. If those men were going to tell scurrilous tales about us, the gossip would already have spread throughout the *ton*. Since it has not, we may assume they are men of honor, whose word can be relied upon."

Cassie was not reassured in the slightest. "I am not worried about gossip," Cassie said, hanging on more tightly to her step-mother's arm. "But Mr. Hawke frightens me."

"Really, Cassie, you surprise me. I had not expected you to be so missish."

"It is not missishness. The way he looks at me, he makes me feel—" She broke off, not able to reveal to Ellen the turmoil she felt every time she met Mr. Hawke's eyes.

"Have you no common sense at all? Have I taught you nothing? Mr. Hawke is said to be as rich as Croesus, and he can do nothing but add to your consequence if it is seen that you have attracted his interest."

"But I fear his interest in me is serious, and I do not at all wish to marry him."

"Marry? Pray, are you not putting the cart before the horse? The man has not even asked you to dance with him, and already you have him on his knees? I had not thought you so conceited. Besides, no one is going to force you to marry where your heart is not given."

"Geoffrey intends to choose my husband for me," Cassie said baldly.

For a moment even Ellen's optimism seemed dented, but then she rallied. "Well, your brother is the head of the family, after all, and as such he has the right to approve or disapprove of your suitors."

"But he has already told me to my face that I shall be allowed no say in the matter," Cassie said, desperately wishing that somehow for once her step-mother would show a little backbone. "It is intolerable! I cannot allow him to ruin my entire life."

"Well, after all, arranged marriages are not so uncommon. Why, my own father picked the man I was to marry. And I am sure he chose wisely, since it is quite . . . quite pleasant to be a countess." Ellen's voice wobbled a bit at the end, and her smile became almost a grimace.

"Oh, my dear," Cassie said, instantly sorry she had put so much pressure on her step-mother, who was indeed a frail reed.

But Ellen was equally unable to withstand pity. At the first sign of sympathy, she affixed her social smile firmly in place. "It is not as though that man is a duke or an earl—why, he is just plain Mr. Hawke, without even a sir to add consequence to his name. I am sure you can attract numerous suitors who are vastly superior to him. Since you are the daughter of an earl, I cannot believe even Geoffrey would force you to marry a man with no title, no matter how rich he might be. So pray let go of my arm and come along, do, before Lady Letitia decides we have forgotten all about her."

Releasing her hold on Ellen's arm, Cassie hesitated only a few seconds before following her step-mother. It will not be so bad, she repeated over and over to herself. I shall smile at Mr. Hawke and dance with him, but I need not be afraid of him, because Geoffrey will never allow me to throw myself away on a nobody, even if he is a rich nobody. Surely I will have other suitors whom Geoffrey will find more suitable.

Indeed, within minutes after they joined Lady Letitia, the men began flocking around, seeking an introduction to her, and by the time she had danced two country dances, her card was filled for all but the waltzes, which she could not dance until after she had been given permission to waltz at Almack's. It was one of the sillier rules, but in this case she was quite thankful for the restriction, since it meant Mr. Hawke must limit himself to signing his name beside two of the country dances.

What she had not anticipated was that he would be seated beside her for all the waltzes. She wished desperately that he would show some attention to another young lady, but he did not budge from his chair, except to rise courteously to his feet whenever her partner returned her to her chaperone.

Halfway through the evening, she realized that in some subtle way, he was staking a claim on her—making it appear that the other men were returning her to *him*, rather than to Ellen.

With added dismay, she noticed what had escaped her attention before—that the first dance he had put his name beside was the supper dance, and the second one was the last dance of the evening. How could she have allowed him to claim her for two such significant dances?

How could she have prevented him, was more to the point, she thought, reluctantly accepting his arm and allowing him to lead her down to supper. He was a master of small talk, and as tongue-tied as she was every time she was near him, she knew she must appear to be shy in comparison. But was it shyness that caused a partridge to flee before a hawk?

She had a moment's reprieve when he seated her at a small table and went to fill plates for both of them. Moments later, Ellen took one of the other three chairs.

"Is he not handsome? Oh, my dear, I could not credit it. He swears he has never forgotten me, and now he is a widower and quite free to marry again, as am I."

Puzzled, Cassie looked at her step-mother. "Who are you talking about?"

"Why, Mr. Arthur Dillingham, of course. I introduced him to you not an hour ago. Did you not remark how handsome he is? And still quite smitten with me. I remember once he wrote a poem about me, and it was quite well done—everything rhymed beautifully."

Vaguely Cassie remembered being introduced to a tall man with a rather florid complexion, who was already inclining toward fat. Apparently this was a former beau of Ellen's, from the days before her marriage to Cassie's father.

When their two escorts joined them, it was quite obvious that Mr. Dillingham was indeed smitten with Ellen's charms, as he alternated bites of food with fulsome compliments.

Cassie could only be grateful that Mr. Hawke was not given to uttering such flowery phrases.

"I have been wanting to ask you for advice," he said to her instead. "As payment for a debt, I have recently come into possession of a tin mine in Cornwall. Unfortunately, I am as yet at the mercy of my manager. Knowing nothing about mining, I must accept blindly anything he tells me, which makes me rather nervous. I have learned over the years that the more one knows, the less likely one is to be cheated."

Richard had intended it merely as an opening conversational gambit, but Lady Cassiopeia looked positively stricken. "You are the owner of a mine?"

"Yes," he repeated, wondering at her distress. "It appears to be a good investment, although I have not yet had an opportunity to inspect it as thoroughly as I might wish. The manager, who has been handling everything for the previous owner, has assured me that he is capable of running things without any attention from me, but—"

"There is nothing more disastrous than an owner who takes no interest in the running of his mine," Lady Cassiopeia said firmly. "All of the worst abuses occur in such cases."

"Abuses? My manager has said nothing about abuses, only about ways to increase profits."

It was as if he had struck flint against steel—before his eyes she was transformed from shy young lady into fiery reformer.

"Of course he says that, but what he will never tell you is that the easiest way to increase profits is to pay the men such a pittance that they cannot support their families." She had begun in a low, indignant voice, but with each word she uttered, the volume rose. "Then their wives are forced to work in the mines also, except that even then there is not enough money to support the family, so soon the children are also sent to work in the mines. Babies of four and five years are undoubtedly crawling on their hands and knees in your mine, Mr. Hawke, pulling carts of ore through low tunnels, because children are found to be cheaper than ponies and also more expendable, and therefore *profits* go up!"

Before she had finished, her step-mother was frantically

trying to shush her, finally in desperation clapping her hand firmly over Lady Cassiopeia's mouth.

"Really, Cassie," the older woman hissed, her eyes darting around the room to see who was watching, "you are making us the center of attention. You must not talk about such subjects in polite company! Why, people will think you are a Methodist!"

Richard could not contradict Lady Blackstone, who was right about the notice they were attracting, nor yet could he abandon such a promising topic of conversation. Thinking fast, he said quietly, "I would learn more about this subject, but indeed, your step-mother is correct. This is not the ideal place to talk of tin mines. May I take you for a drive tomorrow afternoon, say at three, so that we can continue this discussion?"

Lady Cassiopeia was clearly torn between the desire to avoid him and the desire to reform him. In the end, her concern for the tin miners won out, and she nodded her agreement.

For the rest of the supper, he allowed Mr. Dillingham and Lady Blackstone to carry the weight of the conversation, only now and then tossing in a platitude where one was required.

In general, he was not dissatisfed with the evening's work. He had an assignation with the woman of his choice . . . and he also had the names of several men who had been particular in their attentions to her. Tomorrow Tuke could start investigating and see which of them constituted a serious threat.

Chapter Seven

The red-headed maid who opened the kitchen door regarded him with a baleful eye. Not that Digory could blame her. He had done his best this morning to look as disreputable as possible. The part of his face not hidden beneath his low-pulled cap was adequately covered by a four-day's growth of beard, and his clothes looked as if he had been wearing them night and day for a month.

He had not, of course. It had taken great artistic skill to achieve the level of grime and stains that his jacket and trousers were now displaying. But as Cassie had pointed out to him, all cleaned up he bore a remarkable resemblance to the late Lord Blackstone, and Digory's life would become truly complicated if anyone in London noticed the similarity of features.

Still and all, as much as he sympathized with the maid, he could not let her slam the door in his face, which she seemed inclined to do. Deftly inserting his foot, which was safely clad in a heavy boot, into the opening, he growled, "I'm here to see Piggot. He's expecting me."

There was a string of violent curses from inside, and the maid was roughly shoved aside. Piggot, apparently, had used a more time-honored method of acquiring his patina of grime, because he was not only disgusting to look at, but also offensive to the nose.

"You got the keg?" the earl's factotum said with a scowl.

"If you've got the money," Digory countered.

"My master's credit is good."

"That ain't what I heard."

"You ain't seen the quality of the merchandise he's got his hands on." Piggot's description of Cassie was so crude, he almost earned himself a broken jaw, but Digory was well trained in dissembling, having sat in many a tavern in France drinking to the health of the Emperor with spurious bonhomie.

"I'll sell you this keg on credit, though the price'll be half again as much as we agreed upon, but before you get another, I'll ask around again and see if you're telling the truth."

"Fetch in the keg then and be quick about it," Piggot said with a snarl.

Cassie was sitting up in bed reading the latest novel from the Minerva Press—or rather, she was staring at the pages, trying unsuccessfully to take her mind off Mr. Hawke. Whyever had she agreed to drive out with him, when he was the one man in all of London she wanted absolutely nothing to do with?

And more important, how could she get out of the appointment? She could not feign an illness, because her step-mother would not allow that. The evening before, when they were all returning from the party, Ellen had positively crowed at the thought of Mr. Hawke's being one of Cassie's admirers.

"He is as rich as Croesus, and it is quite a feather in your cap that he is paying you so much notice," she had insisted. "Not that you would want to marry someone like him, who has been wandering around in America, no doubt picking up heathenish habits, but still and all, it adds to your consequence to be seen with him."

Cassie had pointed out that as she was an earl's daughter, it seemed unlikely to her that such a man could add to her consequence, but Ellen had merely laughed and said that there were earls' daughters and then there were earls' daughters, and a rich suitor must always be a welcome addition to a young lady's train of followers.

Unfortunately, the wretched man had already cost Cassie a night's sleep. Every time she had dozed off, she'd had dreams—no, nightmares—that she was sitting beside him in his carriage, but instead of merely driving to the park and back, the carriage had kept going on and on, carrying her farther and farther away from the people she loved . . .

Suddenly, her solitude was interrupted by the maid's entering in a huff. One glance at Annie's face was enough to tell Cassie the maid had not come up to fetch the breakfast tray.

"This used to be a respectable house to work in." Annie cast a fulminating eye at Cassie. "But very much more and I shall decide starving in the streets is preferable to continuing in service here."

"Has my brother . . .?" Cassie asked, not sure how to express her question politely.

"His ardor has cooled considerably since I let him feel the point of my knife," Annie replied, "although I still have to be alert to keep from getting pinched. And that Piggot is worse, because he's got a fouler mouth than ever I heard when I was following the drum, and he never misses an opportunity to bump up against me. But as bad as the two of them are, I draw the line at having a smuggler in the kitchen."

Could it be? Cassie felt hope for the first time since she had left Cornwall. "A smuggler?" Oh, perhaps there was yet a chance that she could avoid driving out with Mr. Hawke!

"Yes, a smuggler! I'll bet a quarter's wages not a shilling was ever paid to the king for that keg of brandy he delivered just now."

"Never mind about the brandy," Cassie said quickly, throwing back the covers and rolling out of bed. "Tell me about the smuggler. What does he look like?" If it was Digory, then he would certainly be willing to help her this time when she explained about Mr. Hawke. Surely her brother could not approve of such a suitor.

"He looked like the scum he is," Annie said, beginning to pace the room. "Like something thrown up by the sea to rot on the beach. Like—"

But Cassie interrupted. "Did you hear his name? Tell me!"

Annie stopped her pacing and looked at Cassie suspiciously. "His name?"

"Did you hear Piggot mention his name? 'Tis most important that I know—oh, please, think hard."

Although still scowling, Annie thought for a minute, then said, "I think Piggot called him Randall or—"

"Rendel?" Cassie asked quickly.

Annie nodded, and Cassie threw her arms around the Scottish maid. "Oh, Annie, that is the most wonderful news."

"Since when do you number smugglers among your friends?"

"Since . . . since . . . oh, Annie, I am sure the man is my brother, Digory Rendel."

"Brother?"

"Born on the wrong side of the blanket, but still a most wonderful brother. He has taken care of me ever since my father died, and I know he has come to London just to see if I am all right. I must talk with him, but . . ." She paused, suddenly realizing the difficulties. "Annie, can you help me? I must speak to Digory, but it will be disastrous if Geoffrey or Piggot learn his identity. I cannot meet him in this house, lest we be seen or overheard. Perhaps a note? Could you . . . ? It is much to ask, I know, that you go down to the kitchen again and risk being insulted by Piggot, but I cannot go myself, and there is no one else to send."

"Are you sure this man is your brother? He looks so . . . so . . ." Annie made a look of disgust.

Cassie smiled. "He is quite good at disguises. But if you ignore the clothes and the scruffy beard, then you will see he bears some resemblance to Geoffrey, although Digory is a little taller, and his shoulders are broader, and he is much stronger. To be sure, he is not as pretty as Geoffrey, but Digory is trustworthy and honest and—"

"An honest smuggler? Is that not a contradiction? Or is he only pretending to be a smuggler?"

"No, he has made his living for years by smuggling, and I shall relate it all to you later if you promise never to tell a soul, but not now—he may be leaving at any moment, so I must get word to him."

"There's no need for a note," Annie said. "I shall go back to the kitchen and flirt with this paragon of virtue and entice him into carrying my basket to the market for me. If he is your brother, he will come with me because he will wish to have me make arrangements for you to meet with him. And if he is not your brother, then I still have my knife. As soon as possible, you slip out of the house and meet us in the alley beside the butcher shop. Wear your plainest dress— one of those you brought with you from Cornwall will do— because in a fancy London gown, you will attract too much attention. And cover your head with a shawl, and pull it forward so that it shadows your face, and—''

"I know what to do," Cassie said, pushing the maid out of the room.

Entering the kitchen where the two men were conversing in low tones, Annie took her shawl from its hook and picked up her market basket, whereupon the stranger immediately stood up from the table and swaggered over to block her path.

"Where are you going with such a big basket, girlie?" he asked with a leer for her and a wink for Piggot.

Yet despite the crudity of his manner, he made no attempt to touch her, which was, as she had learned on numerous occasions, quite out of character for such a man. As unbeliev- able as it had seemed at first, she began to suspect Lady Cassie was right about his identity.

"I'm merely going to the market, sir," Annie replied softly, doing her best to act as if she were flustered by his approach, even though she could easily have evaded him and darted through the door.

Sweeping his cap off, the man bowed in a mock-courtly fashion. "Never let it be said that Digory Rendel allowed a young lady to carry a heavy burden when he was around to assist her."

Relieved to hear his name and know he was in truth Cassie's brother, Annie handed over the basket. Seeing what she had done, Piggot, who had made numerous unsuccessful attempts on her virtue, gave an angry growl and started to get to his feet, but the smuggler casually brushed back his coat so that the handle of his dirk was clearly visible, and with a muttered oath, Piggot sank back down on the bench.

When they were well away from the house, the smuggler

cast off his rough manner as easily as he could have shrugged off the ill-fitting coat he wore. "I assume Cassie told you who I was," he said, his voice now well modulated instead of coarse.

"She said you were her brother."

"*Bastard* brother," he corrected absently.

"Those were not her exact words," Annie said, reasonably sure that his casual tone hid pain at his situation in life—deeply buried, perhaps, but real pain. Still, her years of following the drum had taught her not to pry into other people's feelings, so she did not press the point. "Lady Cassie is meeting us in the alley beside the butcher shop."

They walked side-by-side for a few minutes, then he asked, "Why have you stayed on in that house? You have undoubtedly discovered for yourself what manner of man the earl is. I would think you would have resigned your position before now, not but what I am happy for Cassie's sake that you have not."

Dispassionately and succinctly Annie described her situation in life, concluding with a brief description of the ways her husband had taught her to defend herself.

"I am afraid your knife may not be adequate if the earl becomes determined," Digory said. "In which case you may come to me for protection."

Involuntarily she stiffened. Although more subtle and charming, he was unfortunately cut from the same cloth as all men.

"Excuse me," he said with a grin, "but I fear I did not express myself properly. I shall try again: If you are ever in need of assistance, financial or otherwise, you may count on me to take care of you as if you were my own *sister*. There, have I made my meaning plainer?"

His smile was infectious, and for the first time since her husband had died in her arms, Annie tentatively began to let down her guard.

"Do you have any brothers of your own?" Digory asked casually.

It took her a moment before she could answer. "I had three," she said simply. "But none of them lived to reach the age of ten years."

"And your parents?"

"They died when I was sixteen, so I married Jamie, he took the King's shilling, and I spent the next several years following the drum in Portugal and Spain."

"Why have you never returned to Scotland? Are you not homesick?"

She thought for a moment. "Home for me was wherever Jamie was. There is no one and nothing for me now in Old What." At Digory's look of inquiry, she added, "Old What is in Aberdeen, in the parish of New Deer."

Before he could question her further, they reached the butcher shop and found Lady Cassie there before them, well disguised in an all-enveloping cloak. Seeing them standing side by side, Annie could detect little family resemblance between the two of them except for the color of their eyes and hair. Cassie threw her arms around the "smuggler," and for a half moment Annie wondered if they might both have conned her into assisting with an illicit assignation, but there was nothing lover-like in the way they spoke to each other.

"Oh, Digory, you have come to rescue me after all! And just in the nick of time!"

"Rescue you? What is this nonsense? You don't need rescuing. I have been reading of your successes in the *Gazette*. You have already been declared an Incomparable. You should have no trouble catching a husband." He kissed her affectionately on the forehead, but even to Annie's suspicious eyes, it was in all respects a brotherly kiss.

"I have told you before, I do not *want* a husband." Cassie pulled away from him and, hands on hips, positively radiated indignation. "If you are not going to help me avoid the future that Geoffrey is arranging for me, then you might as well go back to Cornwall."

Turning to Annie, Digory asked with a smile, "Tell me, is marriage so bad a fate for a woman?"

"No, it can be wonderful," Annie replied. "With the right man, of course."

Cassie scowled and made a humphing noise, but Digory remained quite cheerful. "If you truly want me to go back to my boats, I shall, but I rather thought you would like me to make sure that your future husband is the right man for you.'' He waited, but Cassie refused to look at him or reply. ''Sulking will get you nowhere. You would do better to tell me who your most persistent suitors are, so I can investigate them.''

With a slight shudder, Cassie said, ''As yet there is only one who stands out from the others, but I do not think my brother will find him an acceptable candidate for my hand. Although the man apparently has great wealth, he has no title.''

''And his name?''

''Hawke—Richard Hawke. He is a friend of Lord Westhrop, who is the grandson of Lady Letitia. I do not know why, but there is something about Mr. Hawke that frightens me.''

''Is he disrespectful? Does he seem cruel?''

Cassie thought for a moment. ''No, he has always treated me with great respect, even kindness. But . . . Oh, I cannot explain. There is such an intensity about him, he quite unnerves me. Even when he is sleeping, he looks forbidding.''

No one, Annie decided, could look more forbidding than Digory now did. There was open anger on his face and undisguised menace in his voice when he spoke.

''Even when he is *sleeping*? You had better explain yourself, Cassie, or I shall have this Mr. Hawke explaining to the point of my dagger.''

Her account of the stage coach journey was unobjectionable, but Digory was not satisfied, and at his insistence, Cassie related in complete detail everything that had happened between her and Richard Hawke on each and every occasion they had met. ''As I said, I do not think Geoffrey will allow him to be a suitor for my hand,'' she concluded, ''but, Digory, you must do something to help me avoid driving out with him—you must!''

''A drive in the park will do you no harm. And as for the rest, what Geoffrey allows and doesn't allow may not matter in the slightest. Men like the man you have just described to me do not generally allow anyone else to make the rules for them," Digory replied, and all the blood drained from his sister's face.

"I cannot marry such a man," she whispered.

"As I said, I shall investigate further. If you have need of me, send a message to the Clarendon." He turned to leave, but Cassie caught his arm.

"I mean it, Digory," she said, her voice trembling with emotion. "I cannot marry such a hard man."

"You need a man strong enough to protect you from your brother."

"But I need a husband who— No, no, I mean *if* I needed a husband, which I do not, I would want a man who was gentle."

Digory smiled. "A man has to be strong before he will allow himself to be gentle. You will find that it is generally the weakest men who take delight in being cruel toward those who are weaker than they are."

"No matter what you say, I shall not marry Mr. Hawke," Cassie said, but she was speaking to Digory's back. He had turned and was sauntering out of the alley. Within seconds, he lost himself in the crowd that was passing. Turning to Annie, she repeated, "I shall not marry Mr. Hawke, no matter what either of my brothers says."

"This brother has the right of it," Annie said. "Every soldier and every soldier's wife learns early on that weakness aligns itself with cruelty and cowardice."

"But he frightens me, Annie." Cassie pressed both hands against her stomach. "Every time he looks at me, I feel . . ."

The look in her eyes said more than her words, and Annie abruptly realized what the real problem was with Mr. Hawke. It was not anything he was doing that was frightening her mistress—it was how he was making her feel. As sometimes happened with young girls, Cassie was afraid of the womanly emotions he was arousing in her.

How could Annie tell her that these very emotions could lead to one of the greatest pleasures in life? At two and twenty, Annie was barely two years older than her mistress, but the gulf between them was too wide to cross. Annie had shared a marriage bed for four years before her husband had been killed, whereas Cassie had doubtless never even been kissed—except on the forehead by her brother, which was not at all the same thing.

Next week, Cassie thought. She should have told that wretched man that she was not free to drive out with him until next week. That would have given her an additional seven days to think of some way to avoid the forthcoming meeting entirely.

"Mr. Hawke," the butler announced—or rather it was the footman, who was filling in as butler, since the real butler had decamped with the majority of the other servants.

Footsteps approached her, but Cassie did not look up. Her heart, in fact, felt as if it had sunk down to her half-boots.

"Good afternoon, Lady Blackstone," her unwelcome suitor said in his deep voice, which had become entirely too familiar to Cassie in the last few weeks.

Talk to him, Ellen! Cassie thought. Tell him every bit of gossip you have heard since you arrived in London—anything, everything—if only to postpone the inevitable for another fleeting moment.

But Ellen did not cooperate. "The weather has turned so beautiful, I shall not detain you a minute longer. Fetch your bonnet, Cassie. You will not wish Mr. Hawke to keep his horses standing."

Fie on his horses, Cassie thought rebelliously. She sneaked a peek at the man who was standing in front of her, and it was even worse than she had feared. The minute their eyes met, she got the same sick feeling in her stomach, only this time it was even worse than when he had danced a country dance with her.

"I shall go . . . I shall just . . . my bonnet," she finally managed to say. Maybe, she thought desperately, she could throw all her bonnets out the window, and then she would not be able to drive out, because no lady could set foot outside her house without a bonnet. That was another of those idiotic rules society had made expressly to plague young ladies, or so it seemed to Cassie, who was accustomed to going about the Blackstone estate bareheaded.

But again, she was not given a chance to procrastinate even another few precious moments. Annie was waiting in the hallway, the chosen bonnet in her hands. Adjusting it on Cassie's head and tying the ribbons in a bow, the maid said in an undertone, "You will survive a drive in the park. You will discover within yourself more strength than you ever knew you had. When it is over, you will wonder at how foolishly you are behaving now."

There was no reproof in the maid's voice, but Cassie felt herself deeply ashamed that she was, in truth, acting the coward. How Digory would scoff if he saw her being such a timid little mouse—she, who had bragged she could take care of herself.

Stiffening her back, she turned to face the man who had followed her out into the hallway. The bonnet, she discovered, was perfect. Chosen, or so Ellen thought, because it suited the gown, it had actually been picked first and the dress decided upon only because it required this particular piece of headgear. Its particular attraction for Cassie was its most ridiculous brim, which extended so far forward that unless she looked directly up at Mr. Hawke, he would not be able to see her face at all.

Richard looked down at the young lady standing so demurely beside him, and he could not keep his mouth from curling up in a smile. Remembering how fiercely she had argued with the landlord on the journey to London, Richard did not believe she was as meek as she was now pretending to be.

Nor did he believe for a moment that she had just "happened" to be wearing headgear shaped like a coal scuttle—a bonnet, moreover, which could only have been designed by a woman who hated men. But he had never backed down from a challenge, and even now he did not despair in the slightest. Before their drive was over, he would somehow coax her into showing him her face.

He offered Lady Cassiopeia his arm, and as always, she hesitated, as if afraid to allow the slightest physical contact between the two of them. And as always, he had the urge to remind her that she had already slept with her head resting

on his shoulder, but he was too much the gentleman to speak
of that time.

Finally she allowed her hand to rest gently on his arm,
her touch still tentative, as if at any moment she might jerk
her hand away. The best thing to do, he decided, would be
to distract her with conversation, so that she could become
accustomed to him gradually, and perhaps, maybe,
possibly—no, definitely—if he were patient enough, some
day she would begin to feel comfortable in his presence.

"This morning I had my secretary, John Tuke, produce
for me some articles about the newest technology available
for mining. Tell me, what do you think of Humphry Davy's
invention? I believe he calls it a safety lamp and claims it
will prevent gas explosions in mines."

After two days of cold, biting wind, the weather had turned
balmy and the park was crowded with those who had come
to see and be seen. Such was the congestion along Rotten
Row that even though Lady Letitia's coachman was quite
good at avoiding certain specified people, on this occasion
he could not take evasive action when another landau moved
into position beside her carriage and a cloyingly sweet voice
bid her good afternoon.

It was with regret that Lady Letitia turned to speak—
briefly, she hoped—with the woman, a certain Lady
Potherwick, who was distantly related to Lady Letitia's third
husband. The daughter of a cit who had married well above
his station, she was herself the mother of six vapid daughters.
With her two eldest already of marriageable age, Lady
Potherwick was pathetically obvious in her attempt to make
it appear that her connection with Lady Letitia was closer
than it was.

Her efforts along that line were futile, did she but know
it. No matter what gambit she used to try to make Lady
Letitia feel an obligation to help her dispose of her
daughters—no matter how blatant her "hints"—Lady Letitia
was far too clever to allow herself to be trapped into doing
something she had no desire to do.

She would long ago have ended the matter by giving the

woman the cut direct except that it was mildly amusing to watch Lady Potherwick's thinly disguised attempts to impose in an outrageous manner—attempts which were, of course, suitably tempered by her obvious and completely justified fear of the dire consequences that would result if she offended Lady Letitia completely.

Today, however, Lady Potherwick had other things on her mind than acquiring a notable sponsor for her daughters.

"Really, my dear Lady Letitia, without wishing to set myself up as an arbiter of your actions, as it were, yet my conscience demands that I speak to you on what may be a painful subject. Doubtless you recognize the man in that carriage over there? The one escorting Lady Cassiopeia? He calls himself Richard Hawke, and I know you have received him in your home, but I must warn you that he appears to me to be an impostor—nothing more nor less than a deliberate fraud."

Lady Letitia gave the woman an icy stare, but Lady Potherwick rattled on, blissfully unaware of the dangers along the path she was treading.

"Indeed, I have asked all my acquaintances and searched through every page of Debrett's and have not found any family he could be attached to. Granted, Mr. Hawke may be rich," she said with a sniff, "still, I suspect he is some opportunist battening himself on your grandson. Either that, or it is Lord Westhrop himself who is engaged in some sort of practical joke, attempting to foist some American riff-raff off onto an unsuspecting public."

Holding back her anger at the woman's presumption, Lady Letitia uttered a total falsehood, deliberately using her most imperious tone of voice. "Richard is the grandson of one of my dearest friends, who was compelled by unfortunate circumstance to emigrate to America with her husband years ago. I stood godmother to her daughter, Mr. Hawke's mother, and I shall take it amiss if anyone begins to spread *scurrilous* rumors about the dear boy, who is almost like another grandson to me."

Ignoring Lady Potherwick's profuse apologies, Lady Letitia rapped coachman on the back. Luckily, by this time the congestion had eased, and they were able to move away from the other carriage. The cut direct from now on, Lady Letitia mused. Definitely, the woman had ceased to be tolerable the moment she decided to instruct Lady Letitia on proper behavior.

Chapter Eight

"I shall certainly take your advice, Lady Cassiopeia," Richard said, pulling his horses to a stop in front of the house being occupied for the season by the Earl of Blackstone and his family. "In fact, I shall not only send one of my own agents to investigate the situation at my mine, but I shall also instruct him to go incognito so that the manager will have no reason to disguise the true conditions there. Will that be adequate, do you think?"

Cassie tipped her head way, way back so that she could see his face. It had amused him to note that halfway through their drive her bonnet had ceased to be her defense and had become instead merely an obvious inconvenience—and undoubtedly a strain on her neck.

"I think that would be a very good plan," she said. Never before had he seen her look so happy. Her eyes positively glowed, and he felt a ridiculous urge to buy up all the mines in Cornwall and pay all the miners outrageous salaries if only it might give her pleasure.

Then she seemed to realize she was smiling at him, and she immediately ducked her head. "Not that I know anything about the manager of your mine, but it has been my experience with other managers that they tend to resort to any stratagem that will increase their profits. Nor do the owners in general care one way or another, as long as they can squeeze every possible penny out of the misery of others."

"I care, Lady Cassiopeia," Richard said in a low voice.

For a moment he thought she was going to look up at him again, but then she seemed to think better of it and stared instead at the house. He would have given a thousand pounds to be able to see her expression, or ten thousand to know her thoughts.

Lacking that ability, he instead signaled a small boy standing nearby to go to his horses' heads. Then he climbed down and walked around the carriage to help Lady Cassie descend. She was as light as a feather in his hands, and he wondered how such a tiny body could contain such a large heart and such a valiant spirit.

Despite the temptation, he did not let his hands linger on her waist a second longer than politeness dictated. Releasing her as soon as her feet touched the ground, he offered her his arm.

"Will you be attending the Heathertons' ball this evening?" he inquired.

There was a silence beside him as they mounted the steps, then a murmur of assent that was so soft that he was left with no doubts about her reluctance to let him know her plans for the evening. He had hoped that their drive—and more importantly, their discussion of mining conditions in Cornwall—would have lessened her fear of him, but she was obviously still uncomfortable in his presence. Reaching the door, he raised the heavy knocker and rapped loudly to summon the butler.

Despite her unspoken desire to have nothing further to do with him, he nevertheless asked politely if she would save the first waltz of the evening for him. She gave him no answer, but her hand, which had been resting lightly on his arm, suddenly tightened its grip.

His attention was focused so completely on her that it took him a moment to realize the door had opened on well-oiled hinges. Looking up, he saw a man standing in the doorway staring at him—an elegantly dressed young man, who was still handsome despite the lines of dissipation that were already carved into his face.

Although he had never before seen the man in person, Richard had no trouble recognizing the notorious Earl of Blackstone.

"I had not realized you were home, Geoffrey," Lady Cassie said. "May I present Mr.—"

"I wish to speak with you in the library," Lord Blackstone said curtly, cutting her off before she could complete the introductions. Then without in any way acknowledging Richard's presence, the earl turned on his heel and disappeared into the bowels of the house.

Richard could feel the tremors that shook Lady Cassie's entire body, and he wished he could simply whisk her back into his carriage and carry her away from this house—and more important, far, far away from her brother. Alternatively, he wished he could at least wrap his arms around her and hold her close until she stopped trembling.

But the rules of society demanded that he do nothing when she finally released her grip on his arm and followed her brother into the house.

You were rude just now, Cassie wanted to say. But for some reason—something she could see in her brother's expression—she could not bring herself to utter the words that would doubtless only serve to antagonize him further and put him in a worse mood than he was in already.

"In the future," Geoffrey said, his voice little more than a snarl, "you will not waste your time driving out with such men." He picked up a piece of paper from his desk and threw it at her face.

Startled, she flinched away, and the paper dropped harmlessly to the floor.

"That is a list of the men I have chosen as potential husbands for you. Pick it up," he ordered when she made no move to do so.

She met his gaze defiantly, but again, something in his eyes frightened her, no matter how brave she tried to be, and after a few moments, she bent and picked up the piece of paper.

Three names were inscribed upon it in her brother's scarcely legible scrawl: the Marquess of Fauxbridge, the Earl of Rowcliff, and Baron Atherston. The names were familiar, so she had undoubtedly met the men at some society function, but despite her best efforts, she could not put faces to the names.

"You will, of course, concentrate your efforts on Fauxbridge, since he is a marquess. But you must also encourage Rowcliff and Atherston, in case Fauxbridge fails to come up to scratch."

Cassie's hand shook so much, the names on the paper blurred before her eyes. Then to her dismay, a tear fell on the paper, causing the ink to run. She could only be thankful the brim of her bonnet hid her face—and her tears—from her brother.

These were the men who were going to bid for her—Geoffrey was going to sell her to one of these men. One of them was going to own her, body and soul, and there was nothing she could do about it except pray that whoever he was, he would treat her kindly.

"Well, what are you standing here for?" her brother snapped out.

Withoug deigning to answer him, Cassie turned and left the room, going in desperate search of Ellen, hoping despite all evidence to the contrary that her step-mother would do something to help her.

She found Ellen in her room, unpacking the latest batch of new gowns, and at the sight of all the bright colors and beautiful fabrics, the lace and beadwork, the ribbons and flounces, Cassie admitted to herself that Ellen would even sell her own daughter to the devil if it meant she could stay in London and continue to dress herself in the latest fashions.

"Oh, Cassie, look at my new blue lutestring—is it not lovely? I think I shall wear it tomorrow night to the opera. Dear Lady Letitia has invited us to share her box. But come, why the long face? Was your drive with Mr. Hawke so unpleasant then? I vow, if he is going to give you frown lines, then by all means you must do your best to avoid him."

"No," Cassie forced out, "it was not anything Mr. Hawke did. I have just had an interview with Geoffrey."

For a second Ellen's hands shook, and her eyes flitted desperately around the room, as if seeking a way to escape, but then she fixed a smile firmly on her face and asked in an overly bright voice, "And what did your brother wish to speak to you about?"

"He informed me . . . ." Cassie's own voice wavered, and she had to pause and start over again. "He told me which three men he finds acceptable as purchasers."

"Purchasers? Whatever are you talking about?"

"The men who shall be allowed to *buy* me," Cassie snapped out, finally losing control of her temper. "The men with pockets deep enough to satisfy Geoffrey."

"Your suitors, you mean? Oh, Cassie, this is so exciting! Show me the list."

Before Cassie could stop her, Ellen had snatched the piece of paper out of her hand and was reading aloud. "Faux-bridge, Rowcliff, Atherston—oh, this is marvelous beyond anything I had hoped for. A marquess! Imagine that. It is indeed unfortunate that there are no dukes of a marriageable age, but a marquess is almost as good."

Without warning, she threw her arms around Cassie and hugged her tightly.

Standing stiffly in her step-mother's embrace, Cassie said coldly, "I do not even know the man."

Ellen pulled away and looked down into her face. "But of course you know him. Why, you danced with him just last evening."

"I do not remember him."

"But you must remember—he is a marquess! Do, pray, cast your mind back. He was wearing a bottle-green waist-coat with roses picked out in seed pearls, and his cravat was tied in a *trone d'amour*—"

Jerking free of Ellen's arms, Cassie began to pace the room. "I am to marry a man because of his waistcoat and tie?"

Ellen gave a peal of laughter. "No, silly, because of his title. And his money, of course."

Cassie stopped directly in front of her step-mother and glared up at her. "Do you know, they have a name for women who sell themselves to men, and that name is *whore*!"

With no warning, Ellen's hand came up and slapped Cassie across the face, hard enough to make her stumble sideways. For a moment they both stood there staring at each other, then Ellen burst into tears. Automatically, Cassie embraced her and began patting her on the back, soothing her until her sobbing died down.

Pulling away, Ellen dried her face and without meeting

Cassie's gaze directly said, "I think I shall lie down now." Still sniffling and dabbing at her eyes, she crossed to the chaise longue, where she reclined gracefully, a woeful portrait of abject misery. "I suppose now you will refuse to go to the party this evening, and Geoffrey will be angry with me also."

"No," Cassie said tiredly, "I will go and dance with Fauxbridge and smile at Rowcliff and flirt with Atherston."

Without uttering another word, Cassie left her step-mother and returned to her own room, where she threw herself down on the bed. But the tears did not come—or rather, they remained locked in her heart—so when Annie later came to help do her hair, at least Cassie's eyes were clear, with no puffiness or redness to give an outward sign of her distress.

After a day of moderate success at investigating the men who appeared to be courting Lady Cassiopeia with serious intent, John Tuke was relaxing in an easy chair in the sitting room of their hotel suite, a bottle of Madeira on the table beside him, waiting for Richard and Perry to return with news of their day's activities.

Richard was the first to arrive, and John welcomed him with a smile and a lift of his goblet. "Welcome back, Richard. And how was your drive? Have you succeeded in winning the hand of your fair lady? Or has she at least ceased to tremble at the sight of you?"

Richard did not answer, but stood silently, clenching and unclenching his hands, looking as if he would like to smash everything in the room. Apparently his courtship of the Lady Cassiopeia was not progressing smoothly.

"That bad?" Tuke said mildly, trying to hide his smile. "It appears you need some liquid refreshment." Standing up, he fetched another goblet from the mantel and filled it with the sparkling amber liquid. "Here," he said, extending the drink to Richard, who took it and stared down at it.

Before he could lift it to his lips, however, his hand gripped the fragile crystal so tightly that it shattered, spilling its contents on the carpet.

Mutely, John handed him a handkerchief, and Richard wrapped it around his hand to stop the bleeding.

The cuts from the broken glass were little more than scratches, John was relieved to see, but it would appear that whatever was bothering Richard was no minor matter.

"Do you wish to tell me what has occurred?" John asked finally, the smile gone from his face.

After a short pause, Richard said simply, "I have met Lord Blackstone."

"And?"

Richard looked up at him and said bleakly, "He quite reminds me of Mudgeley."

Richard did not need to say anything further. At the mention of that name, John felt his own hands begin to tremble, and he quickly sat down again in his chair before his knees could fail him.

As overseer, Mudgeley had been the most hated man on the plantation where they had been slaves, because he had issued the daily orders and given out the job assignments. He had also been the most feared, since it had been his arm that had wielded the whip when they failed to finish the impossible quotas he had set for them.

But it had not only been control over their lives, which even now, years later, made John's heart pound in his chest. It was the fact that Mudgeley had taken a perverse pleasure in causing pain to others—in thinking up new and novel ways to torment and torture the slaves under his control.

"Dear Lord," John murmured. "If what you say is true, it would appear the earl has undoubtedly earned his nickname, 'Lord Blackheart.' "

"You spoke to me earlier about evil," Richard said. "Today I looked in the earl's eyes and saw a blackness of the soul that he could not hide—indeed, it appears he makes no effort to disguise it."

For a moment they both were lost in their thoughts, shaken by their memories. Then John said, "At least we can be thankful we are not in the earl's power."

"Lady Cassie is," Richard replied, his voice scarcely more than a whisper.

"But you will rescue her," John said, forcing a smile. "I have great confidence in your abilities."

"But I failed to rescue Molly. She died waiting for me

to return for her," Richard said, his voice now so soft John had to strain to hear him. But his friend's words, quiet as they were, felt to John like bullets smashing into his flesh.

Richard's courtship of an earl's daughter had seemed like a game to John—merely another challenge testing their combined abilities and ingenuity. But now that they knew the kind of man her brother was, it had indeed become a serious matter.

What fate might befall Lady Cassiopeia if Richard were too slow to win her for himself?

The Heathertons' ball was a tolerable success, Lady Letitia decided. Not because it was a "sad crush," which was every hostess's dream, nor was it because Lady Letitia's little machinations were all proceeding on schedule.

Due to her cousin's granddaughter having come down with the measles, and her third husband's grandniece being in mourning for one of her grandparents, Lady Letitia had ended up with the task of marrying off only three young ladies this Season, which was rather fewer than usual, and she had assumed it would be a bit boring this year with so little to occupy her time.

But that was before her grandson had returned from the Colonies, obviously in need of a wife. Not only was he the perfect age for matrimony, but there was a chance—however remote—that if he fell head over heels in love with an Englishwoman, he might not be so eager to sail back to America again.

Strangely enough, however, if she were to be honest with herself, Lady Letitia had to admit that she was even more intrigued by the prospect of helping Richard Hawke win the hand of Lady Cassiopeia.

As if her thoughts had conjured him up, Richard reappeared at her side, bearing two goblets. "It is rather inferior champagne, I am afraid," he said, handing her one of the glasses. "Remind me the next time we attend an affair hosted by Lord Heatherton, and I shall contrive to smuggle in a bottle of something that is a little more palatable."

He seated himself beside her, and as always, his eyes

immediately sought out Lady Cassie, who was dancing with Oliver Ingleby.

"You need have no worries about my grandnephew, at least," Lady Letitia said. "Although he is far from being a pauper, his pockets are not deep enough for Blackstone to consider him as a suitor for Cassie's hand."

"It is a pity she is so beautiful," her companion mused. "As it is, Tuke is hard-pressed to investigate all of her assorted suitors."

"Ah, the redoubtable John Tuke. I have also heard many tales of his fearlessness and his physical prowess. But I had not realized he had accompanied you back to England. Why have you not brought him to meet me? I would also wish to thank him in person for the care he has extended to my grandson."

"He is . . . shy about going out into company."

"Shy? You may give him my word that I shall not bite his head off."

"No, no," Richard said with a smile. "I am sure he has no fear of you."

"Of what then?"

"He fears evil incarnate, or at least that is the way he has explained it to me. He claims that he feels safer with me as his shield and defender." Richard smiled wryly, and it was easy for her to believe that it was a role he was not entirely comfortable with.

"I see," Lady Letitia said, but her mind was already busy considering this new challenge. Who could she find to be a wife for John Tuke? Not a woman who would protect him from evil, but a woman he himself would need to defend, that much was obvious.

"Tell John Tuke that he is to call upon me tomorrow afternoon at two o'clock, so that I may thank him in person." Then lowering her voice, she added, "And you may also tell him that the only three men whom he needs to investigate are Lord Fauxbridge, Lord Rowcliff, and Lord Atherston. Of all the peers who are currently in the market for a wife, they are the only three who are also rich enough to attract Lord Blackstone's interest. And they have all three signed

Lady Cassie's dance card this evening. I can, if you wish, point them out to you.''

Richard was not slow to take her up on her offer, and she not only indicated which three men were his rivals, but also gave him a thorough description of their character and a brief history of each man.

As always when he was with her, Lady Letitia could not help feeling a twinge of regret that Richard was young enough to be her grandson, since he appeared to possess all the traits she usually looked for in a husband. His only flaw was that he simply did not have enough years behind him.

Or she had too many.

Pshaw! That was the type of depressing thought she had resolved to give up when she passed her fortieth birthday and decided to stop counting her years. In spirit she was still younger than many of the women here who were half her age and one of these days she might even bestir herself and find a fifth husband.

In the meantime . . . ''I believe my grandson was to accompany you this evening?''

''Perry? Ah, yes. We were actually coming out the door together when Stanfrew arrived to discuss the sale of a filly. The horse in question being a particularly fine specimen, Perry exclaimed to me that the opportunity was not to be lost. He did send his regrets, however,'' Richard said, the hint of a smile tugging at his mouth.

''Did he now?'' Lady Letitia said mildly, and Richard's smile deepened.

''He has, of course, no real objections to the Heathertons' ball—''

''Just that there is a dearth of four-legged females here,'' Lady Letitia concluded.

''Exactly! He shall be so happy to hear that you understand completely.'' Richard's smile was now full-blown, and grinning like that, he looked years younger than the age she knew him to be.

''Oh, I understand full well what his intentions are. But tell me—and please be honest—just how long is he planning to stay in England?''

"He has not set a date for his departure, but he has indicated his willingness to stay until the end of the Season. After which, I believe, he intends to travel in Ireland for a while, buying up more good breeding stock."

"I am surprised to discover that he has the necessary funds for such purchases."

There was a long silence before Richard spoke again. "I have offered to lend him the necessary capital as an investment."

For the first time in years, Lady Letitia felt herself in imminent danger of losing her temper. How could Richard not only refuse to help her keep her favorite grandson in England, but also actively promote Perry's departure?

"I regret that I cannot do what you requested of me," Richard said, "but I have a strong aversion to forcing people to do what they do not wish to do. Coercion is linked so closely in my mind to slavery, and slavery is something I must always fight against, no matter how it seeks to disguise itself."

His tone of voice was so bleak, and there was so much pain in his eyes, that Lady Letitia could not remain angry with him. "I understand why you feel as you do, but for myself, I can only regret that you were not here sixty years ago, when I could have used your support in my own struggles for freedom."

Ponderous. That one word described Lord Fauxbridge perfectly, Cassie decided. Although not precisely fat, there was a thickness about his torso and limbs that was decidedly off-putting. Even his fingers, which now held hers in too tight a grip, were pudgy, and she had to fight off the urge to jerk her hands away from his touch.

Still, as unappealing as he was to her physically, it was his conversation that she found most disheartening. His words were all so weighty and uttered with such deliberation, that she could picture them dropping one by one like stones out of his mouth, falling to the floor to trip up the unwary. Somehow, he made every sentence he uttered sound like the most solemn pronouncement, as if he were the Bishop of London preaching a sermon to the King himself.

Despite his bulk, Lord Fauxbridge knew every step of the country dance, which was lucky for her, as he would surely have crushed her foot if he trod upon it. Still, there was no grace in his movements, only a mechanical perfection.

Worst of all, he appeared to be totally infatuated with her, and she could tell that with the slightest sign from her that she favored his suit, he would rush posthaste to her brother to ask for her hand.

Could she do it? Could she give him that encouragement? If she did not, her brother would be so angry there was no telling what he might do. On the other hand, could she bear to spend a lifetime with such a ponderous companion?

She could not suppress a feeling of deep relief when the music finally ended and Fauxbridge escorted her back to her step-mother, who was sitting and chatting with Oliver Ingleby. But Cassie had not long to savor her release from the weight of Lord Fauxbridge's company.

"Thank you for the dance, Lady Cassiopeia." The marquess bowed formally over her hand but did not release it, not even when she tugged gently, trying to free her fingers from his grasp. "Would you do me the honor of driving out with me tomorrow afternoon?"

Cassie opened her mouth, but she could not say the words that would seal her fate.

"Why, Lord Fauxbridge, what a marvelous idea." Ellen rose to her feet and put her arm around Cassie's shoulders. Batting her eyes wildly at the marquess, who was still attached to Cassie's hand, she said lightly, "And I can see that my step-daughter is so overcome by your flattering attention, she is unable to express her delight properly."

To Cassie's amazement, the marquess did not boggle at the notion that a young lady might be rendered speechless by an invitation from him.

"Shall we say four o'clock then?" He smiled down at her—except to Cassie, it looked more like a leer than a smile.

She could not bring herself to agree until Ellen pinched her on the arm. "Yes, four o'clock," she finally managed to squeak out, and was rewarded by the return of her hand, which Lord Fauxbridge had squeezed so tightly, her fingers had all gone quite numb.

The minute he was out of earshot, Ellen began to scold, her voice low enough that no one would be able to overhear her. "Have you no sense at all? How could you play such coy games with Fauxbridge? Do you think he is so infatuated with you that you can dangle him like a puppet on a string? He is well aware of his own worth, and if you toy with him, you will lose him."

"I was not being coy," Cassie whispered back. "I find the marquess quite repellent."

"Do not be a nodcock," he step-mother replied, tugging her down into her chair. "He is rich and he is a marquess, which makes him quite the most eligible bachelor of the Season. It will be a real feather in your cap if you catch him."

"A title cannot make up for deficiencies of character."

"Yes, it can," Ellen said, smiling determinedly. "A title can make any suitor palatable."

"Even my father?"

For a moment Ellen's polite smile faltered, but she made a quick recovery. "I shall be eternally grateful that my parents were wise enough to arrange such an advantageous marriage for me."

It was hopeless. No one was going to help her escape the horrible fate Geoffrey had arranged for her. Ellen would not, Digory would not, and there was no one else Cassie could turn to.

Feeling like a rabbit caught in a poacher's trap, Cassie looked wildly around the room, searching for an escape even while she knew none was to be found.

Then her eyes made contact with those of Mr. Hawke, who was openly staring at her. For a moment she was tempted to appeal to him for help, but a brief reflection made her realize how ridiculous such a notion was. That would be akin to asking the fox to help guard the chicken house.

Chapter Nine

Sisters were a plaguey nuisance, Oliver Ingleby decided, pacing back and forth in the entrance hall of his town house. As dearly as he loved Cecily, right now he could not help feeling exasperated with her. If she did not hurry, they would miss the entire first act of the opera.

Finally, too impatient to wait any longer, he took the stairs two at a time and was soon rapping on the door of his sister's bedroom. Hearing her voice bidding him enter, he opened the door to discover she was fully dressed in a glittery gold gown, several ostrich feathers in her hair. She was standing in front of her cheval glass, studying her reflection.

"Thank goodness you are finally ready to go. Where is your cloak? I have had the horses put to a good half hour ago."

"Just a minute, Oliver. I am not quite sure I like the fit of this gown. I am considering whether I should change into my green one, even though I have already worn it once before. But if Betty sews some new ribbons on it, perhaps no one will—"

Grabbing his sister's hand, Oliver began dragging her protesting out of the room.

Behind him Betty, the maid, squeaked out, "Wait, Miss Cecily needs her cloak," but Oliver was beyond waiting.

"Brothers," Cecily muttered under her breath, even though she followed him docilely enough. "Since when have you become such a fan of the opera that you cannot bear to be the merest bit late?"

Reaching the foot of the stairs, Oliver was forced to cool his heels a few minutes longer, while the maid hurried down and draped a russet cloak around his sister's shoulders.

"Oh-ho," Cecily cried out abruptly. "I know what it is.

You are not in a hurry to listen to the caterwauling of a parcel of well-endowed sopranos and overweight tenors. It is obvious that you must be impatient to see a woman—a particular woman!''

Oliver felt his face grow hot, and he knew he must be blushing from ear to ear.

"You are in love," his sister crowed. "At last you have thrown your heart over the windmill."

Betty was gazing up at him, her mouth agape, while James, the footman, was staring straight ahead, doing an imitation of a statue carved out of marble. But Oliver well knew that as soon as the door closed behind him and his sister, the maid and the footman both would be off like a flash to the servants' hall, there to report what they had overheard.

Unfortunately, there was no way to call his sister a liar— or at least no way that he could probably convince her she was mistaken, since what she had deduced was nothing more nor less than the truth: He was in love, head over heels in love, as agonizingly in love as a callow youth in the first throes of calf-love. And love makes fools out of all men.

Turning on his heels, he stalked out to the waiting carriage, not bothering to make sure his sister was following. She was forced to scramble into the vehicle without any help from him, but she managed with the same ease with which she had as a child climbed trees on their estate. She had apparently not outgrown all her hoydenish ways, even though her London manners were in general quite above reproach.

Seating herself opposite him, she smiled like a cat and said smugly, "I can guess who you have fallen in love with."

His heart sank, and he considered the possibility of bribing his sister to guard her tongue. But honesty compelled him to admit to himself that it would take more than gold to achieve such a longed-for outcome. Having learned to talk when she was barely a year and a half old, Cecily had been chattering ever since. In short, it would take a miracle to keep her from broadcasting his affairs all over town.

It was enough to make a man flee the country. But if he did, he would never see his beloved again, never look down into eyes that were lifted so appealingly to his, never feel the curves of her waist beneath his hand when they waltzed, never hear the sound of her voice—

"Oh, I shall dearly love having a sister at last. But do you honestly think you have a chance?"

Of course he did not have a chance. It was not only the disparity in their ages, but dearest Ellen, Lady Blackstone, was every bit as much in love with Dillingham as he, Oliver, was in love with her.

"I have heard that Lady Cassie's brother is determined upon snaring a rich peer for her."

Ladie Cassie? For a moment Oliver's mind went blank. Then he realized to his vast relief that his sister had misconstrued the entire situation. She thought he was haunting Lord Blackstone's residence because he was interested in Lady Cassie. Cecily did not even suspect that he had given his heart to Lady Blackstone the first time she had smiled up at him.

Ignoring his sister's continued chattering, he allowed his mind to drift backward. With feelings of joy that he would be seeing her again, mixed with despair that he would never win her hand for himself, one by one he pulled out all his most treasured memories—each word dear Ellen had said to him, each smile she had bestowed so casually on him, every touch of her hand on his sleeve . . .

Tonight she would be attending the opera with her dearly beloved Arthur for the first time in fifteen years. Ellen felt bubbles of excitement racing through her veins. Her late husband had never wished to attend any musical event, nor indeed any form of entertainment that did not involve eating massive amounts of food and imbibing great quantities of wine.

Arthur, however, was cut from altogether different cloth. Why, the last time he had escorted her, when she was but a young girl of seventeen, he had not even spared a glance for the opera dancers showing off their charms on the stage. And the next day he had told her that when she spoke, her voice was more musical than anything written by some Italian composer.

But the day after that, her father had informed her that Lord Blackstone had offered for her hand.

With a sigh for those few magical days so long gone, Ellen rapped on her step-daughter's door. When there was no answer, she opened the door and peered inside. Her mood of mellow reminiscence vanished in an instant.

Instead of being occupied with putting the finishing touches on her toilette for the evening, Cassie was lying flat on her back in bed, a folded cloth over her eyes.

Well! If her step-daughter thought she was going to indulge in another fit of the megrims, she was sadly mistaken.

Marching resolutely into the room, Ellen snatched away the damp cloth. She was so upset that she did not trouble to keep her voice well modulated, but snapped out, "What on earth are you about? Arthur will be here any minute, and you are still in your shift!"

"I am not feeling up to attending the opera tonight," Cassie replied in her mulish tone of voice that always made Ellen want to shake her. "Lord Fauxbridge has already given me a headache, and since you were so *helpful* as to inform him where we would be this evening, he has announced that he will be sure to seek me out during the intermission. He did not, of course, stop to discover if I *wished* to set eyes on him twice in one day. If he had, I would have told him point-blank that one hour in his company is more than adequate for a single day—indeed, for an entire week!"

"He actually said he would visit you during the intermission?" When Cassie scowled petulantly and nodded her head, Ellen clapped her hands in delight. "How marvelous! At the rate matters are progressing, I should not be surprised if he soon takes you to meet his mother. What a feather in your cap that will be!"

Cassie sat up in bed and glared at her. "How can you possibly say it is marvelous? The man is a pompous, ponderous, posturing popinjay. I would not wish to meet his mother if she were the Queen of England."

Ellen again felt the palm of her hand itch with the urge to slap her step-daughter. How could the chit be so unreasonable? So impossibly stubborn? It was all Geoffrey's fault, of course, for leaving them to rot in Cornwall. Isolated from society for so many years, Cassie just could not be brought to understand which things were important and which were not.

"But physical violence had never been the way to win Cassie's cooperation, and cooperate she must, because it was not every day that one received an invitation to watch the opera from Lady Letitia's box.

Smiling instead of slapping, Ellen grasped her step-daughter's hands and pulled her from the bed. "Of course he is a pompous, posturing, and . . . what else did you call him?"

"Ponderous," Cassie muttered, but at least she appeared to have accepted the idea that she must attend the opera, headache or no.

Feeling quite relieved that the crisis was over, Ellen laughed. "Ponderous—yes, that is exactly the word for Lord Fauxbridge." She pulled a new white dress embroidered with clusters of red rosebuds over Cassie's head and quickly fastened it up. Picking up a hairbrush, she began vigorously dragging it through her step-daughter's black tresses.

"But what you must remember, my dear, is that he is a marquess, and not only a marquess, but a very *rich* marquess. Think of how wonderful it will be when you can command an army of servants, when every modiste in town is competing to win your patronage, when you can wear the Fauxbridge jewels, which rival the Crown jewels, or so I have been told."

Cassie muttered something about not caring about such things, and for a moment Ellen wondered if her step-daughter's mind was deranged. But time was of the essence, so she could not afford another quarrel. Without giving the recalcitrant chit an opportunity to voice further objections, Ellen continued in a bright, cheerful voice that was deliberately designed to bring Cassie into the proper mood.

"Why, every young lady in London for the Season will be positively *green* with envy if Fauxbridge does seek you out during the intermission. The gossips report that *dozens* of ambitious mothers have made a push to capture him, but he has never before shown such a *marked* partiality for any eligible maiden, although he has been known to pursue the more *racy* widows.''

Ellen abruptly became aware that her wayward tongue had gotten her into deep water. Such scandalous *on-dits* were not at all suitable for the tender ears of an unmarried maiden like her step-daughter. And more important, knowing about such liaisons, which were, after all, quite normal among gentlemen, was only likely to make Cassie even more reluctant to accept Fauxbridge's suit if he did come up to scratch, which Ellen had every reason to expect he would.

Tossing down the brush, she hurried to the door, where she paused only long enough to utter a feeble explanation for her hasty retreat. ''I find I must, after all, summon Annie to finish your hair. It is not responding to my efforts in the slightest.''

So, thought Cassie, watching her red-faced step-mother flee the room, My Lord Fauxbridge is not only ponderous, it appears he is also a womanizer.

What a bargain she would be getting. No, she corrected herself, the gains would all be on Geoffrey's side. Once she was safely wedded to Lord Fauxbridge, her brother could raid the marquess's purse with impunity, since Fauxbridge was too stiff-rumped to allow the slightest hint of scandal to besmirch his family name. Never would he allow a brother-in-law to be cast into debtor's prison.

Cassie blinked back tears at the thought and wished that she could bestow her unsuitable suitor on one of the multitude of young girls supposedly pining after him. Although when she thought about it, the image of Fauxbridge surrounded by a sea of adoring females was completely ludicrous. More than likely it was only the matchmaking mamas who considered him an eligible parti.

The door to her room opened again, but this time Cassie was relieved to see it was Annie, the only member of the household Cassie considered a friend.

''What did you say to Lady Blackstone to put her in such a taking?'' Annie asked, coming over to where Cassie sat and picking up the discarded brush.

"All I did was tell her my honest opinion of the ponderous Lord Fauxbridge," Cassie replied vehemently. "I wish certain people would understand that I would truly rather starve in the gutter than marry such a—such a jackass as Lord Fauxbridge!"

Twisting Cassie's hair up on top of her head and pinning it securely in place, Annie said quite prosaically, "I have tried starving in the gutter. If I were you, I would sooner accept an honorable proposal, because in the gutter all you will be getting are dishonorable propositions."

"That does not matter. I shall simply tell them all no also."

"A fine plan indeed. But unfortunately men do not willingly accept a refusal from a defenseless woman in the gutter. They would consider you fair game—a tasty morsel to be gobbled up without a second thought."

"How can you talk that way?" Cassie protested. But even as she said the words, her eyes met Annie's steady gaze in the mirror, and Cassie had to admit the justice of the Scottish girl's statement, unpalatable as the truth might be. Cassie had only to remember several unfortunate women she had known in Cornwall to accept that a female was powerless to protect herself when a man decided to use his superior physical strength against her.

Cassie's heart went out to the Scottish girl, who must have suffered terribly after her husband died. "Were you . . ." Cassie did not know how to phrase the question in such a way that it would not cause offense—or additional pain.

Instead of being embarrassed, however, Annie smiled broadly. "You needn't worry about me. My husband taught me to defend myself. Used properly, a small dagger can compensate for a large difference in size."

Eagerly, Cassie jumped to her feet. "But that is the answer! Do you not see, Annie? If you teach me to use a knife, then I can also defend myself—then I will not need a husband."

"No," Annie said flatly, "that is not what you need to learn."

Feeling betrayed by her one and only friend, Cassie balled her hands into fists and glared up at Annie. "Why does everyone assume that I am totally incompetent and incapable merely because I am smaller than the average woman? You just told me yourself that a knife is a great equalizer, so why will you not teach me to use one? Do you think I am incapable of learning anything?''

"Oh, no, I think you are quite capable. You can undoubtedly learn how to conceal a knife about your person, and I can teach you the proper way to hold it. And it is not difficult to learn where to slice a man if you wish to maim him permanently, or where to slip in the blade if you wish to kill him instantly.''

Cassie felt herself growing faint at the images that Annie's words conjured up, but she did her best to hide her weakness from the other girl. "So, what is the p-problem then?''

"The problem is,'' the Scottish girl continued relentlessly, "that I cannot teach you or show you or give you the resolution necessary to actually use those skills against another human being.''

"Oh, Annie,'' Cassie said, swaying on her feet.

A moment later Annie was hugging her. Cassie fought against the tears that were forming in her eyes. "You are right. I could never bring myself to hurt anyone. But there must be some way out—some other alternative to marrying Lord Fauxbridge—because it is all I can do to avoid shuddering when he even touches my hand.''

"I cannot believe your brother would—''

"My brother? Geoffrey has told me he will sell Seffie to a white slaver if I do not comply with his wishes.''

For a moment Annie's hand, which had been patting Cassie's back, was still. "I was referring to your other brother, Digory Rendel.''

Immediately, Cassie felt better—strong enough even to move out of the comforting circle of the other girl's arms. "Of course! How could I have forgotten? Digory himself said that he came to London specifically to make sure that Geoffrey did not force me to marry the wrong man. And despite his title and his wealth, no one but a featherhead like Ellen—or a greedy, grasping, selfish pig like Geoffrey— could think that Lord Fauxbridge would make *any* woman a good husband.

"Oh, Annie, please help me. Find Digory and explain what has happened. Ask him to meet me in the kitchen garden after we get back from the opera."

The opera was like a symbol, showing him how far he had come, Richard thought. Many times as a skinny, always very hungry young boy, he had stood hidden in the shadows of Covent Gardens, watching the elegantly clad gentlemen escorting beautifully gowned ladies into the theater. And now tonight, for the first time, he would be entering those majestic portals—entering the world of beauty and fantasy that lay behind the stone walls and heavy wooden doors.

He had, of course, already seen numerous other theatrical productions in America, even operas. But somehow the Covent Garden Theater was different—more special—because he still saw it through the eyes of the child he had been.

Would it live up to his expectations? Would it still seem a magical place, or would the layers of skepticism and cynicism that had grown around his heart prevent him from enjoying the pageantry and glamour? Would he see that the gold was merely gilt? That the velvets and satins worn by the actors were undoubtedly stained by sweat and make-up? That the houses and trees on the stage were merely painted canvas?

More important, would he see that the ladies and gentlemen in the audience, who all those years before had seemed godlike, were mere mortals? That like people everywhere, some of them were admirable and some were not. Some of the "ladies" had the souls of courtesans, and some of the "gentlemen" were as uncivilized in their habits as any longshoreman.

Adjusting the folds of his cravat, Richard surveyed himself in the looking glass. One thing he did not doubt—this time, instead of wearing dirty rags, he would be as elegantly dressed as anyone there, and his clothes could hide his true nature as well as anyone else's. No one would suspect that he was not a gentleman—that he had not been born with a silver spoon in his mouth and a family standing stalwart behind him.

Staring at the mirror, he observed the connecting door behind him open, and Tuke entered, a glass of brandy in his hand. Although John had reluctantly paid a call on Lady Letitia, he had resisted all of her and Richard's entreaties to attend the opera.

"I wish you would change your mind and come with us," Richard said. "There will be room for you."

"It is not a matter of overcrowding the box," John replied mockingly. "But if I came, I would be odd man out, and the numbers would be thrown off. Only consider, as it now stands, you will be escorting Lady Letitia, Perry is matched up with his cousin Cecily, Dillingham is paired with Lady Blackstone, which leaves young Ingleby to do the honors with Lady Cassiopeia."

Knowing from years of experience just how stubborn his companion could be, Richard did not point out the obvious, namely that Lady Letitia could quite easily have found a female partner for John, also. Instead, Richard changed the subject.

"Have you succeeded in learning anything about Fauxbridge?"

"Everything and nothing," John replied. "Everything about his family, his estate, his habits, his horses, his women. But nothing that will be of the slightest use for our purpose. As boring a bag-of-wind as he is, I have not yet been able to find a weakness we can exploit."

Richard uttered a colorful oath.

"Do not despair so easily," John chastised him gently. "As they say, Rome was not built in a day, and even God required six days to create the universe. I have been investigating the man for less than twenty-four hours. Only give me a little more time, and I will find the key to ending his courtship of Lady Cassiopeia."

"I am sorry to be so lacking in patience, but I cannot help feeling the need to proceed with great dispatch." Picking up his top hat and cane, Richard did not give John a chance to question the reason for his anxiety, which would have been hard to explain, consisting as it did merely of feelings, rather than logical thoughts. "Is Perry ready for the opera, or has he again slipped away to see a man about a horse?"

"I have seen to it that he is wearing proper evening attire, but from the glint of mischief in his eyes, I would say he has already prepared a last-minute excuse."

Turning away from the mirror, Richard looked John straight in the eye. "As much as I am opposed to coercion, tonight I think we must see to it that Perry does not disoblige Lady Letitia."

"Of course. 'Twould be the height of incivility if he put a four-legged filly before his own grandmother."

"Or even more appalling to contemplate, if he is allowed to slip away, the numbers would be thrown off, and you would doubtless be required to attend the opera in his stead."

John grinned. "In that case, I am sure I can persuade the reluctant viscount to do his filial duty, even if I have to carry him bodily to his grandmother's side."

Never, since the day she had first left Cornwall, had Cassie wished so desperately to be back home. She might have actually enjoyed the singing and the fancy costumes if anyone else in the theater had been paying attention to what was transpiring on the stage. Unfortunately, all the eyes in the theater were trained on her, or at least so it seemed.

The evening at the opera had not started out poorly, to be sure. But gradually everyone had become aware that Lord Fauxbridge, whose box was almost directly opposite Lady Letitia's, was doing nothing but ogle her through his opera glasses. As a result, one after another of the occupants of the other boxes—followed in due course by the young bucks in the pit—had also begun craning their necks to see what the attraction was.

Or rather, *who* the attraction was. At first Cassie had felt herself blushing at being the center of attention, but she had assumed—wrongly—that when the performance began, everyone's eyes would be on the dancers and singers. Now she was beyond blushing. Staring fixedly at the stage, she tried to avoid looking at the other boxes. Actually, all she really wanted to do was find a small, dark place to hide. It was unfortunate that no one had ever built a priest's hole in an opera box.

Just the thought of such a thing made Cassie smile, and

as soon as she did, a ripple of sound and movement swept through the crowd. Risking a glance around the theater, she saw to her added dismay that now people were not only still looking at her, but also talking about her—the "ladies" whispering behind their fans, the "gentlemen" talking about her openly, smirking with their friends, even pointing at her.

"Do you realize, my child, how much money most of the ladies here tonight would pay to be in your shoes?" Lady Letitia's voice was a quiet murmur in her ear. "To be the center of attention at the opera is every woman's dream. To that end, Lady Ermyntrude has festooned herself with every jewel and bauble she owns, the Mulrooney sisters have nearly bankrupted their brother to pay for their outfits, and Mrs. Hennings, among others, has come this evening in the sheerest of muslin gowns, dampened to reveal every one of her overabundant charms. Yet all their stratagems have failed, because it is you who has captured the fancy of the crowd."

"They care nothing about me," Cassie whispered back out of the corner of her mouth. "They only wish to see whether Lord Fauxbridge will be obtaining good value for his money."

"It might help, my dear, if you were to picture Lord Fauxbridge standing in front of you at this moment."

Cassie turned her head and looked directly at Lady Letitia, who, she discovered, was smiling seraphically, like the cat who has eaten the cream.

"Then you could imagine yourself placing both hands against his chest and giving him a mighty shove."

The thought of the pompous Lord Fauxbridge tumbling head over heels into the pit was so ridiculous, Cassie had to bite her lip to keep from laughing out loud. Instead, she resolutely stiffened her back and fixed her most serene expression on her face.

Looking around the theater quite openly now, she felt her fear and cowardice melt away. Who were these people, to think they could stare her out of countenance? She was the daughter of an earl, after all. And not only that, she could cope with anything.

These people, however, were like delicate hothouse flowers. They would wilt if exposed to the biting wind of Cornwall—they would doubtless fall into hysterics if someone told them to skin a rabbit or muck out a horse's stall.

Actually, if Ellen and Cecily were anything to go on, these ladies would probably have the hysterics if asked to iron their own ribbons or brew their own cup of tea.

When her glance reached Lord Fauxbridge's box, she paused, once again seeing him in her mind's eye tumbling over and over, like a child's toy. The image made her smile, and at once the ponderous lord lowered his opera glasses. Then the fool held up his hand and wiggled his pudgy fingers at her, and again a murmur of sound swept the opera house.

Really, Cassie thought with disgust, the man has no common sense whatsoever. Deliberately wiping the smile from her face, she turned her attention back to the stage, but it was too late. The curtain was coming down for the intermission.

Glancing back at Lord Fauxbridge's box, she was dismayed to see it was already empty. She would have wagered pounds to pence that she knew where he was headed, but she would have had difficulty finding any takers.

"Is it not wonderful?" Ellen spoke from directly behind Cassie's ear. "I am positive Lord Fauxbridge is totally besotted with you. Now remember, if he asks to take you to meet his mother, you *must* say yes. Now is not the time to insult the man. He could still slip out of our grasp."

I hope someone will let me know when it is the proper time to insult him, Cassie thought to herself. More practically, if she bestirred herself, she might still escape from the box before Lord Fauxbridge arrived. Standing up, she turned toward the door, but her step-mother seemed to have read her mind. Moving to cut Cassie's escape, Ellen glared at Cassie, and it was obvious she was ready to go to any extremes to ensure that Cassie complied with her wishes.

Even knowing in advance it would be futile, Cassie looked around desperately for an ally, for anyone who might help her avoid the upcoming meeting with Fauxbridge. Her nominal escort for the evening, Mr. Ingleby, had already vanished from the box.

Then her eyes met those of Mr. Hawke, and she could see he fully grasped her predicament. The only thing preventing her from asking him to help was Digory's words—"Men like you have described to me do not generally allow anyone else to make the rules for them."

She had made a pact with Mr. Hawke once, back in that little inn in Cornwall, and she had survived unscathed. Dare she accept the offer she could now read in his face? Or would it be tempting fate once too often? Would he this time demand her soul?

Chapter Ten

Cassie's desperate desire to escape from Lord Fauxbridge warred with her need for self-preservation. As a result, she was still staring mutely into Mr. Hawke's eyes when the door to the box opened to admit Lord Fauxbridge.

Mr. Hawke raised one eyebrow in silent question. It would appear that the time had come for her to stop waffling around like a silly pea-goose and make up her mind. Deciding the devil she knew was safer than the pompous peer she had no desire to know, she nodded her head an infinitesimal degree. Mr. Hawke immediately bent and said something to Lady Letitia.

What it was, Cassie had no way of knowing, but before Lord Fauxbridge could do more than bow over her hand and begin to spout the most fulsome of compliments, Lady Letitia bellowed out, "Ah, Humphrey, dear boy. Come sit beside me and tell me how your dear mama is getting on. I have not seen her in an age."

The "dear boy" was clearly torn by indecision, but Cassie deftly extracted her hand from his grip, and Lady Letitia took care of the rest. "Richard, do not stand there in Lord Fauxbridge's way. Make yourself useful and take Lady Cassiopeia out for a walk in the salon. She is doubtless parched, and there is no need for her to stay cooped up in the box with an old woman like me. Dear Humphrey can keep me tolerably entertained until you return."

Leaving behind a red-faced Lord Fauxbridge looking about as miserable as a grown man could look, Cassie laid her hand on Mr. Hawke's arm and allowed him to escort her out into the corridor, which was now jammed with other theater patrons, some obviously intent upon securing refreshments, while others were merely using the opportunity to meet with friends.

As crowded as it was, a path cleared before them as if by magic, and Cassie's smile gradually faded. For a moment she had forgotten how dangerous the man beside her was. She sneaked a peek up at his face. Well, perhaps dangerous was not the proper word, since he had always treated her with the greatest kindness and respect. But still, there was definitely something about him that set him apart from the other gentlemen. Something that caused other people to move aside when he approached where they were standing.

It was not his clothing, which was in all ways a model of elegance and good taste. It was perhaps the intensity of his expression . . . as if he were a man who was accustomed to getting his own way. But no, that made it sound as if he were an overgrown, spoiled baby, like Lord Fauxbridge. It was rather . . .

Cassie's heart skipped a beat when it came to her that Mr. Hawke looked like a man accustomed to *taking* what he wanted from life. Just as she realized this, he looked down at her and their glances met. Gazing deep into his eyes, she could read quite plainly that what he wanted this time—what he was intent upon having . . . was her.

How long they stood there, she had no way of knowing, because it seemed to her as if all the world stood waiting, as if time itself paused. Then he raised his eyebrows again, this time silently asking her if she would . . . would what? Would go with him? Would trust him enough to give herself into his keeping? Would marry him?

"Would you like some champagne?" he asked.

At the sound of his voice, the strange spell he had cast over her was broken. Lowering her eyes, she felt no relief at his polite question, however, because it was not the question he had been asking with his eyes, and there was no way she could pretend that she had misunderstood the message he had conveyed so clearly without words.

Releasing his arm, she said merely, "Yes, please. I find I am indeed quite parched."

He had scarcely moved away from her side when someone else spoke to her.

"But my dear Lady Cassiopeia, what is this? Have you

been abandoned by your escort? Shame on him for treating you so cavalierly.''

Turning, she saw the smiling face of her second official suitor. ''Good evening, Lord Rowcliff. Mr. Hawke has not actually abandoned me. He is merely fetching me a glass of champagne.'' Although she knew Lord Rowcliff was several years older than herself, his face still had a boyish quality about it that made her feel as if she were his elder.

''The fortunate Mr. Hawke—how I envy him that he is your lucky escort this evening. Would that I were granted such a favor.''

Unformed, yes, that was the word for Lord Rowcliff. His expression was so open, so guileless, so carefree, it seemed to her as if he were newly created—as if life and fate and fortune had not yet set a single mark upon him. Where Mr. Hawke was an enigma, with hidden depths to his character that she was afraid to explore, Lord Rowcliff, on the other hand, was an open book, whose pages could be riffled and perused by anyone.

''Mr. Hawke is not actually my escort,'' she was quick to respond, lest the gossips should spread their tattle tales around town, linking her name with Mr. Hawke's. ''We are both merely members of Lady Letitia's party this evening.''

She was not sure why she was so worried about word of Mr. Hawke's interest in her getting back to Geoffrey. Did she simply wish to avoid an unpleasant confrontation with her brother—a scolding for not obeying his direct command? Or was she . . . no, that was patently ridiculous. She could not possibly be trying to protect Mr. Hawke from Geoffrey's wrath.

Watching the said Mr. Hawke approach her carrying two glasses of champagne, she could not picture his requiring anyone's protection. In fact, she could not imagine his ever needing any woman, period. He seemed too self-contained, too sure of himself, too thoroughly in control of his life.

So forceful was his personality, it seemed to her that she could have closed her eyes and still have known he was approaching. On the other hand, even when she had her eyes open and was staring right at him, Lord Rowcliff did not seem completely real. With only a minimal response from her, he chattered away quite charmingly, but somehow his words conveyed no meaning to her.

Unformed, insubstantial, inconsequential, he was like a figment of someone's imagination—like a hero in a novel by Mrs. Radcliffe, possessing all the gifts of the gods, such as good looks, wealth, and an inoffensive manner. Unfortunately, Lord Rowcliff had no more depth of character than those paper heroes.

Which induced Cassie to pose the as yet hypothetical question—assuming she could somehow discourage Lord Fauxbridge from offering for her—would she be any better off married to Lord Rowcliff?

Digory Rendel watched his sister pace back and forth in the shadows of the kitchen garden. It was too dark to see her face, but her whispered words left no doubt in his mind as to her emotions. She was as angry as he had ever known her to be.

His sister. He rather liked the sound of that—his sister. Never, not in all the years he had taken care of her, had he allowed himself to call her that. Even in his own thoughts he had always been careful to think of her as Lady Cassie. But now, he decided, convention be damned, she was his sister and he loved her more than anyone else on the face of the earth. Even though he could never acknowledge their relationship publicly, at least in his own mind he could claim her.

"And then," she now concluded indignantly, "after all my efforts to prevent Lord Fauxbridge from having an opportunity to speak with me privately, I returned to Lady Letitia's box only to find that Ellen had accepted for me!"

"Accepted?" Digory asked. "Surely he did not make a formal offer for your hand at the opera?"

"Of course not, but it was almost as bad. He arranged with Ellen to take me to meet his mother tomorrow afternoon. Do you realize what that means? Arthur was quick to point out to me the significance of such an invitation, as if I were too green to recognize the trap I am being pushed into."

"Arthur?"

"Dillingham. Ellen's old beau. Although I am surprised he was even awake long enough to notice what was going forward. He was snoring through most of the opera."

"Quite a romantic evening you have had," Digory said with a chuckle.

"Do not laugh at me! It was the worst evening of my life. Oh, why do people think titles are so important? Why? Tell me, Digory, because I cannot understand it."

"Can you not? Have you yourself never felt proud of the fact that you are Lady Cassiopeia, the daughter of the Earl of Blackstone? Can you honestly say you have never been glad that you were not just plain Miss Anderby?"

She caught her breath with a gasp, and he realized his voice had sounded harsher than he had intended. It was, after all, not Cassie's fault that he was a bastard—that their father had tricked his mother into lying with him and had then abandoned her.

"But my name is all I have to be proud of."

The darkness hid her tears, but he could tell from her voice that she was crying. Pulling her into his arms, he held her close and whispered, "Your strength comes from inside you. It is not your title or your father's title that makes you strong."

They stood there together a long time, and he wished he could know what she was thinking. Finally she stopped shaking and moved out of his arms. He offered her a handkerchief, and she wiped her face, then said quite matter-of-factly, "I agree. It is not my title—or at least not *only* my title—that is making so many men throw themselves at my feet."

"No one can fault them for admiring your beauty," Digory commented mildly. "Men have always been susceptible to a pretty face."

"Then men are all fools! Tell me, if I were ugly, would you be here in London helping me? Or are you like all the rest?"

"If you were not so beautiful, I would not be here," he said, and she gasped as if he had struck her. "But you could be skinny as a rail and have spots and a dreadful squint, and I would still think you lovely, because you have a beauty of the soul that can never be diminished, no matter how old and wrinkled your face may become. Your mother was the same, God rest her soul.''

''Oh, Digory, I wish I had known my mother. Sometimes—'' there was a catch in her voice, then she went on, ''sometimes I need her so much.''

There was nothing he could say to that—no words of his that would help her.

Finally she spoke again. ''Tell me about your mother. Is she still living?''

''She was laid to rest in the churchyard when I was six,'' he said. ''But she died before I was born. Our father killed her. She did not have the strength of character to survive after he rejected her. But I was fortunate, because my great-aunt raised me. She was a very plain woman, who never in her life managed to attract a man's attention, but when it became necessary, she defied convention and willingly shared our lot as social outcasts. She supported my mother and me by doing fine sewing. She was even strong enough to endure the degradation of accepting work from the assorted wives of the Earl of Blackstone, who was the cause of all our misfortune.''

''I am surprised you do not hate me.''

''Why should I hate you? Because of the sins of your father? That would be as pointless as loving you because you have fair skin and enchanting dimples.''

There was a slight sound somewhere in the darkness, and for a moment they both froze, but nothing more was heard. Finally he whispered, ''You had best get back to your room now before you are missed. And do not fret yourself unnecessarily about Lord Fauxbridge.''

She moved away into the darkness, but then her voice came out of the shadows, and every word she spoke tore at his heart. ''Is it too much to ask then, that I marry a man who loves me for myself?''

Her question lingered in the night air even after he heard the sound of the door to the house opening and then closing behind her. There was no answer he could give her, but in his heart he promised her that he would lay down his own life before he would allow her to be forced into marriage with a man who did not appreciate her inner beauty.

As he slipped through the garden gate into the mews, every one of his senses was alert, yet even so, the attack was so swift and so silent, he was caught off guard. One minute he was feeling his way along the fence, and the next moment he was lying face down on the ground, someone's knee on his back, the pressure so great it felt as if his chest were being crushed.

Before he could draw a breath to cry out, he was gagged and his hands were bound, not only quickly, but most efficiently. Then as if he weighed no more than a child, he was picked up and carried away effortlessly. He could only wonder at the strength of his attacker, because he himself was not at all a small man.

Being dangled head downward over a very hard shoulder, Digory had ample time to consider the irony of his situation. All those years of smuggling and spying, he had escaped capture by Napoleon's soldiers and the English preventatives, only to come to grief in the heart of London. Despite his present danger, he could not keep from being amused at the thought. If his crew ever got wind of this night's events, they would razz him until the end of his life.

Strangely enough, he did not for a moment consider that the end of his life was now at hand, partly because if killing him had been desired, it would have been much easier to accomplish than kidnapping him.

And also because no one in London had a motive for killing him, especially not the man he suspected was behind this abduction.

Beside him, Perry waxed eloquent about the attributes of a hunter he had purchased that day, but Richard paid him scant attention. Sitting in a comfortable chair in front of a cheerful fire, his thoughts were neither comfortable nor cheerful, which was unexpected, given the progress he was making with Lady Cassiopeia.

He should, in fact, have been overjoyed that she had once again turned to him for help. He should have been celebrating as enthusiastically as Perry, because unlike the earlier occasion in Cornwall, this evening she had not even attempted to bargain with him.

Richard's thoughts went back to that low-ceilinged tavern where he had first made the decision to marry Lady Cassie—a decision he had made without even knowing who she really was. At the time, he had merely wanted a wife who would love him as fully and as completely as Molly had once done.

What he had not wanted, and what he had never expected, was to fall in love himself.

The pain of losing Molly had been so great, he had sworn an oath never again to give his heart to anyone—man, woman, or child.

To be sure, he was fond of Perry, and as for John Tuke, the bond between them was strong, but it could not be called love. No, John was like another part of himself—a better part—his conscience, as it were. Moreover, John was strong enough that Richard was never going to lose any sleep worrying about his friend's safety and well-being.

But ever since he had realized that he loved Lady Cassie, he had been tormented by thoughts of what might happen to her. He had looked into her eyes and then into his own heart and had recognized how easy it would be to lose her. Despite her courage, she was so terribly vulnerable. So many things could happen to her—even a chill or a fever might carry her off.

In his heart, he knew that if she died of an accident or illness, he would surely curse God and thereby damn his own soul to an eternity in hell.

And if she married someone else? Then the hell for him would be here upon this earth. But that at least, he was confident he could prevent.

"I love her, Hawke, I absolutely love her. She is the sweetest, dearest thing I have ever seen!"

Perry spoke so vehemently, his enthusiasm pulled Richard out of his trance.

"You are in love? Your grandmother will be happy to hear

that. Unless, of course, the object of your affection is an opera dancer.''

''Opera dancer? Hawke, I swear, you have not heard one word I have been saying! I was telling you about a mare I saw today that Charles Neuce was riding.'' Chuckling to himself, Perry got up to fetch another bottle of brandy from the table by the window. ''I have told you before, a good horse is worth more than any woman. Unfortunately, it appears you have once again seen fit to disregard my advice, since you show all the signs of a man who has fallen in love with a two-legged filly. Well, despite your example, I shall use better sense and reserve my heart for the four-legged variety.''

Perry was correct—at least partially correct. His vow notwithstanding, Richard had to admit to himself that he loved Lady Cassiopeia more than life itself. And he was also forced to acknowledge that he had already made himself vulnerable.

In the Bible, had Samson lost his strength because Delilah cut his hair? Or had he become a weakling simply by giving his heart to a woman?

Before Richard could pursue this line of thought, there was a light knock at the door, and Perry opened it to admit John, who was carrying a trussed-up body over his shoulder.

Dropping his burden onto the chair recently vacated by Perry, John moved only a step away, obviously ready to stop his prisoner if the man made a move to escape.

''Who have you brought us?'' Richard asked.

The ''body'' was very much alive, but oddly enough, the man's eyes held no fear, only intelligence . . . and amusement, Richard realized with surprise.

''I caught this fellow, whoever he is, having a secret tryst with Lady Cassiopeia,'' John said, and the tone of his voice was such that most men, tied up or not, would have been cowering away from him in abject terror.

Studying the stranger's face carefully, Richard began to suspect that he knew why the prisoner was not struggling to get free of his fetters. Something about the man's eyes was familiar . . . but no, the idea was too preposterous . . . and yet . . .

Richard removed a penknife from his pocket and, leaning across the small space that separated the two chairs, he cut through the strip of cloth John had used to gag the man.

"What the deuce are you doing?" John asked.

As Richard had anticipated, their visitor did not immediately begin screeching for help, but merely stood up and turned his back so that Richard could also cut the cords that bound his hands.

Once released, the man seated himself again, crossed his legs as casually as if he were in the habit of being abducted, picked up the glass of brandy Richard had been toying with, and drained it to the dregs.

With no further ado, he said, "I have been meaning to make your acquaintance, but I had planned to seek a more normal introduction."

"Who are you, then?" John growled, obviously not pleased with the man's sangfroid. "Are you a Bow Street runner or some such?"

"I am a retired smuggler," the stranger replied, not even bothering to hide the laughter in his voice. "And may I say, I have never tasted such wretched swill as you are drinking this evening. I can supply you with real brandy, and undoubtedly at a lower price than what you have paid for this."

"Blast the brandy, you insolent jackanapes!" John interrupted, obviously incensed by the stranger's audacity. "Who the devil are you and what business have you in Lord Blackstone's garden in the wee hours of the morning? And do not try to persuade me you were selling Lady Cassiopeia a keg of brandy, because I am not so easily gulled."

Rising to his feet, the stranger doffed an imaginary cap and bowed extravagantly. "Digory Rendel at your service, my kind sir." He held out his hand, but John refused to take it.

"So, you are a retired smuggler, and I think you may also be . . ." Richard paused until he had the attention of the three other men in the room, then continued, "Lady Cassiopeia's . . . cousin perhaps?"

"Half-brother," Rendel corrected. "Born on the wrong side of the blanket, to be sure. And you, my oversized abductor, must be John Tuke, and your young friend by the window is undoubtedly Lord Westhrop. And from what my sister has related to me," he continued, looking straight into Richard's eyes, "you must be Richard Hawke."

"What has she said about me?" Richard could not resist asking, even though he knew the other man might well interpret such open curiosity as a sign of weakness.

With a smile, Rendel seated himself again. "She said you looked fierce even when you were sleeping. I tell you openly, when I heard her say that, you were as close to dying as you have ever been in your life."

The smuggler was smiling when he spoke, but his eyes were completely serious. Looking at him, Richard could well believe that this man would make a deadly enemy.

"Before this discussion becomes any more dangerous," Richard said, "I feel compelled to assure you that my intentions with regard to your sister are completely serious. I am resolved to marry her."

"And I may even allow you to do just that, provided you can convince me that you are the right husband for her."

"Convince you?" Perry moved away from the window to glare down at the smuggler, who did not seem the least bit perturbed by the display of youthful bravado. "What makes you think we'll leave the decision up to you? There are three of us, after all, and only one of you."

Rendel looked up and said mildly, "In a fair fight, I have no doubt but that the three of you could whip me soundly. But you see, I would not hesitate even a moment to make use of unfair, even dishonorable tactics."

Responding to the other man's deliberate baiting, Perry started to bluster, but Richard cut him off.

"You err in your assessment of the situation, my good sir. Only two of us are handicapped by inconvenient scruples or notions of honor and fairness."

A slow smile began to spread across the smuggler's face. "In that case, I begin to think that perhaps you will make an adequate husband for my sister, assuming you can dispose of the three men chosen by Lord Blackstone as suitable pigeons for the plucking."

"Are you with us then, or against us?" John asked impatiently.

"Why, neither," Rendel replied, rising to his feet. "If Mr. Hawke here cannot overcome three such petty obstacles without my help, then he is not the man for my sister. Be assured, I shall watch the proceedings with great interest, and if my decision goes against you, why then my sister and I will vanish and you will never see either of us again. I bid you good evening, gentlemen."

With those words he moved toward the door, and Richard signaled to Perry and John that they should not try to prevent the man from leaving.

Once they were alone again, Richard turned his attention to more practical matters. "Well, John, when you have not been busy with abducting people, have you learned anything more of importance about Lord Fauxbridge?"

"Oh, yes, I managed to speak to Captain Rymer this evening. He is in London still, waiting for some minor repairs to be completed on his ship, and he provided me with some very interesting and useful information about our noble friend. It seems that you and Fauxbridge have something in common, Richard. He also owns a plantation in the West Indies."

"Does he indeed," Richard murmured, already beginning to see the ideal way to dispose of the inconvenient Lord Fauxbridge.

Chapter Eleven

"Really, Cassie, I am ashamed to call you my daughter. I vow, I have never seen you behave so rudely." Ellen began scolding the minute Lord Fauxbridge returned them to their domicile.

"If you wish to accuse someone of being rude, then I suggest you start with Lord Fauxbridge and his mother." Cassie jerked her bonnet off her head and cast it aside.

"That is utter nonsense. To my way of thinking, they were both very complimentary, praising your looks as highly as they did."

"Complimentary? I beg to differ with you. The two of them sat there discussing me as if I were a piece of furniture they were thinking of buying for their drawing room." Cassie stalked up the stairs, followed by her step-mother.

"Be that as it may, nothing they said gave you any excuse to be rude. Why, you contradicted virtually everything Lord Fauxbridge said. I vow, if you had deliberately set out to offend the marquess, you could not have done a better job of it."

As a matter of fact, it had been deliberate, although Cassie was not about to confess that to her step-mother. Ten minutes of having the man smile at her in a proprietary manner, as if he had already purchased her, and Cassie had determined to ignore Geoffrey's threats and do everything in her power to give the marquess a disgust of her.

Unfortunately, Lord Fauxbridge was so set up in his own esteem, he had acted as if her insults were compliments. Could anyone truly be that obtuse? Or had he merely not listened to a word she was saying? One did not, after all, pay too much attention to what a sofa might say, or heed the complaints of a Chinese vase.

"Have you considered, Ellen, that if I marry Lord Faux-bridge—" Cassie could not control the shudder that shook her at that horrible thought, "you will either be forced to live with him and his dear mama, or you must return to Cornwall."

Pausing outside the door to her room, Ellen smiled so sweetly that for a moment she looked like a young girl of two and twenty, rather than a widow of two and thirty. "Actually, I think dear Arthur is about to pop the question. He has been dropping rather broad hints." Then her smile faded, and she said more sharply, "And I am not so foolish as to contradict his every word. Men do not like to be crossed, you know. You would do well to consider that."

"Well, Mama, what did you think of her?"

"She is a trifle scrawny, do you not think?" Lady Faux-bridge helped herself to another bonbon. "And she does not have the look of a good breeder. Her mother died in child-birth, and you know the saying: Like mother, like daughter."

Rubbing his hands together, Humphrey began pacing back and forth the length of his mother's sitting room. "She is well enough endowed where it counts—quite well enough." He chuckled to himself.

"And I noticed a tendency toward levity on her part. In fact, there were times when her remarks bordered on rudeness."

"She is young and still a bit high-spirited, but I am sure I can train her well enough to suit my tastes once we are married."

"Well, if you wish for my advice, I strongly recommend you forget about this gel and marry Lady Ermyntrude. She is all compliance, and not only is she the daughter of a duke, but I have heard from reliable sources that her marriage portion is in excess of fifty thousand pounds."

She could be the daughter of a royal duke and have a million-pound dowry, Humphrey thought, but it would not make up for the fact that she also had a squint and the figure of a cow. No, he was determined to have Lady Cassiopeia. He had always prided himself on being a connoisseur of beautiful things—a gourmet, as it were. He smiled to himself. Even if it cost him one hundred thousand pounds to pay off Lord Blackstone's debts, that was a small price to pay for such a delectable morsel. He could hardly wait to gobble her up.

Observing Perry moving gracefully through the patterns of a country dance, Lady Letitia asked, "How have you persuaded my grandson to attend the Craigmonts' ball? Have you perhaps overcome your reluctance to apply coercion?"

Beside her Richard smiled slightly. "It was not precisely coercion. I merely offered him a choice—either he accompanies you to at least five social activities of your choosing each week, or I cease to supply him with the funds he needs to buy up every bit of prime bloodstock he can lay his hands on."

"And you do not call that coercion?"

"Not at all. He is quite free to choose his course of action. It can hardly be laid on my doorstep if his fanatic desire to set up his own stud compels him to accede to my wishes."

"Five social activities per week," Lady Letitia mused. "In that case, I must lay my plans well, think through carefully which events we should attend—or to be more precise, consider carefully which young ladies to throw in his path." For a moment she was silent, considering what her best strategy should be. Then she said, "Speaking of plans, are you making any progress toward ridding yourself of your rivals?"

"Actually, I am intending to take the initiative this evening. By enlisting the aid of Lady Blackstone, Lord Fauxbridge has managed to secure Lady Cassiopeia as his partner for the supper dance. He is quite pleased with his success, little knowing that it is the last time he will ever dance with her," Richard said. Without taking his eyes off Lady Cassiopeia, who at the moment was dancing with Lord Atherston, he added, "If you would care to have an unobstructed view of his downfall, then you have but to allow me to escort you down to supper."

"With pleasure," Lady Letitia agreed with alacrity, her

curiosity aroused. Would Richard use finesse to accomplish his ends? Or intimidation? Or brute force? That he was a master of all three, she could not doubt for a moment.

An hour later she was seated beside a very subdued Lady Cassiopeia at a small table for four. The opening barrage was fired moments after Lord Fauxbridge and Richard returned with four plates of food, but the shots came from a totally unexpected quarter. It would appear that finesse was the weapon Richard had chosen.

"I understand you own a sugar plantation in the West Indies, Lord Fauxbridge," Richard said, his voice indicating nothing more than idle curiosity. "Tell me, what is your opinion of the anti-slave-trade law?"

The look of self-satisfied complacency vanished from the marquess's face. "That has to be the most accursed, ill-advised bill that Parliament has ever passed," he blustered. "The day will soon come when England will force out of office the fools who supported such badly conceived legislation."

If Richard were trying to kill off Fauxbridge with an apoplectic fit, he might very well succeed, Lady Letitia thought. The marquess was quite red in the face and looked ready to burst with indignation.

"But surely, my lord, merely cutting off the importation of new slaves will not noticeably affect the larger landowners, such as yourself. Owning hundreds of slaves already, you should have no trouble breeding a sufficient number of new ones to keep yourself well supplied with field hands."

Lady Letitia noted with interest that Lady Cassiopeia's face was now as white as the damask tablecloth, her lips positively bloodless. If Richard's aim was to give the girl a disgust of Fauxbridge, then he had already achieved his goal.

Stuffing half a lobster patty into his mouth, Fauxbridge waved his fork at Richard while he chewed. "It is clear to me, Mr. Hawke," he said, once he had finally swallowed the mouthful, "that you do not understand in the least the economics involved. It is far more expensive to raise a slave than to buy one fully grown and ready to work. Why, the way things stand now, I have to pay out good money to feed and clothe the little pickaninnies for at least four years before they are big enough to start working in the fields. And I cannot show a significant profit on them until they are at least ten or eleven—''

At the word *profit,* Lady Cassiopeia leapt to her feet and began to speak quite loudly—no, Lady Letitia amended, Lady Cassiopeia was actually shouting, in a voice that immediately stilled the entire room. All eyes were upon her and everyone listened in rapt attention when she told Lord Fauxbridge her opinion of men like him who owned slaves, who employed child labor, who lived in luxury bought at the price of other people's misery, and who thought only of profits.

Clearly, Lord Fauxbridge could not have been more astounded if his walking stick had suddenly come to life and started beating him about the head and shoulders. But by the time Lady Cassiopeia had finished her condemnation of his character and stalked out of the room, his shock had been replaced by anger.

Standing up, he attempted to salvage what little dignity he had left by formally excusing himself to Lady Letitia. Unfortunately, the whispering that started in the back of the room quickly grew to a murmur. The marquess stammered on gamely until a woman tittered and a man guffawed, at which time Lord Fauxbridge's composure broke entirely.

Red-faced, he hurried from the room, walking faster than Lady Letitia had ever seen him move before.

His departure was the signal for a mass exodus. Like rats fleeing a sinking ship, the other guests abandoned their plates of half-eaten food in a mad rush for the door, each one obviously determined to be the first person to spread the news of this delightfully scandalous contretemps.

"Have some of the pheasant in aspic," Richard suggested, his appetite apparently not the least bit impaired by the recent furor. "It is quite well prepared."

"And your little drama was quite well planned, also," Lady Letitia complimented him truthfully. "But now you have made me curious. What technique do you intend to use with Lord Rowcliff? He is too lacking in self-consequence to take umbrage at anything you or Lady Cassiopeia might say."

"Lord Rowcliff has the devil's own luck, or so I have been told," Richard said with a smile. "But then, perhaps he has never yet actually gambled with the devil."

"Cut for high card, double or nothing." Lord Rowcliff's optimism remained intact, even though after several hours of playing piquet all the gold coins on the table were in front of Richard. Scribbling a note on a scrap of paper, the earl tossed it onto the middle of the table. "My credit is good with you, I assume?"

Nodding his head briefly, Richard handed over the deck of cards. Although they had both been drinking heavily, neither of them was yet in his cups. The same could not be said for the crowd of young bucks who had gradually gathered behind Lord Rowcliff as the stakes became ever higher. They were for the most part rather badly foxed.

No one stood behind Richard except John Tuke, who had already privately expressed his disapproval of gambling for exorbitant amounts.

" 'S useless," one of the observers pronounced rather thickly. "Got the devil's own luck, Rowcliff does."

"He'll come about. Always does."

"Ace of clubs—what did I tell you. The man can't lose."

Without commenting, Richard turned over his card and held it up for everyone to see. It was the ace of hearts.

"Double or nothing, my good sir." Without pause, Rowcliff scribbled his name on another piece of paper and tossed it onto the table.

"Rowcliff's never yet greeted the dawn a loser."

"Nor never even had to turn his coat inside out."

"Fifty pounds says he wins this cut."

There was a flurry of side bets, then Richard turned over his card. "Six of diamonds, my lord," he said, pushing the deck of cards toward the younger man.

A murmur of triumph ran round the room, and one of his friends clapped Lord Rowcliff on the back.

"You can beat a six of diamonds easy as spitting on the ground."

After first shaking his fingers to loosen them, Lord Rowcliff carefully and with great precision turned over a three of spades. There were groans behind him, but his smile did not falter. "Double or nothing. I'll not quit until I win, gentlemen."

"Until dawn," Richard said quietly. The murmur of voices in the room died down. "The game ends at dawn."

The silence was absolute, and for a moment Rowcliff's smile wavered. Then with a cocky wink to his companions, he accepted the challenge. "Agreed."

"But who's to say when it's dawn?" someone muttered.

"First cock's crow."

"Ain't no roosters on this street."

"First milkmaid calling out her wares," someone else suggested.

The crowd immediately agreed to the proposal, and the contest resumed.

"It is fortunate indeed that your luck was in tonight. Had it been running the other way, you might have lost all," John commented.

Richard pulled handfuls of coins, bank notes, and slips of paper out of his pockets and dumped them all unceremoniously onto his dressing table. "My luck, as you call it, consists solely of having made the acquaintance of Raoul Pironquet years ago," he said, smiling wryly.

"The Natchez gambler?"

"None other."

"He is the one, then, who taught you to play so well?"

"He is the one who taught me to *cheat* so adeptly," Richard corrected calmly.

"Cheat? Richard, you cannot have cheated this evening! Why, that is dishonorable!"

"Surely you have lived with me long enough to know that the concept of honor has not played an important role in my life."

"But cheating? No, Richard, this time you have gone too far."

"Alas and alack, I do believe my faithful follower has finally noticed my feet of clay."

"Will you stop joking? This is a serious business."

"I agree. It is much too serious to have risked everything on the vagaries of chance."

"I had not thought you so amoral. Have you then no twinge of conscience at what you have done?"

Richard shrugged. "It was the lesser of two evils."

"Two evils?"

"Have you forgotten the object of the game, which was to prevent Rowcliff from making Lady Cassie an offer? I assure you, I never lost sight of the stakes. But perhaps you would have preferred it if I had forced a duel on him and put a bullet through his heart?"

"Dueling is illegal."

"But still considered to be an affair of honor, you must admit. Which poses an interesting theological question: whether 'tis more righteous to kill a man in an honorable fashion or merely to ruin him financially by totally dishonorable means."

Tuke was silent for a long time.

"Well, John, have you come up with an answer to my thorny question?"

"What I have come up with is another question." Tuke looked at him with suspicion. "Do you make it a habit of cheating at cards?"

"Ah-hah! What you are asking now is whether or not I have been fleecing you all these years."

"I am not worried about myself, since I would freely give you anything of mine that you wished for. My concern is for the others you have gambled with."

"You may rest easy, oh would-be conscience. In the past I have always made it a rule not to risk more than I can afford to lose, and so I have been content to rely on my skill and the smiles of Lady Luck. But in this case, I could not afford to lose, and so I took what measures I deemed necessary to guarantee that I would win."

"The end justifies the means—is that what you are saying?" his friend asked bitterly. "You realize that by stooping to such dishonesty, you are lowering yourself to the level of all the other people who manage to find reasons to justify their wicked actions."

"Ah, John, forgive me, but I have never claimed to be better than other men. You are the one who has been working to secure my canonization, not I." When his friend did not answer immediately, Richard continued in a soft voice, "You did not object when Molly stole food for us."

"That was different. That was a matter of survival."

"Which means the end justifies the means? It was *stealing,* John. It was breaking one of the Ten Commandments. How can you possibly say that stealing then was any different than stealing now by cheating at cards? Should we make some effort to judge—to differentiate between honorable stealing and dishonorable stealing? Are we then to set our judgment above the laws of God?"

"Blast it all, Richard, you know the cases are not the same! It was a matter of life and death then—"

"And you think it is any less important now? I was gambling for a life tonight—Lady Cassie's life. Would you have had me risk her entire future on the turn of a card?" As he watched, Richard could see the anger drain out of his friend.

"There are times when I question whether you are to be my salvation or my damnation," John said with a smile on his lips that did not, however, quite reach his eyes.

"Have you considered that if Rowcliff were to marry Lady Cassiopeia, Lord Blackstone would beggar him over the years? Considered in that light, I have actually done my lord a favor."

"No matter what your rationalizing, I cannot like it, Richard."

"Then if it will ease your mind, I shall set aside the money that I have won this night and return it to that unfortunate young man—after Lady Cassie is safely wed to me, of course."

"You would do that?"

Richard shrugged. "The money is no real part of the affair. It means nothing to me."

"Rowcliff may refuse to take it, being under the mistaken impression that you have won it fair and square," John said doubtfully.

Richard could not hold back a laugh. Clapping his friend on the back, he said, "Not all men have your scruples, John. Rowcliff will take the money when it is offered, and I will wager a shilling to a hundred pounds that he does not make even a token protest."

"There . . . there . . . what did I tell you." Ellen rustled the newspaper indignantly, but Cassie did not raise her eyes from her breakfast plate. "Lord Fauxbridge has become engaged to Lady Ermyntrude—a duke's daughter, and her father is wealthy as a nabob. You are well served for your impertinence, you ungrateful girl. How you could have whistled away a chance to be a wealthy marchioness, I shall never understand."

"You are rapidly running out of suitors," Geoffrey's voice sounded unexpectedly behind Cassie, startling her so much she dropped her fork. "Rowcliff left town this morning. He lost half a fortune at White's last night gaming with the mysterious Mr. Hawke. Which leaves only the baron. If you cannot bring Atherston up to scratch, then you will be spending the summer in Leeds."

"What a strange thing for him to say," Ellen commented after Geoffrey had left as abruptly as he had arrived. "Why on earth would we wish to visit anyone in Leeds? To my knowledge, we do not know a soul who lives there. I should much prefer Brighton. How very odd of your brother. But then, I have never truly understood that boy." Laying her newspaper aside, she began to peruse the pile of invitations that had arrived that morning.

"The Nethertons are having a rout party tomorrow night. Shall I accept, or would you rather go to the theater with the Spencers?"

Cassie made no reply. She could not utter a word without breaking into tears—or casting up her accounts, she was not sure which would occur. Unlike her step-mother, she knew precisely what her brother had meant—he was again threatening to auction her off to some rich mill owner or merchant in Leeds. She wanted to flee the house—run away as far as she could from London. But where could she go? And what would happen to Seffie if she did such a cowardly thing?

"I think the Nethertons' party will be more fun. I am not at all impressed with Shakespeare, despite what the critics say about his writing. He is much too gloomy to suit me." Ellen laid aside several more invitations unopened, then with a squeal of glee snatched up a cream-colored missive and broke open the seal. Scanning it quickly, she let out a sigh of satisfaction.

"Oh, how delightful. Lady Letitia has invited us to go on an outing to Wimbledon tomorrow. Mr. Hawke is thinking of buying a small estate not too many miles from there, and he wishes to inspect it personally. Apparently she has arranged a rather large party, since her grandson and the Inglebys will be going, and she has invited dear Arthur and—oh, Cassie, how fortuitous! Lord Atherston is included. That will give you ample opportunity to engage in a flirtation with him, especially if you play your cards right and manage to ride beside him."

She looked up, a frown wrinkling her brow. "Whatever you do, Cassie, do not allow that flirt Cecily Ingleby to cut you out. I would not put it past her to try to steal one of your beaux. She must have some ulterior motive for dragging her brother over to our house virtually every day. At first I had thought that Oliver was dangling after you, but he is content to chat with me and has made not the slightest push to win your affections. Indeed, I should not be surprised if Cecily has her eye on Atherston himself. It is a pity that she is Lady Letitia's grandniece, else I would be tempted to instruct the footman to tell her we are not at home."

Moderate. That was the word to describe Lord Atherston. During their ride out from London, Cassie had quizzed the baron as covertly as possible, and as far as she could discover he did nothing to excess. He was not a heavy drinker, nor did he gamble for anything other than chicken stakes. Moreover, she had carefully sounded him out and learned that his feelings on the subjects of absentee landlords and child labor were exactly in line with hers.

His clothes were quietly elegant without being extravagant,

his features were well formed, his intelligence was above average, and his comments revealed a surprising degree of common sense. To add to his suitability, he did not feel it necessary to shower her with flowery compliments. Beyond remarking on how her blue riding habit brought out the color of her eyes, he had said nothing of a personal nature, but had instead kept the conversation on a more general level.

In short, when she evaluated his suitability as a husband, everything she had learned about him so far seemed to indicate that he would make a very congenial spouse.

Without volition, her eyes strayed to where Mr. Hawke was riding on a large chestnut horse next to Lady Letitia's carriage, which was being driven by Mr. Tuke. One thing Cassie knew for certain—it would be far, far better to marry a rather ordinary gentleman like Lord Atherston, who did nothing to disturb her equilibrium, than to marry a dangerous man like Mr. Hawke.

Even after all these weeks of acquaintance, he had only to turn his dark eyes in her direction and frissons of fear raced through her veins. She could only be thankful that Geoffrey did not consider him a suitable candidate for her hand.

Although if she failed to bring Lord Atherston up to scratch, might not her brother see in Mr. Hawke a way to avoid the expense of a prolonged stay in Leeds?

Clearly, the time had come to do as she had been instructed and give Lord Atherston a little encouragement. Smiling at him as sweetly as she knew how, she said, "This mare you have loaned me is so beautifully trained. Did you raise her yourself?"

Nothing, she had discovered during her stay in London, was a more surefire topic of conversation with the gentlemen than horses. Nor was she mistaken this time, since Lord Atherston managed to spend the next half hour describing to her the horses he owned, the ones he had owned, and the ones he planned to purchase someday, including a team of grays suitable for a lady to drive, he added, giving her what was apparently meant to be a significant glance out of the corner of his eye.

She knew she should seize such a perfect opportunity and

respond to his hint with a warm smile at the very least, yet something made her resist taking that fateful step. Feeling unaccountably reluctant to commit herself, she avoided meeting his glance and instead kicked her horse into a gallop.

Her step-mother's advice to the contrary, Cassie felt more comfortable once she joined Cecily and Perry, who were riding at the front of their little cavalcade. Unfortunately for her peace of mind, she received a black look from Ellen, who was seated beside dear Arthur in his carriage. There was sure to be a scolding when they returned home, and Cassie resolved not to make any further attempt to escape the attentions of Lord Atherston. With luck, he would ascribe her abrupt flight to maidenly shyness.

The estate, Richard was happy to discover, was everything he had been promised. The graveled drive was free of grass and weeds, the shrubs were well trimmed, the flowerbeds a riot of color, and the lawns had an evenness that bespoke two hundred years of being perfectly tended.

Morwyle House itself was not the least bit pretentious. A lovely example of late Elizabethan architecture, it was beautifully maintained. The sunlight glanced off the mullioned windows, making them sparkle like diamonds. Just such a house had he dreamed of when he was sweltering in the heat of that cursed island.

Leading the party around to the stable block, which fortunately came fully staffed, as did the house, Richard helped the ladies dismount, then offered his arm to Lady Letitia. "If none of you objects, we shall begin the tour with the house. Then, since the weather is so lovely today, I have arranged for a luncheon to be served *al fresco.*"

Everyone proved amenable to his plan, and Mrs. Beagles, the housekeeper, met them at the door. She was a wellspring of information about the history of the manor, having served there all her life, as had her mother before her, and her mother's mother before that.

With the amused cooperation of Lady Letitia, Richard managed about halfway through the tour to detach Lady Cassiopeia from the arm of Lord Atherston, who could not quite hide his chagrin when he discovered that somehow he was now expected to escort Lady Letitia. In the end, good manners prevailed, and he did not object openly to the switch in partners.

To Richard's relief, neither did Lady Cassiopeia, whose opinion of the house he was not slow to solicit.

"I cannot think of any way it could be improved," she said, looking around her with delight. "Indeed, I marvel that anyone living here could bear to part with it."

"The owner died childless," Richard explained, "and his only heirs are two nieces whose husbands already own vast estates in Canada. Since they have no intention of returning to this country, they prefer to sell the house and furnishings as they stand." He paused, then asked casually, "You do not think this house is a bit too small, then?"

"Well," she considered the matter carefully, "that would depend, of course, on how much entertaining you might wish to do. The dining room can easily seat thirty, and there are enough bedrooms for a large family plus a dozen or so house guests. Were you planning on getting—"

She broke off, obviously abruptly aware that she was straying into dangerous territory. Taking pity on her delightful confusion, he pretended to misunderstand her. "I plan to entertain frequently, but not on a grand scale."

"And this," Mrs. Beagles said, throwing open a set of double doors, "is the picture gallery." She began with great assurance to name not only all the distinguished members of the Morwyle family who were hung there, but also the well-known and less well-known artists who had painted them.

"There is one change in the house that I would recommend," Lady Cassiopeia said in an undertone.

"And what is that?" Richard asked, looking down at her.

She smiled up at him. "I have never before seen such a depressing collection of sour frowns and homely visages. They are not at all in keeping with the cheerfulness of the rest of the house. I suggest you crate up all these fine people, pack them off to Canada, and replace them with pictures of your own ancestors."

Caught off guard, it took him a moment to regain control of his emotions before he could reply. ''What makes you think my ancestors are any pleasanter to look at than these? I am not noted for my beauty, nor beloved for my charming smiles.'' He spoke lightly, as if joking, but for the life of him, he could not look down for fear she might read the pain in his eyes—pain caused by what to her had doubtless been only a casual remark.

Not even when he married her would he be able to tell her of his humble origins. That information must remain a secret until the day he died.

Even Lady Letitia would doubtless withdraw her support were she to learn that he did not even know the name of his father, nor did he have the slightest memory of his mother.

Chapter Twelve

"I am only sorry your daughter could not be with us this afternoon, Mr. Shuttleworth," Richard commented politely. Besides inspecting the property itself, he had decided it was desirable to make the acquaintance of his neighbors before committing himself to the purchase of the estate, in order to ascertain if any of them would be actively hostile to him.

To that end he had invited the cream of local society, namely the Reverend Mr. Philip Shuttleworth and his daughter, Squire Fanning and his wife, and Admiral Tucker, late of the Royal Navy, to join them for lunch. So far they had all—or at least, the four who were present—expressed quite freely their delight that Morwyle House would again be opened, since the previous owner had been an invalid for years and so had done no entertaining to speak of.

"As to that," the vicar now replied apologetically, "my daughter is shy and retiring and does not feel comfortable going about in society. She is quite the little homebody, in fact. It is all I can do to persuade her to attend services on Sunday."

"Well, I shall doubtless make her acquaintance there," Richard responded politely.

"Have you decided to purchase this place then, Richard?" At Lady Letitia's question, all conversation ceased and everyone listened attentively to hear what his answer would be. She had asked nothing more than what he knew the others were wishing they could ask.

"I would be a fool to pass up such an opportunity," he said with a broad smile, "and whatever else I may be, I am not lacking in common sense. As soon as we return to London, I shall instruct my man of affairs to execute the option to buy Morwyle House."

He was heartily congratulated on all sides, and such was the cheerful confusion that it took everyone a few minutes to realize that Arthur Dillingham was attempting to speak. Reluctantly they quieted down so that he could be heard.

"Ladies, gentlemen, on this happy occasion, I wish to propose a double toast. First to you, Mr. Hawke, and may you enjoy a long and prosperous life here at Morwyle House. And secondly, although it is not quite proper form for me to propose it myself, I wish you all to drink a toast to my wife-to-be, Lady Blackstone, who has today agreed to marry me."

Oliver Ingleby sat frozen, his glass halfway to his lips. He had been about to drink the proposed toast to Morwyle House and Hawke's purchase of the same when Dillingham had uttered those fatal words.

Mercifully, he was at first too numb with pain to speak, to cry out his denials. But all too soon the reality of his situation penetrated to the very core of his being—his beloved Ellen was going to marry someone else. She was going to be forever beyond his reach.

Setting his champagne down without tasting it, Oliver rose abruptly from the table and left the assembled company without the slightest explanation. He could not bear to listen to everyone wishing his dearest Ellen happiness, not when all he himself wanted to do was grab Dillingham around the neck and squeeze the life out of him.

It was fortunate that the rest of the company were too preoccupied with their own affairs to notice his departure, since he was too agitated to think of any polite excuse to offer for absenting himself.

Margaret Shuttleworth stood hidden behind the heavy plum-colored curtains in the library, staring through the window at the group of people eating and talking so cheerfully out on the terrace. Oh, that she could be there among them! If only . . .

Behind her the door opened and Mrs. Beagles quietly slipped into the room and joined her at her observation post.

"Jim, the footman, told me he heard Mr. Hawke announce that he is going to buy this place. I have already sounded that gentleman out as to his intentions with regards to the servants. Saints be praised, he has assured me privately that he will have need of a full staff. Not only will he retain all of the present servants, but he intends to hire additional help."

"That is indeed wonderful. I know what a worry it has been to you all, not knowing if your continued services would be required." As happy as she was with the others' good fortune, Margaret could not keep from hoping that her life was also going to change for the better. "Tell me, did you also perchance discover if . . . if Mr. Hawke is a bachelor?"

"That he is, although it appears he is already contemplating marriage in the near future," the housekeeper replied. "Howbeit, there are two other bachelors in the party. Lord Westhrop is not yet leg-shackled, and Mr. Hawke's secretary, Mr. Tuke, appears to be likewise unattached."

"Lord Westhrop looks to be younger than I am, and besides, I could never aspire to wed a peer of the realm. But a gentleman's secretary . . . that would not be aiming too high, would it?"

Mrs. Beagles, who had been her only friend for as many years as she could remember, was now strangely silent. Finally the housekeeper spoke, but what she said came as a complete shock to Margaret.

"As to that, I think you should know . . . ." She turned her head away and did not meet Margaret's eyes. "I have held my tongue all these years, knowing if I told you truth, it would cause you nothing but pain. But I cannot keep silent any longer."

The truth? Margaret felt faint with apprehension. Was there something wrong with her? Something she herself did not perceive when she looked into her mirror? Some fatal flaw about her person that had made her father deem it best to shut her away from the world and deny her the right to go out into company?

Folding her arms across her ample bosom, Mrs. Beagles said bluntly, "Squire Fanning's eldest son, Manfred, offered for you when you were eighteen, but your father turned him down flat. Said you were still too grief-stricken over your mother's death to think of marrying anyone.''

Feeling herself begin to tremble, Margaret immediately stiffened her muscles, lest Mrs. Beagles notice and offer her sympathy, which would be her undoing. One word of pity would doubtless cause her to lose control and break down completely, which was too embarrassing to contemplate.

''I see,'' she said finally, once she felt herself able to speak again. ''That would explain so much.''

The housekeeper did not need to ask what it explained— she knew, as did everyone else in the village, that from the time she was eighteen, a full three and a half years after her mother had died, Margaret had withdrawn completely from society.

Being in Margaret's confidence, however, Mrs. Beagles was the only person in the parish who knew that it was the Reverend Mr. Shuttleworth himself who had decreed his daughter's withdrawal, and that Margaret had not only protested vigorously, but had also begged and pleaded to be allowed to continue making social visits. Unfortunately, neither tears nor reason had availed her one whit.

''My father explained to me that since we did not have the necessary funds to allow me to be presented in London and since the local society was beneath our touch, I would find it easier to adjust to my lot in life if temptation were removed from my path, lest I contract a *mésalliance.* As my father, he knew what was best for me, and as a dutiful daughter, I was to obey him in all things. He quoted from the scriptures at great length to justify his position.''

''There is more,'' Mrs. Beagles said apologetically, ''but perhaps it is better if you do not know everything.''

With effort Margaret forced the necessary words out. ''Tell me. Please, if you are my friend, do not hold anything back.'' She bowed her head and listened with increasing pain while the housekeeper revealed the extent of her father's perfidy.

''Do you remember Lord Kormly? He visited here at Morwyle House when you were three-and-twenty.''

"I remember him. He spoke to me once at church. He seemed a very pleasant man."

"Indeed he was—he made a most favorable impression on all of the servants here. And . . ." The housekeeper's voice faltered, "and while he was here, he asked your father for permission to call on you."

"I must assume . . . that my father denied him permission." So many wasted years, Margaret thought with agonizing pain in her heart. She might have been married seven years by now—might have three or four children—if only . . .

"Yes, and I was that angry with your father, if I'd've been a man, I would have eloped with you myself," Mrs. Beagles added.

That would explain why Lord Kormly had cut short his visit after specifically mentioning to her that he planned to spend the summer. And why her father had decreed that she henceforth wear bonnets with concealing brims and not speak to anyone after services were over.

Raising her eyes, she looked out the window at Mr. Hawke's secretary. John Tuke—a strong name for a strong man. But his eyes were too clear, his expression too open, for her to hope that he might be her rescuer. Even were he to notice her, which was an unlikely circumstance, given the rules her father had laid down for her conduct, it was most unlikely that he could penetrate her father's defenses.

"You do not suppose my father may have mellowed somewhat through the years?" she said, unable to keep the wistfulness entirely out of her voice. "After all, it is not as though he enjoys my company of an evening. He rarely speaks to me over dinner, and then he invariably locks himself in his study afterward. Surely he could easily hire a housekeeper to take over my chores, and it would cost him no more than my keep does now. Perhaps, now that we have such exalted neighbors, he might allow me to accept an occasional invitation. Do you not think it possible?"

Mrs. Beagles did not reply. Turning to look at her, Margaret saw tears in the housekeeper's eyes.

"Child, child, do not get your hopes up. You were invited here today, but your father made your excuses."

"Without telling me anything about it. I see. If that is the way it is, then I must resign myself to my situation." Holding her head up straight, Margaret turned away from the window. "I should be getting home now, lest my father discover I have played the truant and punish me for it."

Her father had never struck her in his life, but then he had not needed to. He was adept at the cutting remark, the stinging rejoinder, the annihilating look. His cruelty was too subtle, too refined, to give her something solid to protest against.

Trudging down the lane toward the vicarage, she made no effort to conceal herself. Due to her father's efforts, no one in the village would tip his hat to her or in any other way acknowledge her existence. But on the other hand, none of the villagers had ever betrayed her by the slightest word when she occasionally escaped her father's watchful eye. Which was little enough to be thankful for.

"Why do you wish to dally so long amongst the vegetables?" Lord Atherston asked. "The roses are a much prettier setting for a beautiful woman such as yourself."

Cassie could not very well explain to him that years of hunger made her see more beauty in a well-developed cabbage than in the finest cabbage rose. Thinking quickly, she invented a plausible explanation for her abnormal interest in edible plants.

"I find a kitchen garden can be most revealing if one wishes to ascertain the true condition of an estate. Neglected carrots and turnips are significant, and should alert one that the management of the estate is not as it should be."

"But you should not bother your pretty little head about such matters," the baron said, a trace of condescension in his voice. "That is a subject for Mr. Hawke to concern himself with, and as he has pronounced himself satisfied with the condition of the estate, so should we all be. I would not be so impatient, my dear Lady Cassiopeia, except that I have been wishing to speak to you in a more romantic setting.

On the other hand, since we have achieved a measure of privacy here amidst the broccoli, perhaps 'twere best that I seize the moment, so to speak.''

Something of her shock must have shown on her face, because he immediately began to reassure her. "Please, you must not think that I am being forward. I would never dream of speaking to you directly before I have received permission from your brother. Indeed, such action would be reprehensible on my part. But I do feel it is entirely allowable for me to inform you that I have arranged an interview with your brother for tomorrow morning at eleven.''

Apparently he thought she was going to say something, because he held up one hand, palm toward her. "No, no, do not think that I am expecting you to make known your sentiments at this time. That would be pushing things beyond what would be seemly. But you need have no fear that I shall spend the night in an agony of suspense. I am sure enough of your feelings that I am willing to wait until tomorrow to hear what your answer will be.''

Cassie was surprised to hear that he was sure of her feelings, because she was not. She should, of course, be quite content to marry such an amiable man, especially considering the men Geoffrey had threatened to sell her to.

She doubted even Digory could find anything offensive about Lord Atherston. He was all amiability and was even displaying an amazing degree of sensitivity, and she knew she had nothing to fear from him.

Taking her hand and placing it gently on his arm, he began to lead her back through the gate to the formal gardens, where the others were still strolling about, enjoying the auspicious weather.

"I know you will be delighted to learn that the kitchen garden at Atherston Hall is quite well tended.'' He chuckled at his own cleverness, and she smiled up at him.

Strangely enough, her smile required a great deal of effort. Although by rights she should be as happy as Ellen was, Cassie felt almost . . . sad. But that could not possibly be. Knowing that she was going to be the recipient of an unexceptionable offer was no reason for her to be cast down in the dumps. More than likely she was merely fatigued by the ride out from London and by all the walking about under the hot sun.

John Tuke moved away from the shrubbery that had concealed him from Lady Cassiopeia and her suitor. Although John's eavesdropping had been unintentional, it was nevertheless fortuitous.

As quickly as was possible without attracting undue attention, he sought out Richard, who was ensconced on a wrought iron bench beside Lady Letitia.

"Might I have a word with you privately, Richard?" he asked. "Something has come up that you should know about as soon as possible, assuming it is not already too late."

"If it concerns Lady Cassiopeia," Richard replied with a smile, "then you may talk freely in front of Lady Letitia. She is privy to my plans, and has even offered sound advice in the past."

"As you wish," John said. Then he quickly related what he had overheard.

"Less than twenty-four hours," Richard said calmly, no sign of emotion visible on his face. "That gives us little time to formulate a plan, much less carry it out." Turning to Lady Letitia, he inquired, "Do you perhaps know a way Atherston could be discouraged from wishing to marry?"

"I doubt anything anyone might say would persuade Atherston to remain a bachelor. In fact, he feels it is imperative to marry as quickly as possible. He has three younger brothers, you know, and he is quite determined to cut them out of the succession." She paused, then said bluntly, "And if you are too much of a blockhead to use that information, then I must tell you, Richard, I wash my hands of your affairs."

Despite her white hair and lined face, her smile was so engaging, it was easy for John to see how she had managed to ensnare four husbands—although ensnare was not the correct term. Doubtless each of them had considered himself to be the most fortunate of men:

"So, my Lord Atherston wishes an heir, does he?" Richard mused.

"And a spare," Lady Letitia said quite tartly. "In fact, I would imagine only a household of sons will satisfy him."

"Then we must arrange to celebrate his forthcoming nuptials with him, John. This evening would not be premature, would it?"

Catching on at last to what his friend was planning, John smiled also. "One should never postpone celebrating, lest the cause of the celebration likewise be postponed."

Sitting beside dear Arthur, Ellen could not keep from smiling as they drove back toward London. Betrothed, and to such a handsome man. She sneaked a peek at him. Yes, she would be the envy of all her contemporaries, some of the more catty of whom had warned her that lacking a son, Arthur was falsely raising her hopes—in the end he would choose a much younger woman to take for a wife.

But he had not—he had chosen her! Oh, how he must love her! Her heart felt as if it would burst in her chest, so happy she was.

"Morwyle House is pleasant enough," Arthur broke the silence, "but I should not choose to live there myself."

"And why is that, my dear?"

"Too close to London. Why, everyone and his brother will be thinking of an excuse to drop by and wangle an invitation to stay for a few days or even a few weeks. For my own part, I much prefer living in Northumberland. I shall not be sorry to shake the dust of London off my feet forever."

"But . . . but . . ." Ellen frantically cast around in her mind for some plausible explanation. Surely dear Arthur did not mean what he had just said. He must have been joking— or had he been? "What about . . . what about my daughter Persephone? It is only a few years until she must be presented in court—and of course, she must have a London Season."

"Oh, as to that, I have it all thought out. We can take her to a few assemblies in Newcastle-upon-Tyne, and I am sure we can find her a suitable gentleman there who will count himself fortunate to marry an earl's daughter. Then after they are firmly buckled, it will be up to her husband to see to such things as court presentations." He chuckled. "And I shall thereby save a pocketful of brass. I hope you appreciate, my sweet, that you are marrying a very frugal man, who knows how to hold household. I shall not fritter away a fortune by riotous living, or gamble it away like young Rowcliff did."

With every word he spoke, Ellen felt her disquiet grow. Indeed, what she was feeling already went far beyond what could be termed disquiet. Panic was a more suitable word.

"Would we . . . that is, do you plan to entertain much once we are back in Northumberland?" she asked hesitantly. Maybe she was jumping to unwarranted conclusions? Maybe life there would not be as bad as it was beginning to appear? Maybe there was something she could still look forward to, even if she had to give up London shops and London balls and London theater and the opera, and . . . and everything that made life worth living.

"I have no time to waste on such things, nor any inclinations along that line. My father was never one to socialize much, and the older I become, the more I realize the wisdom of his ways."

Why had she never seen it before? Dillingham was cut from the same cloth as her late unlamented husband, the Earl of Blackstone.

"It is fortunate that you already have so many gowns, so we will not need to postpone the wedding while you purchase your bridal clothes. I shall arrange to have the banns called immediately, so that we can be married in St. George's without delay. A pity that we have to wait three weeks, but it is better than the expense of a special license."

He patted her knee, then squeezed it hard enough to bring tears to her eyes. Ellen felt herself shrinking away from him. Just three weeks before she would have to marry this . . . this provincial oaf! It did not bear contemplating. In fact, if she allowed herself to think about being sequestered—no, imprisoned!—for the rest of her life in Northumberland, she would lose control of the tears that were even now threatening to spill out of her eyes. Oh, she was trapped—horribly, awfully, revoltingly trapped! No one could possibly help her now.

For the first time since they had left Cornwall, she understood how her step-daughter felt—except that no one, not even her despised step-son, had forced her to say yes to Dillingham's offer. She had walked blindly into his trap with no one pushing her, and thus she had no one to blame but herself.

It was not the slightest consolation.

Although obviously unaccustomed to such surroundings, Atherston had not raised an objection when Richard had suggested celebrating his impending marriage—or, rather, his impending proposal—in a tavern near the wharves. In fact, it had been Perry who had turned up his nose when he had seen what a low dive Richard was leading them into.

After the first round of ale had been drunk and the second round called for, Richard clapped Atherston on the back. "You are indeed fortunate to be in a position to marry Lady Cassiopeia. If I had a younger brother, or even a cousin, I should not hesitate to make a push to cut you out."

"I am no fool," Atherston replied. "I am fully aware that her brother will cost me a pretty penny before all is said and done. But if he expects to get aught from me beyond the marriage settlement, he will have to toe the line. He who pays the piper, calls the tune, as the saying goes. He will find I am not an easy man to chouse out of what is rightfully mine."

Richard and Perry exchanged deliberately meaningful looks, and like a trout rising to a fly, Atherston snapped at the lure.

"Here, here, what is the meaning of the odd looks? If there is something I should know, then out with it. I already know the earl's estate is heavily encumbered, and the man himself is nothing more than a dashed loose screw."

"Something else," Perry muttered. "But don't know as I should tell you. Thought you knew, but it 'pears like it's a secret."

"It is quite all right," Richard was quick to reassure him. "I am sure that neither Lord Blackstone nor Lady Cassiopeia has engaged in a deliberate attempt to trick Atherston." Turning to the baron, who was fortifying himself from his tankard, Richard said quite matter-of-factly, "You were doubtless already informed, were you not, that Lady Cassiopeia can never bear a son?"

The baron choked on his ale, and Perry quite helpfully pounded him on the back until he waved his hands in a signal to desist.

"What are you talking about?" he finally managed to croak out.

"Why," Richard replied, his composure still intact, "it is common knowledge among the *haut ton* that there has never been anything but girls in her family."

"Never was, never will be," Perry contributed.

"A brother—she has a brother," Atherston said, his voice still a little husky.

Looking suitably mournful, Perry and Richard shook their heads. "Half-brother," Perry said.

"Totally different mothers," Richard added.

"And *her* mother never had no sons."

"And her grandmother never had any sons."

"And *her* mother . . ."

"And her mother's mother . . ."

"None of them ever had a boy."

Atherston looked first at Perry, then at Richard. "This cannot be true."

"Not a single son born to them, all the way back to the beginning," Richard said, wondering if it would occur to Atherston to ask just how the beginning was to be determined. "But you were properly informed of this, were you not?"

Atherston swore with a fluency Richard had not heard since Raoul Pironquet had discovered that someone had added a second set of markings to his own marked cards.

"On the contrary, my dear sir. I have heard no mention of this."

"That'll have been my grandmother's doing, I expect," Perry drawled. "Doubtless she advised the chit to keep mum on the subject."

"Lady Letitia—my word, it never occurred to me. I had no idea she was involved in finding a husband for Lady

Cassiopeia. If I had known, be sure I would have suspected something havey-cavey right from the beginning.''

"Probably why she didn't acknowledge her connection to the chit," Perry added.

"Connection? I was not aware that you were related to Lady Cassiopeia.''

Perry waved his hand dismissingly. "Doubt if I am. But that don't mean anything. Can't keep track of my own blood relatives, much less sort out the miscellaneous connections my assorted step-grandpapas have dragged into the family.''

"But this is all beside the point," Richard said with assumed bonhomie. "We are here to celebrate your forthcoming nuptials. You will have to make the best of a bad bargain. Having already offered for the girl, you will look a proper cad if you back out at this late date.''

"That is where you are wrong," Atherston declared with ill-concealed rage. Slamming his empty tankard down on the table, he stood up. "I have not yet offered for the chit. Only told her brother I had something I wished to discuss with him. That is not the same as making an offer.''

"Still and all," Perry was quick to point out, "he'll do his best to keep you from shabbing off. Why, doubtless he's already spread the word among his creditors that his hand is soon to plunge deeply into your pockets.''

"He can try whatever he likes," Atherston replied in a cold voice. "But first he will have to find me. Even if he learns I have flown the coop, I own a half dozen large estates and any number of smaller properties. With only a little effort, I can avoid the earl for months.''

"That's the proper spirit." Perry clapped him on the back.

"You do not intend to explain to the earl in person then?" Richard asked.

Trapped for a moment by the invisible bonds of what a gentleman may and may not do, Atherston vacillated, but soon his face brightened. "I shall write him a letter—tell him I have been called away unexpectedly.''

The landlord was summoned and a sheet of paper was soon produced, along with the necessary pen and ink.

Atherston scribbled for a few minutes, then folded the

paper and sealed it with some drops of wax from the candle. After pressing his seal into the soft wax, he then handed Richard the missive.

" 'Tis done, and I thank you for your assistance this evening. You will see to it that Lord Blackstone receives my note?"

"I am happy to be of service," Richard replied, although he was hard-pressed to control his smile of satisfaction until Atherston was safely out the door. Blessings on Lady Letitia for having given him the key to the baron's character.

His smile was wiped from his face, however, when a man spoke up from a table in the corner. "Well done, Hawke."

Chapter Thirteen

Turning in his chair, Richard peered through the gloom. To his chagrin, he recognized the speaker: Captain Rymer, and seated beside him was the ex-smuggler, Digory Rendel.

"If I had known I had an audience, I would have written the script with more attention to the humor inherent in the situation," Richard commented. "Although the sport is over, will you not join us?"

The two men obliged, and the landlord brought another round of ale.

"I feel I should warn you," Digory said after he had taken a deep draught from his tankard, "that Blackstone intends to extract the maximum payment for my sister. Now that you have disposed of her three official suitors, I hope your pockets are sufficiently well lined to pay his price."

Richard was silent for a moment, then he said, "I shall not pay one farthing for your sister. I am afraid the mere thought of purchasing another human being is totally repugnant to me. But I shall marry her nonetheless."

"In that case, you can be sure that the earl will not part with her willingly," Digory pointed out, his tone reasonable. "Which in turn means you will have to apply a little coercion to persuade him to see your point of view. Or do your principles also prohibit such activities?"

"With so much at stake here," Richard replied, "you will find me quite flexible. The problem as I see it is that having neither reputation nor money, Blackstone is not open to blackmail."

"The only thing he would not wish to lose is his freedom," Perry pointed out. "He knows full well he is in danger of being thrown into debtor's prison. Perhaps you might hurry things along by buying up his outstanding debts."

"It would be far cheaper," Captain Rymer interjected, "if you merely told him that if he does not agree to the marriage, you will have him kidnapped and sold to the Barbary pirates."

Richard rose from his chair. "I thank you for the suggestion, but I cannot pursue such courses. Although I could cheerfully wish him to the devil, I could never actually have a man thrown into prison, nor sell him into slavery, no matter what he has done. But have no fear, gentlemen, I shall undoubtedly think of something effective."

"But listen to what he is saying, Richard." Perry caught his arm and restrained him from leaving. "It would not be necessary to do anything more than convince Blackstone that you are prepared to follow such a course if he refuses. Even if he suspects that you are bluffing, he will never dare risk such a fate."

Richard sat down again at the table. "There is much to what you say. Tell me more details."

Captain Rymer smiled and began to explain just what he had in mind.

"A gentleman to see you," the footman said. "I have put him in the library."

Geoffrey checked his watch—eleven o'clock. It was always gratifying when a man was punctual for his own fleecing. Checking his cravat one more time, he left his room and descended the stairs.

"Well met, Atherston," he said before he realized that the man silhouetted in front of the window was not the expected baron.

"Good morning, Lord Blackstone." The reply was formal and gave no hint of the man's purpose in coming here.

"Mr. Hawke, is it not?" Geoffrey asked. "You will excuse me, I am sure, but I do not have time to speak with you right now. I am expecting a visitor. But please understand, I shall be perfectly willing to see you at some later date if you will make an *appointment.*"

His unexpected visitor did not make any move toward the door. Remaining where he was, he said, "Atherston has taken to his heels. He asked me to deliver this note.''

Doing his best to disguise his anger, Geoffrey took the piece of paper Mr. Hawke was holding out to him. Perusing it quickly, he crumpled it into a ball and tossed it aside. Then reaching in his pocket, he extracted a coin and without looking at it, flipped it to the other man, who caught it expertly.

''A little something for your trouble, Mr. Hawke. Or did Atherston already pay you to run his errand?''

Mr. Hawke looked down at the coin in his hand, smiled, and tucked it into the pocket of his waistcoat. Something about the expression on his face made Geoffrey think he had erred when he had tried to insult the man.

''I am here to inform you that I am going to marry your sister,'' Mr. Hawke said bluntly.

Really, the man's insolence knew no bounds. Pressing his lips tightly together to prevent intemperate speech, Geoffrey thought rapidly. That Mr. Hawke had had a hand in sending Atherston away, he had no doubt. And now that he thought on it, this was the same man who had gambled with Rowcliff and won half his fortune. Had he also had something to do with Fauxbridge's defection?

Casting his mind back over what he had heard about that disgusting episode, Geoffrey thought he remembered that Mr. Hawke's name had been mentioned, although he could not recall precisely in what connection.

It did not take much intelligence to realize that the man standing before him had undertaken to meddle in his affairs to an astonishing degree. Geoffrey's immediate thought was to refuse to deal with this man and to make Cassie take her chances in Leeds. On the other hand, that would entail additional expense, and moreover, it was rumored around London that this Mr. Hawke was in possession of a handsome fortune. There might be more profit to be had by complying. Geoffrey spoke quite calmly and politely.

''It appears, my good sir, that you have emerged the winner of the competition, even though you are something of a dark horse. Very well, I shall allow you to marry my sister . . . if you can meet my price.''

And that price would be double what he would have required from any of the three peers, Geoffrey decided, but Mr. Hawke would not be able to complain. If he even tried to dicker like a blasted shopkeeper, Geoffrey would take delight in refusing him outright.

"I will not pay you a single farthing for your sister," Mr. Hawke replied. "But be advised, I mean to have her as my wife with or without your consent."

The man's insolence was intolerable. He would have done well to show a little more humility in front of his betters. Although after what he had just said, he could grovel at Geoffrey's feet without altering the outcome of this conversation.

"You mean to have her?" Geoffrey asked with a smile. "Apparently it has slipped your mind, my dear fellow, that she is under twenty-one and cannot marry without my consent. And I shall see you in Hades before I give you my permission. All you have achieved by your insolence is to destroy forever your chance to marry my sister, which chance I admit was rather remote from the beginning."

"The choice, of course, is up to you," Mr. Hawke replied, his face showing no sign of discomposure. "But before you refuse me, you might bear in mind that if I am not married to your sister within the week, you will be kidnapped and sold to the Barbary pirates. Arrangements have already been made, my lord, and if anything untoward should happen to me or to Lady Cassiopeia, then you will find yourself in the hold of a ship, in chains, being carried off to a place where I have heard it is even hotter than Hades."

With difficulty Geoffrey restrained himself from blurting out something rash. No, he must keep control. If only he had time to think . . .

Suddenly it came to him—the perfect plan. If he let this insolent upstart think he had won, then Geoffrey would achieve a double goal: He would not only have the time he needed to plot Mr. Hawke's downfall, but by his apparent acquiescence, he would throw the man off his guard.

"Very well," Geoffrey said, deliberately scowling and grinding his teeth so that the other man would not suspect he was planning any treachery, "but do not expect me to dance at your wedding."

"I want the permission in writing," Mr. Hawke said in a soft voice, which held so much menace that for a moment Geoffrey considered giving up his plans for revenge.

But no, he would send the encroaching Mr. Hawke to his eternal damnation if he had to shoot the cursed fellow in the back himself.

For once her step-mother was being remarkably subdued, Cassie realized with relief. Waiting for her brother to summon her into Mr. Atherston's presence, her own nerves were totally on edge. She could not have tolerated Ellen's usual chattering.

It was already ten minutes past the hour, and she had heard the faint sounds of the large front door opening and closing precisely at eleven, so it would appear the baron had presented himself precisely on schedule.

How long would it take for Geoffrey and Lord Atherston to come to an agreement as to her purchase price?

She pushed those thoughts out of her mind lest she burst out crying. Deciding that even her step-mother's chattering was better than thoughts of marriage settlements, she asked, "When do you and Mr. Dillingham plan to be married?"

"As soon as the banns have been called," Ellen answered simply.

When there was no elaboration on that bald fact, Cassie looked at her in amazement. Why was her step-mother not chattering away about invitations and parties and . . . and shopping? Why was she even now sitting here instead of being fitted for an entire new wardrobe?

"Which mantua maker are you planning to patronize for your bridal clothes?" Cassie asked, sure that this would start a flow of information.

"Really, my dear, that would be a waste of money, would it not? After all, I already have an extensive wardrobe, which will be more than adequate for Northumberland, where I imagine the styles are at least two or three years out of date."

Cassie was so amazed at her step-mother's words that she

was caught completely off guard when her brother appeared in the doorway of the room and snapped out, ''Your suitor awaits you below, my dear sister.''

Her heart pounding in her throat, she rose to her feet, trying to maintain a calm demeanor. It was difficult with Geoffrey scowling at her.

Scowling? He should have been smirking, now that he had finally sold her for a good price.

He caught her arm as she passed, and jerked her around to face him. ''Do not get any ideas that you can defy me,'' he snarled down at her. ''Your marriage has already been arranged. You will smile sweetly and make yourself agreeable, or you will rue the day you were born.''

''You are hurting my arm,'' she said. ''And I do not know why you are speaking to me thus. I have no objection to Lord Atherston.''

''Atherston, bah!'' Geoffrey thrust her away, and she rubbed her arm where he had bruised it. ''Take yourself down to the library, and remember what I have said.''

All the way along the corridor and down the stairs she wondered what Atherston could possibly have done to put her brother in such a temper. Had Geoffrey not been able to force as high a marriage settlement as he had intended?

Her questions ended as soon as she entered the library and stood face to face with its sole occupant. Her eyes widened, but she bit back all the new questions that popped into her mind.

''Lady Cassiopeia, your brother has given me permission to speak to you.''

How could he? was her first thought. How could Mr. Hawke have betrayed her thus? Betrayed?—an odd word to describe her emotions, but nonetheless the only word. Only now did she realize that she had come to think of him as a friend—only now when he had ruthlessly ripped away the bonds that had gradually been forming between them.

''Lady Cassiopeia, will you do me the honor of becoming my wife?''

He had deceived her—like a fox in sheep's clothing, he had subtly led her to believe that he cared about her, whereas all the time he was no different from the other men who had wanted to purchase her.

How much did it cost you to buy me? she wanted to ask. As much as a new carriage? More? As much as a new ship? Or did you haggle with my brother until you had me for a bargain price?

"Are you all right, Lady Cassiopeia? Has your brother said something to upset you?"

Mr. Hawke reached out a hand toward her, but she flinched away as if he had struck her.

There was a long and not at all comfortable silence while he stared at her, his eyes boring into hers. But she refused to look away. Let him read in her eyes the anger she was not allowed to express with words—the contempt, the disgust, the defiance, the . . . the hatred!

Perhaps he would decide he had not gotten the better of the bargain after all? Perhaps he would withdraw his offer? There was nothing he could do that would please her more. She would much rather be sold to a total stranger than be betrayed by a false friend.

"Will you marry me?" he repeated, his eyes now shuttered, his thoughts well hidden from her.

Her heart aching in her chest, she finally admitted to herself that there was nothing she could do that would alter matters. Her fate had been decided by her brother and this . . . this . . . She could not think of an epithet bad enough to describe him.

"I shall be delighted to marry you," she replied in a wooden voice.

The anger in her eyes could not quite cover up the pain. Richard looked down at Lady Cassiopeia and wished there were some way he could reassure her. But even were he to kneel before her and swear eternal love and devotion, he doubted she would believe a word he said.

Her brother had apparently done something to cause her hostility. Since Blackstone had made very little effort to hide his animosity, it was only to be expected.

There was, unfortunately, no viable option at hand other

than a hurried wedding, even though Lady Cassiopeia deserved a long and ardent courtship.

And a husband of her own choosing?

He pushed that thought out of his head. Given the character of Lord Blackstone, she would never be allowed the slightest say in the matter, even were he himself to withdraw his offer.

"I have procured a special license," he said finally, when he could bear her silence no longer. "We shall be married in St. George's in Hanover Square a week from today."

She nodded her head briefly, but did not utter a single word. On her lower lip, however, a drop of scarlet appeared. Her torment was obvious, and just as painful for him as it was for her. He wanted nothing more than to hold her in his arms and soothe away her hurt. But remembering the way she had earlier flinched from his touch, he kept his hands clenched at his side.

"Do you prefer to—"

Interrupting his question, she said, "Make whatever arrangements you wish. I have no preferences in the matter."

Without meeting his eyes again, she turned and walked stiffly out of the room.

"And when will the wedding take place?" Oliver asked politely. He was a fool to have come—a masochist to torture himself this way. But after a night wandering the streets, unable to sleep, unable to think, unable to eat, his feet had led him to the house of his beloved.

"Arthur wishes us to be married as soon as possible—as soon as the banns are called," Ellen replied, her eyes downcast.

Three weeks—in three weeks she would be gone from his life forever. Another man would receive her smiles, delight in her conversation . . . share her bed. He could not bear this torment any longer. He had to find a place to hide until he could again face the world—a world without his dearest Ellen.

Rising to his feet, he began to take his farewell, when he noticed that a tear was rolling down her cheek. Stricken, he knelt in front of her and took her hands in his.

"You are crying! Has someone done something to upset you? Tell me what is wrong."

Pulling one hand free, she wiped at her cheek, but as soon as she removed the first tear, two more took its place. "I am . . . am . . . all right," she said, sniffling a little.

"Oh, my dearest darling," he said, joining her on the settee and pulling her into his arms. "Tell me what is wrong and I shall fix it."

"I do not . . . I do not wish to marry Arthur," she wailed. "He is the awfullest man I have ever met."

Now that the reason for her unhappiness was out in the open, her words tumbled out faster than her tears.

"He falls asleep during the opera, and he snores, and . . . and he says he is going to shut me away in Northumberland forever—in Northumberland! Why, that is even worse than Cornwall! And he has made it clear I shall never again have a new dress or a new bonnet. He calls it being frugal, but I think he is the veriest nipfarthing! And . . . and he does not intend for Seffie to have a Season. He says he will marry her off to some provincial hick in Newcastle-upon-Tyne!"

Somehow, without precisely planning it, Oliver began kissing away the tears. He met with no resistance whatsoever, and soon his lips met the sweetest, softest lips . . .

His heart was filled with ecstasy when he realized his angel was kissing him back.

"You shall not marry Dillingham," he said firmly. "I shall not allow it."

"Oh, Oliver," she said, looking up at him adoringly. Never had his name sounded so beautiful as when she said it.

"You shall marry me instead."

"Oh, yes, I should love that above all things," she replied. Then clouds again appeared on her face. "But how shall we manage? There will be such gossip, and Arthur will not wish to release me from my promise, and I cannot bear to think of how my step-son will scold me. Why, Geoffrey may even forbid me to marry you. He is quite determined to have his own way in everything, you know. He was always the most deceitful, nasty, boy."

Oliver kissed her again, and she softened against him. With her head resting against his chest, he explained to her how they would manage everything.

"We shall simply elope. I shall take you—and Seffie, of course—to Paris, and we shall have the most delightful honeymoon. I shall buy you dozens of Paris bonnets and we shall attend the opera every night, and when we become bored, we shall move on to Italy or Greece. By the time we return to England, we shall be quite old news, not the least bit worthy of gossip."

"Oh, Oliver, you are so masterful—so . . . so absolutely wonderful!"

He could not argue with her. When she looked up at him with that light in her eyes, she made him feel as if he could do anything.

Lying alone in bed with Annie asleep on a cot in the corner, Cassie thought back over the events of the last few days. The gods must surely be enjoying a good laugh at her expense, because every time it seemed as though her life could not possibly be any worse, events invariably proved her wrong.

It had been four days since she had agreed to marry Mr. Hawke, and three days since Ellen had shocked all of London by jilting Arthur Dillingham and eloping with Oliver Ingleby, a man at least five years her junior. As bad as that had been, two days ago Geoffrey had installed Chloe, his foul-mouthed mistress, in the bedroom formerly occupied by Ellen. That had been such a disgraceful thing for him to have done that the few remaining household servants had resigned in high dudgeon.

Only Annie had remained faithful, but there was little the Scottish maid could do to help. Although she had willingly gone to his hotel several times, she had never found Digory at home, nor had he responded to the notes Cassie had written.

With Seffie safely in France, well out of reach of Geoffrey's machinations, it had immediately occurred to

Cassie that her brother no longer had any hold over her—that she could also simply walk out the door and never come back. She had toyed with the idea of returning alone to Cornwall, where she could live in Digory's secret room in the stable and grow whatever food she needed.

Unfortunately—or perhaps fortunately, she admitted grudgingly—she had mentioned that possibility to Annie, who had told her bluntly that there were any number of men who could be counted upon to take advantage of an unprotected young girl. Men who were, in fact, so totally ruthless and depraved, compared to them Piggot appeared virtually a gentleman.

For better or for worse—and the way her life had been going, it was undoubtedly for worse—it seemed unlikely that anything fortuitous would occur in the next three days to prevent her from standing up beside Mr. Hawke in St. George's and reciting her vows.

"You shouldn't oughta let him cheat you out of what is rightfully yours." Chloe jabbed him in the ribs to emphasize her point. "He's bluffing, that's what he's doing. Hundred to one he ain't made no arrangements to have you kidnapped."

Geoffrey opened one eye and glared balefully at his mistress. Ecod, but she looked raddled by the light of day. He had planned to give her her congé as soon as he was plump in the pocket, and in her place make an arrangement with that feisty red-haired Scottish maid, who was playing hard to get. Unfortunately, the way things now stood, Chloe was better off financially than he was, and he would be lucky if she allowed him to sleep on the floor in her miserable room in Soho.

On the other hand, what she was saying now made good sense. What could he lose by calling Mr. Hawke's bluff? His creditors were already yapping at his heels, and as soon as they learned he had lost his sister and all the potential wealth she represented, they would go for his throat—tear him to pieces in their frenzy to recoup their losses.

"Shut your mouth, woman," he growled, his mind made up. "And send Piggot in to see me. I have work to do."

The perfect plan had sprung full-blown into his head. All he had to do, in fact, was turn the tables—do unto the self-confident, supercilious Mr. Hawke what Mr. Hawke had threatened to do unto him. But he, Geoffrey, planned to do it first, and in such cases, timing was everything.

"Piggot," he said as soon as his minion appeared, "I need you to find me someone who will do anything for money, no questions asked."

Briefly he explained what he intended to do. With every word he spoke, the smile on Piggot's face became broader.

"I already knows just the man we need. Digory Rendel is his name, and he's bound to know his way around the docks, because he's a smuggler by profession. He's got no more morals than a snake, and he'd betray his own crew members to the preventatives if he thought there'd be a profit in it."

"The very man for our purposes," Geoffrey gloated.

"There's only one problem," Piggot continued. "I doubt the man will be hired on credit. Very tough customer, he is—he'll demand cash on the table."

Geoffrey thought for a moment. Cash was as difficult to come by as credit was easy. But then he bethought himself of Chloe. Knowing her miserly ways, she undoubtedly had plenty of brass squirreled away for her old age. Under sufficient duress, she would cough up enough for his purposes.

"Arrange for a meeting with this Rendel, and be quick about it. The wedding is the day after tomorrow. Or rather," he added with a laugh, "that is when Mr. Hawke *thinks* he is getting married."

"There does not appear to be anyone home," Perry said.

"Nonsense," Lady Letitia replied. "I am positive that Lady Cassiopeia has not flown the coop in the disgraceful way apparently favored by her ramshackle relatives. Only rap more vigorously and someone is bound to answer."

Her grandson raised the knocker again and banged it

several times loud enough to wake the dead. A few moments later they were rewarded by the door opening to reveal a red-headed housemaid, who eyed them with suspicion.

"I am Lady Letitia. I have come to escort Lady Cassiopeia to St. George's Church."

The girl made no move to admit them, and after a moment Lady Letitia realized the chit was dubiously eyeing her grandson. Glancing sideways at him, Lady Letitia realized with astonishment that he was staring at the servant girl with the same look of rapt delight that he usually reserved for a four-legged filly with particularly fine conformation.

Well, the maid did indeed have a trim figure, but why could Perry not look at a lady of quality with just such a light in his eye? Why, after all her efforts to strew his path with nubile young ladies, had he ignored them one and all only to be overset by a servant girl?

At least it proved he was not totally blind to feminine charms. Perhaps she had erred in providing only blondes and brunettes? Now who did she know who had hair that looked as if it would burn your fingers if you touched it, green eyes that sparkled like emeralds, and withall not a single freckle? No candidate came to mind, but that did not mean she could not conjure up one if she applied herself.

"Do you intend to leave us standing on the stoop all day?" she asked sharply, and the maid stood aside to allow them to enter.

"I shall tell Lady Cassiopeia that you are here," the girl said, only a trace of Scotland in her voice.

"Close your mouth, Perry, or you will catch flies," Lady Letitia said firmly.

Gripping Annie's hand tightly, Cassie could only wish it were a longer drive to Hanover Square.

"He is not an ogre, you know," Lady Letitia interrupted her thoughts.

Her nerves too overset to allow her to participate in idle chit-chat, Cassie did not reply. She essayed a smile, but doubted that it fooled any of the other three occupants of the carriage.

"If I were thirty years younger, I would not hesitate to marry Richard myself," Lady Letitia added.

And you would be welcome to him, Cassie thought rebelliously.

Lord Westhrop now spoke up. "There are rumors circulating in London this morning that your brother has fled from his creditors. Some are saying he is hiding here in town, while others are saying he is gone to the Continent. That is why my grandmother has prevailed upon me to escort you to the altar."

Cassie felt her stomach lurch. Her brother gone? Fled the country? That would explain why his mistress had hurriedly packed her belongings this morning and left without any explanation. If only she herself had known earlier, in time to—

But she was deluding herself. Even if she had known, there was nothing she could have done—no other options she could have taken. With her step-mother gone to Paris, and her brother Digory inexplicably playing least-in-sight, even without Geoffrey around to force her, she had no choice but to marry Mr. Hawke. Abandoned by one and all—except, of course, by Annie—she had no one to fall back on, no resources of her own, no friend, except . . . perhaps Mr. Hawke, and she was not at all sure he was a true friend. He had, after all, bought her from her brother.

If only . . . but there was no more time for wishful dreaming. She must get her emotions under control—she really *must*—or the only way she would make it down the aisle would be if Lord Westhrop carried her, which would be embarrassing to say the least.

Too soon the coachman pulled the team to a halt. Cassie looked out the window of the carriage and was amazed at the size of the crowd of tradesmen and shopkeepers and passersby who had gathered to see who was marrying whom.

When Lord Westhrop handed her down, a murmur spread through the crowd, and to Cassie it seemed as if everyone were asking, how much? How much had she cost?

Taking Lord Westhrop's proffered arm, she tried to strengthen her knees by reminding herself that she was the daughter of an earl, but what had worked in Cornwall was no longer the least bit effective in London. She had seen for herself how empty of importance a title was, as witness the pompous Lord Fauxbridge, himself a marquess.

Then Digory's words came back to her, almost as if he were walking beside her, whispering in her ear: Your strength comes from inside you.

I *am* strong, she thought. Whatever befalls me, I shall be brave—I shall not give in to any weakness. No matter what people are saying about me, I shall never act the coward.

Walking up the steps to the church, Lord Westhrop commented sotto voce, "In Kentucky there are so few preachers that couples sometimes live together for months before they can be officially married, yet they are treated by their neighbors the same as if they were lawfully wed, and no stigma attaches to their union, nor even to any children born before the preacher's arrival."

He smiled down at her, and Cassie realized he was telling her this for no other reason than to ease her nervousness. Strangely enough, it helped a bit.

Not to be outdone, she whispered back, "In Cornwall not too many years ago, a shopkeeper took his wife to market and auctioned her off to the highest bidder, who was, if what I have heard is correct, a blacksmith."

She heard Lord Westhrop make a sound somewhere between a laugh and a cough. Encouraged, she continued, "Moreover, it is reported that the blacksmith and his wife lived contentedly together for many years and raised a large family."

Unfortunately, at that moment she looked down the nave of the church. Recognizing Mr. Hawke standing by the altar, his friend Mr. Tuke beside him, she could not maintain her smile. Why had she thought it amusing to relate the story of the auctioned wife? Had not women been treated so since time immemorial? Had not Geoffrey, her own brother, offered her up for bids?

The next time she saw Digory—if indeed she ever saw him again—she must remember to tell him he was right. In the end, one must find the courage within oneself. It took every ounce of resolution that she possessed to walk down the aisle, and she could only hope that no sign of her fear was visible on her face.

Chapter Fourteen

Annie stood at the back of the church, watching the ceremony. The words were familiar, but in all other ways this wedding bore little resemblance to her own. Instead of crowds of elegantly dressed ladies and gentlemen, she and Jamie had only had two friends stand up with them.

"They make a handsome couple, do they not?"

The low whisper in her ear made Annie jump with surprise. Turning, she saw Digory Rendel, who was smiling with great satisfaction.

"Where have you been the last few days?" she asked crossly. "Your sister and I have been scouring London trying to find you."

"I was helping Blackstone book passage on a ship bound for North Africa," he replied.

She eyed him suspiciously. The earl had asked for his help? On the face of it, that was not quite believable. "And just why did Lord Blackstone wish to travel at this time? And to North Africa, of all places?"

"Actually he did not. *He* wished me to arrange passage for Richard Hawke and John Tuke. Unfortunately for him, Captain Rymer and I decided to alter the arrangements slightly."

Annie was beginning to understand why Digory was smiling so broadly. "The would-be abductor became the abducted, do you mean?"

"Precisely," the smuggler replied. "And the cream of the jest is that he paid cash for his own abduction."

It was over. She had said her vows, then signed her name in the marriage register, and now the man sitting beside her in the carriage owned her, body and soul. Cassie wished she could hate him for what he had done to her, but she felt too drained of energy. Surprisingly enough, despite the fact that he had betrayed their friendship, she wanted nothing more at this moment than to lean her head against his shoulder and go to sleep.

It seemed very odd—not precisely déjà vu, but more a feeling that events had come full circle—that she had come to London sitting beside this man in a stagecoach, and now she was again seated beside him, jouncing over the cobblestones in a carriage, although this vehicle was much better sprung than the coach had been. And more important, Mr. Hawke was no longer a complete stranger to her.

"Since you did not state your preferences, I have arranged for the wedding breakfast to be at Lady Letitia's house, and I have limited the guests to only our closest friends."

"Thank you," she murmured. She supposed for himself he was referring to John Tuke and Lord Westhrop. But as for her friends? She had been in London for weeks and had made several acquaintances, but no one who could be called a friend, much less a close friend. Well, she could be thankful that she would not have to face dozens of staring, smirking, gossiping strangers.

"Besides the two of us, there will only be four others, in fact: John, Perry, Lady Letitia, and your brother Digory Rendel."

Cassie stared at her husband in astonishment. "You know my brother?"

"I would not claim to know him well, but we have met. He seems a most resourceful fellow."

An ugly suspicion began to grow in Cassie's mind. "Did he conspire with you to—" She stopped herself before she uttered those terrible words, *to help you purchase me.* Her abrupt silence had not gone unnoticed, however, and she felt compelled to finish her sentence somehow. "To persuade Geoffrey to agree to this marriage?"

"No, Rendel did nothing to help me. He did, however, make it quite clear to me that if he decided I was not the proper man to be your husband, he would guarantee that I would never see you again."

Never see her again—for a moment Cassie felt a twinge of pain, but she firmly suppressed it. They drove in silence for a few minutes while she thought about what she had just learned. Then Mr. Hawke spoke again.

"If you have no objections, my dear, I propose we invite the others to join us at Morwyle House in a sennight. It seems fitting to have them be our first guests."

"I have no objections," she replied. She wondered what he would say if she suggested that they not wait a week to have company. He might agree—but at the same time, he would surely guess that she was nervous at the thought of being alone with him, and she did not wish him to discover what a fearful creature she could be.

Besides, she would not be entirely alone. Annie would be with her. Until, of course, it was time to go to bed. Cassie felt her stomach churn at the thought of what this man might do to her—what unspeakable things he might demand of her . . .

She did not precisely know what husbands did to their wives on their wedding night, because Ellen had never been willing to discuss such things. But Cassie had overheard bits and pieces of talk, and none of what she had heard had made her eager to participate in such activities.

I must be brave, she thought. I must never let him know how much he frightens me.

As if he were reading her thoughts, he said, "I am sorry that we could not have had a longer courtship, but your brother's attitude made it necessary to proceed with haste. It is my intention, however, to postpone consummating the marriage until we have had a chance to become better acquainted with each other. I shall therefore not demand my rights as your husband until you wish it."

Cassie could not look at him, lest he read the disbelief that she was sure must be obvious in her face. She found it very difficult—nay, impossible—to give credence to what she was hearing. Surely he did not actually mean for her to take what he had said literally? In her experience, men were not at all inclined to postpone self-gratification. In fact, from the stories she had heard in Cornwall, the surest way for a woman to receive a beating was to deny her husband his legal access to her person.

On the other hand, assuming that Mr. Hawke did mean what he said—at this moment, anyway—how long would it be until he changed his mind and became impatient? How long before he decided to assert his rights?

If only she could somehow force him to abide by his noble intentions . . .

Casting caution to the winds, she asked in as meek a tone as possible, "Do I have your word on that?"

"You have my word," he replied without hesitation.

Now at last she looked up at him, making no effort to hide her satisfaction. "Then I thank you for giving me the decision. I can only hope for your sake, Mr. Hawke, that you are a most patient man, because nothing will ever, *ever* induce me to be your wife in fact as well as in name. Indeed, I fear it will not be many days before you will discover that you have made an extremely bad bargain in marrying me."

Rather than looking discomposed, Mr. Hawke still smiled down at her. "I have learned, my dear, that no one can accurately foretell the future. If I had tried to do so a year ago—even three months ago—it would certainly never have occurred to me to predict that today I would be riding through London with you beside me. Yet here we are, husband and wife, bound together by the laws of God and the laws of men. Since that is the case, I do think it extremely appropriate that we use each other's Christian names, do you not?"

Distractedly, she agreed, her mind preoccupied by the truth of what he had said—no one could, in fact, predict what the morrow would bring.

There was much to be said for being married to a rich man, Cassie thought, snuggling down in the luxurious softness of her new bed. She and Mr. Hawke—that is to say, she and Richard—had been welcomed to Morwyle House by servants who were not only friendly while remaining properly deferential, but who were also models of efficiency.

By the time they had arrived early in the evening, their trunks, which had been sent ahead only that morning, were already unpacked and the clothes hung neatly in the ward-robes. The evening repast, while not elaborate, had been superbly cooked, and their bedrooms had been spotlessly clean.

The door opened, and someone entered the room. Drowsily she asked, "Did you forget something, Annie?"

A man's voice answered, and Cassie was instantly wide awake, all her nerves on edge. Sitting up in bed, she stared across the shadowy room. "What are you doing here, Mr. Hawke?"

"I thought we had agreed that you would call me Richard," he said calmly, beginning to untie the sash of his dressing gown.

Not wishing to discover what a naked man looked like, Cassie hurriedly shut her eyes. "What are you doing in my bedroom, *Richard*?" she repeated. "Does your word mean so little to you that you are breaking it less than twelve hours after you have given it?"

"I have no intention of breaking my word," he said, and she could hear laughter in his voice. "I shall, however, take whatever steps I deem necessary for us to become better acquainted with each other. After all, I can hardly expect you to become accustomed to me if we sleep in different rooms, now can I?"

Become accustomed to him? Even though she wished him in Jericho, curiosity prompted her to peek at him. To her relief, he was wearing a very proper nightshirt.

Before she could protest further, he approached the bed and lifted the covers. As quickly as she could, she moved away. Clinging precariously to the far edge of the mattress, she tried to remonstrate with him. "I have never shared a bed with any other person, not even my sister; I am afraid I shall not be able to sleep. Perhaps it would be better if you returned to your own bedroom."

He chuckled. "If you are troubled by insomnia, I can suggest an enjoyable activity that is purported to relieve tension and to relax one most thoroughly."

She started to ask him to explain when suddenly she knew exactly what he was referring to. So, he was not above using trickery in order to have his way with her! Well, she was not going to ask what that activity was, nor was he going to accomplish a thing by invading her bed, which fortunately was quite large.

"I thank you for the offer, but I believe I shall be able to sleep all night, provided you stay on your own side of the bed," she said rather crossly. If he decided to encroach on her privacy still further, she would know that he was making a mockery of his word.

But he did not protest, merely wished her good night, and not many minutes later she could tell by his breathing that he was sleeping.

Hours later it was obvious that she would never sleep again, at least not while he was in her bed. The situation was clearly impossible—she lay awake for hours, but the harder she tried to put him out of her mind, the more he filled her thoughts.

Cassie was so warm and comfortable when she woke up that it took her several moments to realize she was curled up against Mr. Hawke—against Richard. With her head on his shoulder and his arm around her, she was, in fact, so very comfortable that she continued to lie there for a few minutes instead of immediately moving back to her own side of the bed.

It was a very embarrassing position to be caught in, she realized moments later. Undoubtedly Richard would be quite smug when he discovered her there. Perhaps if she was very careful, she might be able to ease herself away from him before he realized that she was trespassing on his side of the bed? Before he discovered how successful his contemptible tactics had been?

Unfortunately, before she was able to move, he spoke. "Good morning, my love."

After a brief silence, she asked, "How did you know I was awake?"

He chuckled, and so infectious was his laugh that she was hard-pressed not to smile herself.

"You have been cuddled up against me like a soft little

cat, and then all at once you became as stiff as a board in my arms. It seemed reasonable to assume that you had just woken up.''

He was entirely correct—she was absolutely rigid with tension. With conscious effort she tried to relax, and she had achieved a measure of success when he began stroking her arm with his free hand, as if he were in truth petting a cat. It was so pleasant, she felt her firm resolve to abandon his shoulder begin to weaken.

After all, the damage was already done, was it not? Richard already knew she had—however strong her intentions not to—crept into his arms while she was sleeping. So what harm could there be in staying where she was a few more minutes? Thinking it through logically—or at least as logically as she was able to think, given the fact that she was positively groggy from lack of sufficient sleep—there was no pressing reason for her to return to her side of the bed, which at this moment seemed unappealingly cold . . . and lonely . . .

When she awoke again, the sun was high in the sky, and she was the only occupant of the bed. For that she could be thankful, of course, since she did not wish to have Richard observe her when she was not fully clothed, even if he had that right as her husband—and even though she had slept in his arms.

After ringing for Annie, Cassie went over to the window and looked out. The scene that greeted her eyes was so different from London—and from Cornwall. The sky was so blue, the sun so brilliant, she knew she could not possibly waste such a glorious day by staying inside.

If Richard was too busy to ride out with her and explore the estate, she would at least take Annie with her and walk around the garden and home woods. Perhaps the cook would be able to tell her if there were any berries ripe at this time of the year?

Cassie was contemplating her choice of walking dresses, trying to decide which would be the most appropriate for the country, when Annie entered with hot chocolate and scones on a tray. ''You slept late this morning. Did your husband manage to wear you out last night?''

"Annie!" Cassie was shocked at how casually—how crudely—her maid spoke of things that proper ladies never discussed openly.

Setting down the tray, Annie peered at her closely. "It appears I am premature in speaking of such things with you. Your husband has not yet made you his wife, apparently."

Cassie felt as if her face were on fire. "What makes you say that?" she asked, turning away to hide her blushes.

"Your eyes are still those of an innocent maiden—they display no knowledge of what it means to be a woman," Annie replied enigmatically. "It is odd, but I would never have credited that Mr. Hawke was not man enough to bed his own wife."

"There is nothing wrong with my husband!" Angrily, Cassie whirled around, only to discover Annie was laughing silently. With effort Cassie unclenched her fists. "Oh, very well, if you must know everything, Richard has given me his word that he will not consummate our marriage until I ask him to."

"And you have been married more than twenty-four hours and have not yet asked? More fool you."

"That is all you know! I shall never ask—never!"

"I had not thought you hated him so much."

Hate? No, Cassie realized to her own surprise, she did not hate Richard, nor even dislike him. Even more amazing was the growing awareness that she no longer was afraid of him.

"Can you not understand, Annie? He purchased me from my brother. Surely you can understand how that makes me feel? Would you ever stoop so low as to sell yourself to a man? Even if you were starving? I know you would not."

"No," Annie replied, her smile gone, "I never have and I never will. But marriage is different."

"How is it different? What rights do I have as a married woman? My husband has the power to control my every action, to make every decision for me. And yet he himself can do whatever he wishes, and I have no say in the matter."

"Marriage is different," Annie repeated stubbornly. "The bonds between a husband and wife are much deeper than a simple financial transaction."

"Perhaps I would agree with you if my husband loved me."

"Pray, what makes you think he does not? The way he looks at you, I would say rather that he is quite besotted."

"It is simple really." Cassie took a deep breath, then continued. "If he loved me, he would never have bought me as if I were a horse or a cow or a sheep."

"You are being foolish beyond permission," Annie retorted. "Marriage settlements have been around as long as there have been marriages, and most of them are designed as much to protect the woman as the man. Moreover, if you wish to have power over your husband, you have only to welcome him to your bed. You will soon discover that a little loving can bring even the strongest man to his knees."

A series of disconcerting images flashed through Cassie's mind. Thoroughly unsettled, she said quite sharply, "I do not wish to discuss this matter any further."

"Very well, my lady. Whatever you say, my lady." Annie curtsied so deeply, her forehead touched her knee. "We shall say nothing more on the subject."

Cassie could not hold back a laugh. Her bad mood was gone as quickly as it appeared. "The role of deferential servant does not suit you, Annie. You look positively ridiculous, in fact. Now do get up and help me dress; I have already wasted enough of this glorious day."

"And someday you will regret every one of the nights you are so determined to waste, you mark my words."

It still rankled that he had been tricked so easily. Geoffrey stood at the rail of the ship that had carried him away from England—the ship that should have been transporting Richard Hawke to a lifetime of slavery in North America.

So far the winds had been favorable, and they had made good time. Ahead of them, its top lit up by the last rays of the dying sun, loomed the bulky shape of Gibraltar—which he realized full well represented his last chance to make a successful escape.

After their first day at sea, Captain Rymer had not kept his two prisoners in chains, apparently deeming it unnecessary because the crewman assigned as guard was a

full head taller than Geoffrey—who was not a small man—
and the sailor was also extremely well muscled, undoubtedly
weighing more than Geoffrey and Piggot combined. Only
a man wishing sudden death would have attempted a direct
assault on such a giant.

The question Captain Rymer had apparently not
considered, however, was whether or not his oversized
crewman could swim as well as Geoffrey. If he could, then
all was lost. But very few sailors could swim at all, so the
odds in Geoffrey's favor were quite good. As for Piggot,
he was henceforth on his own—Geoffrey certainly owed him
no loyalty, since he was the one who had suggested they hire
that treacherous smuggler, Digory Rendel.

Doing his best to analyze the unfamiliar currents, Geoffrey
waited until he judged the ship to be in the most auspicious
position, then suddenly vaulted over the railing.

The water was warmer here than off the coast of Cornwall,
which was to his advantage. He had also had the foresight
to leave his boots and jacket below deck, so that he would
not need to waste precious moments struggling to take them
off once he entered the water. Surfacing, he could hear cries
above him of "Man overboard!"

Instead of making directly for shore, he swam around the
stern of the boat until he was on the opposite side from where
he had entered the water. Already there were creaking sounds
of winches as a boat was lowered.

At first the growing darkness was his ally, keeping the men
who still stood on deck from spotting his head among the
waves. But after the ship finally vanished into the night, the
darkness became his enemy. Too low in the water to see the
lights along the shoreline, he could only swim in what he
hoped was the proper direction.

By the time the first light of dawn streaked the sky, he
was too exhausted to swim another mile. His arms felt like
lead weights, and it was all he could do to keep his head
above water.

Not that it mattered—in whichever direction he looked,
he could see no sign of land, not even clouds, which
commonly formed where the sea met the coastline.

With his remaining breath, he cursed Richard Hawke, Piggot, Digory Rendel, Captain Rymer, and of course his sister Cassie, who was undoubtedly enjoying her new wealth without sparing a thought for him.

Annie walked into the breakfast room and almost into the arms of Viscount Westhrop, who smiled engagingly down at her.

"So, at last we meet again, Annie Elizabeth Ironside."

Keeping all traces of emotion from her face and voice, she replied, "If you will kindly step aside, my lord, I need to fetch Lady Cassie's shawl, which she inadvertently left here this morning."

Instead of moving out of her way, he took a step toward her, which she matched by taking one step backward. "Why have you been deliberately avoiding me, my love? I have been here for five days already, and this is the first time I have even managed to catch a glimpse of you."

"Beg pardon, my lord, but I have not been avoiding you. I have merely been doing the job that I am paid for." She took another step backward and bumped up against the door she had just come through.

He stopped a mere foot away and reached out one hand to caress her cheek. "Do not utter such fibs, my love."

Quick as a flash, she pulled her knife from its hiding place. "I am not your love, and if you value your life, do not touch me, my lord."

Looking down at her weapon, he merely smiled. "Does this mean I may not kiss you?"

Something about his expression made her think that perhaps she had met her match—he certainly did not seem to fear the naked blade in the slightest.

Tightening her grip on the handle of her knife, she answered as firmly as possible, hoping she could still bluff him. "You may kiss me only at the expense of your life, my lord."

"Then tell my friends I died happy," he replied. Making no effort to seize her weapon, he leaned over and kissed her gently on the mouth, then gasped. Pulling away slightly, he looked down at the blood that was oozing from a cut in his side.

"I warned you, my lord," she said, keeping her tone icy although she felt sick at what she had done. In her heart, she knew she should not have used her dagger, because this man had meant her no real harm—a slap on the face would have doubtless been as effective as sticking a knife in his ribs, and certainly less dangerous for him.

"It is not yet mortal," he commented as serenely as if he were remarking on the weather. "I can perhaps steal another kiss before I expire."

He suited actions to words, pulling her into his arms and kissing her with growing passion, which she found herself reciprocating. Her knife fell from nerveless fingers to land with a soft thud on the carpet.

The blood soaking through her dress brought her back to reality, and she shoved him away. "Oh, stop, stop, before you bleed to death."

"You forgot to say 'my lord' in that prim and proper voice of yours," he said, reaching out to her again.

She batted his hands away. "Do not joke; you are bleeding all over the carpet."

He laughed. "Ah, yes, so I am. I agree, a gentleman should not be so crass as to ruin a carpet with his demise, especially such a magnificent Oriental one as this."

Tears filling her eyes, she said, "You must let me bind up the wound, before the loss of blood weakens you."

He touched her cheek gently. "You are crying—does this mean you care for me? Very well, I shall allow you to bandage my cut, but only if you kiss me first."

Staring into his eyes, which were as blue as a Scottish loch, she said passionately, "You have not the least bit of common sense, my lord; I am surprised you have survived this long!"

"Oddly enough, my cousin, Edmund Stanier, was likewise astounded to discover me still in the land of the living. If I were pressed to come up with an explanation, I would have to say that luck has played a large part in my survival thus far. Now kiss me, my love."

Frustrated beyond measure, she grabbed his face with both

hands and pressed a quick kiss on his lips. "There, I hope you are satisfied."

"Never will I be satisfied, my love. I intend to keep kissing you every day for the next fifty or sixty years."

She was too angry with him to answer. Pulling him by the hand over to the table, she shoved him down into a chair, then began unbuttoning his jacket. With his help, she soon had his ribs exposed.

"Be gentle, I cannot stand pain," he said teasingly.

Going to the sideboard, she found a bottle of brandy. Instead of offering him some to drink, she poured a healthy measure of it onto the cut.

"A—a—a—a—a!" He was gasping for breath, and sweat appeared on his brow.

"Stings, does it, my lord?" she asked sweetly.

"Perry," he finally managed to say through clenched teeth. "You must call me Perry, my love."

Folding a clean napkin into a pad, she pressed it against the cut. "Please hold that in place, my lord."

Fully recovered now from the effects of the brandy, he put his hands behind his head and grinned impishly up at her. "Not until you say my name."

"If you do not do as I tell you, *my lord*, then I shall douse you with brandy again."

He made no move to take the cloth, but instead scrunched his eyes shut and gritted his teeth.

She was tempted to do it just to teach him a lesson, but she had the feeling she had finally met a man who was immune to all her threats. On the other hand, she could not very well stand there all day pressing the napkin against his wound. With a sigh, she gave in. "Please hold the pad in place, *Perry*."

He opened his eyes and smiled up at her, looking quite like a naughty little boy who had just coaxed the cook into giving him another cookie. In this case, looks were deceiving—there had been nothing boyish about his kisses.

Quickly tearing a strip of cloth from her petticoat, she finished bandaging his ribs.

"You do that very neatly, my love."

"I had ample practice in Spain, my lord."

Without warning, he caught her arms and pulled her down onto his lap. "I thought we had settled that you were to call me Perry?"

"We have settled nothing, my lord, except that we both agree you have no sense at all."

"I have quite enough good sense to recognize my own true love when I find her at last. Marry me, Annie Elizabeth Ironside."

In a flash she was off his lap. "That has got to be the most ridiculous thing you have said so far." Without stopping to listen to his protests, she marched resolutely from the room.

Belatedly she realized she should have run; he caught up with her at the bottom of the stairs.

"There is nothing remotely ridiculous about wanting to marry you. I am completely serious."

Fending off his hands, she started up the stairs. "And I am also quite serious. I do not wish to marry you."

"At least have the courtesy to tell me why you will not," he demanded, still following her. She could only be thankful that there did not seem to be any other servants around at the moment—or even worse, one of the guests.

"Because you are a peer and I am only a servant girl," she replied. "It would be most improper for you to marry so far beneath your station."

"Then there is no problem," he said gleefully. "I intend to give up my title and return to America. You can come with me. In America we do not allow titles, nor do people worry about 'stations' in life, their own or anyone else's. Trust the English to worry about such nonsense."

"I am not English, my lord, I am *Scottish.*"

"And I am an *American*, and you will soon learn we do not tolerate such undemocratic ideas."

"I shall learn no such thing," she said firmly. Reaching the top floor, she paused at the door to her room. Something about the look in his eyes made her feel so reckless, she blurted out the words she had always sworn nothing would ever make her say. "If you wish, I will be your mistress while you are here, but I will never marry you."

Her offer made him so angry, for a moment she wished her knife were at hand.

"I don't want a mistress—I want a wife!"

"Then you will have to find someone else, my lord. I have told you—I am not available." Stepping into her room, she slammed the door in his face, then quickly turned the key in the lock.

Chapter Fifteen

"Something must be done at once!" Lady Cassie said, bursting into the drawing room where Lady Letitia was sitting with Perry, John, and Richard. "It is the most appalling situation."

"What is, my dear?" Richard asked calmly.

"Mrs. Beagles has just told me about the vicar. The man is a veritable monster! She says he keeps his daughter shut away like a prisoner! He has turned down two very respectable offers for her and will not even let her visit the squire—"

"I believe she is shy—" John started to explain.

"She is no such thing! Every time we have invited her here, her father has *forbidden* her to come, and then that wretched man has sat here in *our* house, explaining in that *mealy-mouthed* way of his, that she did not *wish* to visit, and all the time she was back in her room in the vicarage, *crying* her eyes out."

"Surely your housekeeper is exaggerating," Perry said. "Even if her father were to forbid her to go about in society, she is of age and so can do whatever she wishes."

Lady Cassie turned on him in a flash. "That just shows how little you know of the world. You make it sound as if women have the freedom to do whatever they wish. But Mrs. Beagles reports that the Reverend Mr. Shuttleworth does not give her even a penny of her own, lest she have some little pleasure in life. Why, the way he treats her, she is little more than a—a slave!"

The possibilities inherent in this situation were beginning to interest Lady Letitia, especially since she had noticed the meaningful looks that John and Richard exchanged when Lady Cassie uttered the word "slave."

"Would this gentleman perhaps be a Mr. *Philip* Shuttle-worth?" Lady Letitia asked.

"Yes," Richard replied, "do you know him?"

"I knew his mother. I have not seen Philip since he went off to Oxford, but as a boy he was the most odiously selfish child I have ever met—never wished to share his toys with his older brothers and sisters. Why, I have seen him spill an entire box of bonbons into the dirt, merely because his mother instructed him to offer some to his siblings."

"You see, it is as I have said—the man is a beast. You must do something, Richard," Lady Cassie said, still so incensed she was pacing back and forth. "We cannot allow the poor girl to be treated so shabbily."

Before Richard could reply, Lady Letitia decided to meddle further. "I do not think it wise for your husband to interfere in the vicar's private business, my dear. It is liable to cause bad blood, which can lead to endless feuding. It is always better to contrive somehow to remain on civil terms with one's neighbors, no matter how sorely vexed one becomes. I suggest instead that John be allowed to handle the whole matter. I am sure we can count on him to be tactful."

John walked briskly along the path through the home woods, hoping that he would be more successful than he had been the last few days—that this morning he would find the woman he was seeking so diligently.

Twice he had paid a call at the vicarage, and twice the vicar had informed him his daughter was lying down with a sick headache and so was unable to entertain visitors. The frontal assault having failed, John had finally turned to Mrs. Beagles for advice.

"Mr. Shuttleworth is quite fond of wild strawberry preserves," she had said, "and the season is not yet over. Try the meadow at the east end of the estate, and you may find Miss Shuttleworth there. Her father is not at all particular about whose berries go into his jams, you see. But Mr. Morwyle felt pity for the poor unfortunate girl, and he instructed all his servants and tenants to let her pick where she might."

After two days of unsuccessfully checking the meadow, it had occurred to John that perhaps Miss Shuttleworth was only allowed out quite early in the morning, before the gentry might reasonably be expected to be abroad. This morning the sun was up, but the dew was still on the grass.

In the time that had passed since Lady Cassie had discovered the situation, he had mulled over the possibilities for the unfortunate vicar's daughter and had decided that the best thing to do would be to settle enough money on her that she could hire a companion and rent a modest house in Bath.

On the other hand, while he was watching the sunrise this morning, it had occurred to him that after thirty years of being browbeaten, the unfortunate Miss Shuttleworth might no longer be capable of managing her affairs on her own. If her spirit had been completely broken, then he might have to hire someone as a caretaker . . . and also, Bath might be too intimidating for her. He might need to find a smaller, less imposing town for her to reside in.

Emerging from the woods, he spotted a woman crouching in the middle of the meadow, her bonnet dangling down her back. At the sound of his approach, she rose to her feet and turned to face him.

She was a strikingly beautiful woman—her face was a perfect oval, her features well formed, her hair like polished mahogany, and even her drab gown, as ugly as it was, could not hide the fact that she had all the requisite curves in all the proper places.

What delighted him the most, however, were the stains of strawberry juice around the corners of her mouth. Despite his fears, he realized with relief that her father had failed to destroy her spirit completely.

"Good morning, Mr. Tuke," she said as politely as if they were meeting under normal social conditions.

He tipped his hat. "Good morning, Miss Shuttleworth."

She smiled and looked at him expectantly, and all his prepared speeches about settlements and companions and little houses in Bath flew out of his head. "I have come to rescue you," he said, feeling not the least bit foolish to be speaking so dramatically.

"I have been hoping you would do so," she replied simply.

So besotted was he by her smile, only now did it occur to him to wonder how she had known his name.

"Mrs. Beagles pointed you out to me several weeks ago," she replied when he asked her, "when you all came out from London to inspect Morwyle House."

"You should have spoken to me then," he chastised her gently. "I could have rescued you that much earlier."

"I am sorry to confess that I am not at all a resolute person. I have learned over the years that it is safer to avoid having a direct confrontation with my father."

"Whereas I am afraid I have no particular talent for subterfuge," John confessed. "So, shall we beard the lion in its den, as it were?"

"If by lion you are referring to my father, at this hour of the day he is still abed, so we may as well pick a few more strawberries first. They are so tiny and so well hidden, it may seem scarcely worth the trouble, but they are much sweeter and more flavorful than the domestic varieties. Would you like to try one?"

He nodded, and she bent down and retrieved her basket. To his delight, instead of allowing him to help himself, she carefully and with great deliberation selected one and fed it to him, her fingers touching his lips in the process.

The strawberry was indeed superb, but he scarcely noticed. Staring intently into her eyes, he caught a glimpse of something that made him realize there had been nothing inadvertent about her actions—she had deliberately used the berry as an excuse to touch him, and the blush creeping up her face merely confirmed his suspicions.

No hired companion would be needed, he decided at that moment. Miss Shuttleworth's charms required a husband—and he did not need Lady Letitia to find the proper man. He himself intended to begin courting her without delay.

Reaching out, he took another strawberry from the basket she was holding, but instead of eating it, he fed it to her. "I have a better idea," he said. "Instead of picking more berries, let us eat the ones you have already picked. Unless you wish to save them for someone else?"

Her blush deepened. "No," she said, her voice quite breathless. "I shall be glad to . . . to share them all with you."

He took off his jacket and spread it out on the ground for her to sit on, then sat down on the grass beside her. "My father was also a vicar," he began.

The sun was quite high in the sky by the time they returned to the vicarage. Approaching it with her hand safely resting on John's arm, Margaret was amazed at how brave she was feeling. She knew her father would rant and rave and scold and likely even call down curses upon her head, but she had enjoyed the morning immensely.

Already she had such faith in John's abilities that she could not conceive of her father's being able to intimidate him or drive him away. Only one little thing nagged at her. When they had first met, John had said he had come to rescue her. Just what had he meant by rescue? The word conjured up such possibilities.

She sneaked a peek up at him. He was so beautiful, it made her heart race faster just to look at him. There was so much nobility in his features, such strength, such courage, it fair made her tremble when his eyes met hers and she could gaze into their depths.

Dare she hope? No, that could never be. But at least he must intend to force her father to relax some of his rules, and if her father would only let her go out into society then she would surely see John again—maybe pass the time of day with him after Sunday services?—perhaps even be allowed to dine occasionally at Morwyle House?

It would not be enough. She sighed.

"Do not fret yourself, Margaret. Your father is only a man. No matter how he has treated you, he is not the devil incarnate."

"I am not worried with you beside me," she admitted, then realized her words made her sound quite shameless.

They were still a few feet from the gate when her father, his hair in total disarray, appeared on the other side of it, looking quite like an avenging prophet from the Old Testament. "So there you are, you wicked girl," he shrieked, completely ignoring the man beside her. "You will go to your room at once and stay there, on your knees, praying for forgiveness, until I decide you have suitably atoned for your flagrant disregard for the rules I have laid down for you."

She did not reply, nor did she release John's arm, and he was the one to answer. "Good morning, Mr. Shuttleworth. I would like your permission to court your daughter."

At his words, Margaret's heart gave a little jump. Her dream, which moments before had seemed so unthinkable, now began to seem quite certain.

Unable to ignore her companion any longer, her father turned his baleful glare on John. "Denied," he snarled. "I shall never give you permission to see my daughter or speak to her again. Why, you are nothing but a hired secretary—virtually a servant. I shall never allow my daughter to demean herself by associating with one of your class."

"As you wish," John replied calmly. Looking down at her, he said, "I had intended to do this properly, but since your father has refused me permission to court you, will you marry me, Margaret?"

Without hesitation she replied, "I shall be delighted to do so."

At her answer, he smiled, and she had a presentiment that delight would be a major component in her life from this day forward.

"No, no, I forbid it!" her father shrieked, jumping up and down. "If you marry this man, I shall disown you! I shall never allow you to set foot in my house again, and you will never receive another penny from me!"

"Good-bye, father," she said, and for once in his life he was totally nonplussed. His mouth opened and shut, but no sound emerged. It was petty of her, of course, but she could not help feeling a degree of satisfaction that for a change he was the one reduced to speechlessness.

"Is there anything here you need or wish to take with you?" John inquired.

She thought for a moment. "No, nothing."

Without a qualm she turned her back on the house that had been her home all her life. "I shall try not to be a burden to you," she said as they walked along. "If there is one good thing that can be said about my father, it is that he has taught me to be thrifty and frugal."

John stopped in the middle of the village street and took her in his arms. Smiling down at her, he said, "Before you offer to take in laundry to supplement my meager income, perhaps I should tell you that I am every bit as rich as my friend, Richard Hawke."

Then before she could reply to that astonishing information, he kissed her quite, quite thoroughly. By the time he had finished, they had acquired a large audience, but she felt not the slightest shame at her wanton behavior.

"Miss Shuttleworth and I shall be married tomorrow in London by special license," John announced to the assembled crowd. "And you are all invited to share in the marriage feast at Morwyle House the day after tomorrow."

A cheer went up from the villagers, and they crowded around her to wish her happy. Not a one of them mentioned her father, or made any comment about the suddenness of this announcement.

"I have heard there is a farmer over near Kingston who has bred a truly superb colt," Richard said.

Perry did not cease his pacing, which was beginning to drive Richard to distraction. "I don't want to see a man about a horse—I want to persuade Annie to marry me. Stubborn, pig-headed girl! Why won't she listen to reason?"

"I thought you were not interested in dragging along such useless baggage as a wife."

"Annie's different. I knew as soon as she stabbed me with that ridiculous knife of hers that she was the only woman for me. She followed the drum on the Peninsula for three years, did you know that? Hellish life for a woman, marching about all the time, lucky if the supply trains can keep up. At least in Kentucky I have a small cabin already built, and I intend to build a much larger house as soon as possible."

He stopped his pacing. "But how am I going to persuade

her to have me? Every time I ask her, she spouts some nonsense about our different stations in life."

Richard smiled. "Can this be the same man who only a few months ago was lecturing me on the evils inherent in marrying a servant girl?"

Perry looked sheepish. "Well, all of us have to grow up sometime. I am surprised you did not box me on my ears for uttering such drivel."

He resumed his pacing. "Really, Hawke, I was there when you needed help courting your wife. Now you are happily married, so the least you can do is give me a little advice—tell me what I can do to convince Annie. She insists I cannot be allowed to give up my title and estates to marry her, because in the future I will surely come to regret it, and then I will resent her. Yet I cannot convince her that I would even willingly give up my land in Kentucky for her, although that would indeed be a painful step to take."

"Have you tried kissing her?"

"Of course I've kissed her!" Perry exploded. "Do you think I am a total lackwit? Oh, blast it all, there is no point talking to you." Muttering to himself, he stalked to the door. "Perhaps she has changed her mind. It can't hurt to ask her again."

"When was the last time you proposed?" Richard called after him.

"Over half an hour ago," came the reply before the door was shut, leaving him alone.

Perry was wrong, Richard thought sadly. He was not happily married. Although Cassie willingly slept every night in his arms, their marriage was still unconsummated.

It could not be that she still feared him, nor did she exhibit the least bit of shyness around him. Although she had not said so directly, her every action proclaimed that she loved him more and more every day. Nor was her nature cold. She was probably not aware of the number of times each day that she found an excuse to touch him.

So why did she still hold back? Why, if she did not wish to be kissed—to be loved—did she look wistful every time she saw John and Margaret gazing adoringly into each other's eyes?

If only he could ask her directly. But if he did so, she might think he was trying to coerce her. In desperation, he had even gone so far as to ask Lady Letitia's advice, but she had merely laughed and said she only meddled before the wedding, not after.

What a wretched business it was. Despite his earlier philosophical discussions with John, in which he had said the concept of honor did not play a role in his life, Richard now found himself bound as securely by his word of honor as by any chains made of iron.

No matter how he wished it otherwise, he could not make love to his wife until she asked him to.

Annie finished pinning up the last curl and stood back to examine her work with a critical eye. Taking a deep breath, Cassie decided the time had come to do what Perry had been begging her to do, namely act as his intermediary.

"I think you should believe Perry when he says he has always intended to give up his title. I do not think he is just saying that to persuade you to marry him. I think he is quite serious about returning to Kentucky."

"You needn't waste your breath trying to convince me," Annie replied. "I fully intend to have him in the end."

"After my experiences with Lords Fauxbridge and Rowcliff and Atherston, I have learned—and you should have also—that a title in and of itself is meaningless and unimportant and . . . what did you say?"

"I said I shall marry him eventually."

"But . . . but . . . if you . . . then why have you turned him down every time he has asked you?"

There was a short pause before Annie answered. "As much as I loved my first husband, I made a serious mistake with him—I let him know how grateful I was that he was willing to marry me. Even though he was a very considerate husband, and I know he loved me and was faithful to me, still he never let me forget that he had done me a favor by taking me for his wife."

She grinned. "This time, my dearest love is not going to take me for granted. I fully intend that every day Perry will wake up feeling lucky that he managed to persuade me to marry him. I do not, of course, plan to waste any of our nights together as a certain foolish girl I know insists upon doing. Some day she will regret every hour she has wasted.''

''I regret them already,'' Cassie said quietly. ''I have grown to love Richard so much—he is so kind and gentle and patient. And every time he looks at me, I feel weak inside—every time he touches me, I tremble. And when he holds me in his arms at night, it is all I can do to keep from crying out with longing.''

Annie looked at her sharply. ''Then why have you not told him you are no longer the reluctant bride?''

''Because no matter how hard I try, I cannot banish that horrible question from my thoughts.''

''I know, you have already told me. You cannot stop wondering how much he paid for you.''

Cassie nodded, tears forming in her eyes. ''I have tried so hard to tell myself that it does not matter how or why— all that matters is that we care about each other and are married to each other. But every time I think about asking Richard to make love to me, I see Geoffrey's mocking face, and I hear him telling me he plans to sell me to the highest bidder, and inside I become so cold, I feel as if nothing can ever warm me again.''

''Can you not make your horses go faster?'' Edmund Stanier clutched the documents his agent had brought back from America—those most precious pieces of paper that would gain him what rightfully should have been his in the first place.

''Certainly we can go faster, if you wishes to end up in the ditch instead of at Morwyle House,'' Jenkins, the man Edmund had hired, said in a bored tone of voice.

To that, Edmund had no suitable reply, so he passed the remaining time dreaming of how Perry would cry and weep and wail when he learned he was no longer Viscount Westhrop.

''And, if you will read this letter, it says that you were

fighting with the American army against England.'' Edmund displayed the piece of paper he had paid so much to procure. It was most gratifying to have them all hanging on his every word. "In short, my dear cousin, you are a traitor to your own country, guilty of the highest treason.''

The groveling that Edmund had expected did not happen. Instead Perry looked positively radiant. "Now she will *have* to marry me,'' he said, dashing from the room.

Edmund looked around at the circle of faces—Mr. Hawke, Lady Cassiopeia, Mr. and Mrs. Tuke, Mr. Rendel, and of course, his grandmother, Lady Letitia, who was smiling in a way that made him begin to feel somewhat nervous.

"I shall have that packet of papers,'' she said calmly, extending her hand.

"But Grandmama,'' he protested, clutching the documents more tightly to his chest. "Perry does not deserve to be viscount, not when he is a traitor.''

"Do not worry; I shall see to it that he renounces the title. But if you will think about it, you will see that it would not be at all the thing for your cousin to be locked up in the Tower. Only consider what the gossips would say about it. We would not wish to have the name of Westhrop forever associated with treason.''

The picture her words conjured up was so horrifying, Edmund shoved the packet at her as if it had suddenly become too hot to touch.

"Thank you, Edmund dear,'' she said. "And now we must consider who to pick as your wife.''

"Wife?'' Truly appalled, Edmund could only stare at her.

"Well, of course,'' she replied serenely. "Now that you are to be the viscount, you must see about securing the succession. Had you not realized that you must marry as soon as possible and start filling up your nursery? But I am sure you know your duty to the family. I confess, I am quite looking forward to hearing the patter of little feet at Westhrop Manor in the near future. Perhaps we should consider Cecily Ingleby. She is, after all, only your second cousin, so we need not worry about consanguinity.''

Flabbergasted, Edmund stared at his grandmother. How

could she have suggested such a horrible thing? If he had to listen to Cecily's chattering every day, he would soon be locked up in Bedlam.

There are times when a prudent man cannot afford to stand on his dignity. This obviously being one of those times, Edmund did not wait to take proper leave of his grandmother. Instead, he fled the house, running faster than he had run since he was ten years old and Perry had decided he needed to be tossed in the duck pond.

In the stable yard, Jenkins was just beginning to unhitch the horses. "Quick, quick, I must get back to London," Edmund screeched, jumping up and down. "Double the money I promised you if we leave this minute!"

Jenkins eyed him impassively, but made no move to comply. "Triple," he said finally.

"Yes, yes, triple," Edmund agreed, looking over his shoulder at the house, where luckily there was not yet any sign of pursuit. "But hurry, my good man—be quick about it. Do not waste any time—this is a matter of life and death!"

Perry found Annie in Cassie's room, hanging up some neatly ironed frocks. Catching her up in his arms, he spun her around the room. "Now you shall have to marry me," he crowed with delight. "For if you do not, I shall be hanged as a traitor."

"What nonsense are you talking now?" She struggled to get down, but he would not release her.

"My cousin Edmund has been snooping around like the little weasel he is, and he has discovered I fought against the British at New Orleans. So, my love, either you marry me and we return to America, or if you still refuse to have me, I shall stay here and be executed for treason."

"If I don't marry you, that does not mean you must allow yourself to be arrested," she protested. "There is nothing to stop you from going back to Kentucky."

Setting her back on her feet, he said firmly, "I swear on my mother's grave that I shall not sail without you. There, you see—if you do not this minute agree to marry me, I shall turn myself in to the local magistrate and confess all. So it is your choice whether I live or die."

"I could not bear it if anything should happen to you," she said softly, "so it appears I must marry you and live in Kentucky with you." Catching his face in her hands, she pulled his head down and kissed him on the lips. "But if you do not treat me with the proper respect, do not forget that I know how to use a knife."

Touching his side, which was still a bit tender, he said, "How can I ever forget? But perhaps someone should warn the bears that you are coming."

When Richard entered his wife's room that night, she was sitting at her dressing table brushing her hair. "Now that Perry has convinced Annie to marry him, I shall have to see about hiring a new lady's maid," she remarked.

Taking the brush from Cassie's hand, Richard began pulling it gently through her hair. "Does it bother you that Perry is marrying a servant instead of a lady of his own class? I am afraid when it is announced, London society will be quick to call it a *mésalliance*."

"I have discovered I have absolutely no interest in what the *haut ton* says and does. I think it is much more important that two people love each other than that their positions in life are equal. And although it happened rather quickly, I do believe Perry truly loves Annie."

She spoke so vehemently, Richard began to wonder if the root of his problem was such a simple thing—that he had not made it clear to her that he loved her. Studying her reflection in the mirror, he could not tell what she was thinking.

"Indeed, he told me that he fell in love with her when she stabbed him with her knife," Richard said, still debating with himself whether he should risk pursuing the subject. Finally, reminding himself that faint heart never won fair lady, he continued, "A strange way for love to begin, and yet when I think back, I would have to say that I began falling in love with you when you bargained with me so bravely in that little tavern in Cornwall. I did not realize it was love, however, until we were at the opera, and you again turned to me for help.''

She did not respond immediately, but sat with her eyes downcast, letting him brush her hair. Finally she asked in a suspiciously calm voice, "When we were at supper that night of the Craigmonts' ball, did you deliberately bait Lord Fauxbridge by bringing up the subject of the slave trade bill?"

"Quite deliberately," he replied, and was relieved when she looked up and smiled tentatively at him in the mirror. "And you may also have heard that I gambled with Lord Rowcliff and won half his fortune. That was also deliberate."

"And then you outbid Lord Atherston," she added, her eyes sliding away from his, "so Geoffrey sold me to you."

His heart stopped beating for a moment. "Where did you get such a notion?" he asked.

"It was never a secret. When he came to Cornwall in February, Geoffrey told me outright that he was going to take me to London and sell me to the highest bidder," she said, her voice trembling and her head bowed.

Laying down the hairbrush, Richard pulled her into his arms. With her face pressed against his chest, she continued. "At first I refused to go along with his plans, but then he said he would sell my little sister to white slavers if I did not cooperate."

"Oh, my love, my love, I had no idea—"

"I know it is quite customary to arrange marriage settlements, but ever since you asked me to marry you—" She hiccuped, but then rushed on, as if she had to get it out before her courage failed her. "Ever since then, I have been tormented by the same question . . . "

Despite her obvious resolve to control her emotions, she was now trembling too hard to continue, so he finished for her. "You want to know how much I paid your brother for you."

She nodded her head.

"Not a penny. I did not buy you from your brother."

She became very quiet in his arms. "You did not? Then how . . . ?"

"I am ashamed to admit that I employed much the same method of coercion that he used with you: I told Geoffrey that if he did not give his permission, I would have him kidnapped and sold to the Barbary pirates. In my defense, I can only say I was bluffing; I would never actually have done it."

Throwing her arms around his neck, Cassie began to kiss him. "Oh," she said, tears running down her cheeks, "you cannot begin to know how happy you have made me. I have been feeling so horrible, thinking you had bought me from my brother. You cannot imagine how bad that made me feel inside—as if I were a thing instead of a person."

But he did know exactly how degraded it could make someone feel.

"Oh, Richard, Annie told me I would regret every one of the nights I have been wasting, and she was right—I do regret them, and I have been wanting to be your wife for so long. Please make love to me tonight."

It would have been so easy . . . and so dishonest . . .

"I cannot do that yet," he said softly. "Not until you know what kind of a man your husband is."

She smiled up at him. "I know what kind of a man you are—you are honorable and kind and patient and resourceful and—"

"But there is much you do not know about my past. And I would be less than honorable if I took advantage of your ignorance."

For a moment he thought she was going to continue her protests, but then she relaxed. "Very well, I shall be happy to listen to the story of your life. But I suggest our bed will be a much warmer place to talk."

A few minutes later she was snuggled up against him under the covers, and the moment he was dreading could not be postponed any longer. Would she still accept him when she knew he was not truly a gentleman? Would she be horrified to discover who was sharing her bed? Would she reject him when she discovered he had married her under false pretenses?

There was nothing to do but start with the worst and hope for the best. "My earliest memories are of fighting for scraps of food in the streets of London. I do not remember either of my parents, nor do I have any idea who they were." He paused, but she did not shriek and push him away, so he continued with growing hope that all was not lost.

"People called me Dickie, but why they gave me that name, I do not know. Then one day, when I was about ten or so, I saw a bird flying high in the sky—a different, much larger and more powerful bird than the sparrows and gulls I was used to. An old lady told me it was a hawk, and I wanted so much to fly free like that bird, that I decided thenceforth my name would be Richard Hawke."

"I think you chose wisely. The name suits you. But before you go on with your tale, I must warn you that if you think it matters one whit to me that you were not born a gentleman, then it is *you* who is being foolish beyond permission, and I should not wish to have a fool for a husband."

He was not a fool. Tomorrow would be soon enough to tell her about his years as a slave. It was strange, but looking back he felt as if his life had not truly begun until the day he had met her; everything else seemed only preparation for that moment.

"I love the man you have been and the man you are and the man you will become," she whispered in the darkness. "But I want to be your true wife. Make love to me, Richard," she again requested.

She did not need to ask him a third time.

Epilogue

"I think I shall be leaving in the morning," Digory remarked to Lady Letitia. They were taking tea on the terrace, the other members of the house party being otherwise engaged. "Watching three pairs of lovers gaze adoringly into each other's eyes is not quite as much excitement as I have been accustomed to."

"Yes, I must agree. As satisfying as it is to view the results of our labors, there is little left for either of us to do here," Lady Letitia replied, setting down her teacup. "But before we take leave of each other, will you not tell me some stories of your adventures as a smuggler?"

"No," Digory replied baldly.

"No?" Lady Letitia glared at him, but he refused to meet her eyes, staring instead at the cloud formations.

"No," he repeated, "you have listened to far too many tales of other people's travels already. The time has come for you to see something of the world yourself." He looked over at her, and she was white as a sheet, but he did not think it was anger that was making the blood drain from her face, so he continued.

"Retired though I am, I can still on occasion be persuaded to go on a smuggling run. So if you are game, we shall send your maid and your luggage back to London, and then we shall drive down to Cornwall, where Jem can doubtless find you some sailor's clothes that will fit."

Lady Letitia was crying now, but smiling through her tears at the same time, so it appeared he had guessed correctly.

"Then we shall sail to France on my boat, *The Wayward Gull*, to Bordeaux perhaps, or if you want more danger and excitement, to Marseilles. We shall take rooms in a flea-infested hotel on the waterfront and sit around drinking in smoky taverns, surrounded by the most disreputable types. Unless you would prefer traveling to Paris to view the latest fashions?''

She shook her head violently.

"Since Bonaparte is safely locked up, we shall not have any legal difficulties in France, but I must point out that if the preventatives catch us when we are landing our cargo in England, you will have to take your chances like any other smuggler.'' He studied her face, but she did not seem the least put off by knowledge that she would be breaking English law.

"Well, what do you say, then?'' he asked. "Do you wish to sign on as one of my crew?''

"The oddest thing, Perry.''

"What's that, my love?''

"Your grandmother is on the terrace—''

"Nothing odd about that.''

"But she is kissing Digory Rendel.''

Perry moved to stand beside his wife at the window. "By Jove, you are right. Well, she always was a lusty old girl.''

Annie jabbed him in the ribs with her elbow. "Don't be disrespectful. Your grandmother is a sweet old lady.''

Perry caught her around the waist and hugged her. "You wouldn't say that if you knew her better. In her heart she's as wild about adventure as I am. Pity she's been stuck here in England all her life—she would love Kentucky. If she were younger, I'd take her back with us, but unfortunately, she's far too old to withstand the rigors of a sea voyage.''

Her legs slightly apart for balance, Lady Letitia stood on the pitching deck of the boat and stared at the dark smudge on the horizon. France! They would be landing soon in Marseilles, where she would rub shoulders with the—how had Digory put it?—with the scum from all the countries of the world.

She was so excited, she could hardly wait to try out the patois Jem had been teaching her, which was not at all like the drawing room French she had been speaking all her life.

To be sure, this little trip was not precisely the same as sailing up the Amazon or searching for the origin of the Nile, but still, it was an adventure, and best of all, it was *her* adventure.

And besides, who was to say where she might be able to persuade Digory to sail next?